PRIME SUSPECT 2

The officers dispersed, leaving through the back garden gate. Tennison stayed. She was glad she did, because a few moments later Gold made an important discovery. He beckoned the photographer over to take several close-up shots of the corpse's wrists, behind its back, beneath the pelvis.

Bream craned forward, speaking softly into a small pocket recorder. 'Hands tied together at the back with. . .'

Gingerly, Gold pulled something out and held it up.

'. . . a leather belt,' Bream intoned.

A movement caught Tennison's eye and she turned to see the little Viswandha boy standing on the top step, all agog.

'For God's sake . . . did no one think to get the family moved?' She went up the steps, ushering him ahead of her. 'It'll be gone soon.'

He wasn't a bit frightened, just filled with curiosity. 'Is it a real person?'

'Let's get you inside, you'll catch cold. You should be in bed.'

'It should have been buried deeper, shouldn't it?' he said, with a child's irrefutable logic. 'Then it wouldn't have come back.'

PRIME SUSPECT 2

LYNDA LA PLANTE

Mandarin

A Mandarin Paperback
PRIME SUSPECT 2

First published in Great Britain 1992
by Mandarin Paperbacks
an imprint of Reed Consumer Books Ltd
Michelin House, 81 Fulham Road, London SW3 6RB
and Auckland, Melbourne, Singapore and Toronto

Reprinted 1992

Copyright © Lynda La Plante 1992
The author has asserted her moral rights in
the television script upon which the novel is based

A CIP catalogue record for this title
is available from the British Library

ISBN 0 7493 1551 2

Printed and bound in Great Britain
by Cox & Wyman Ltd, Reading, Berks

I would like to acknowledge the talent of the writer Trevor Hoyle without whom this book could not have been published.

The young black man was very good-looking. Tall and lithe, with a fine pair of shoulders, he kept himself in shape with regular workouts. He sat at the square wooden table in the interview room, long supple hands clasped in his lap, his bearing erect, his handsome face impassive. His suit was well cut, white shirt immaculate, a neat, precise knot in his tie. He was very calm, very sure of himself. The remote-control video camera high in one corner recorded all this, moved fractionally as he tilted his head back slightly, looking straight into the eyes of the woman opposite with just a hint of lazy insolence.

She stared back unflinchingly. 'I am Detective Chief Inspector Jane Tennison, attached to Southampton Row Police Station. We are in the Interview Room at Southampton Row. I am interviewing . . .' She leaned her elbows on the table. 'Would you please state your full name and date of birth.' When the man didn't respond, she patiently tried again in the same quiet, unhurried tone. 'Will you please state your full name and date of birth.'

'Robert Oswalde. The t'irteenth of August, nineteen sixty-one.'

From his appearance you might have expected an educated voice, but it was a strong Jamaican accent, the t's and d's heavily emphasised.

'You are entitled to speak to a solicitor at any time,'

Tennison informed him, 'and this legal advice is free.'

Oswalde stared back, black man to white woman, the insolence in his dark eyes almost like a blatant sexual challenge.

There was a builder's skip half-filled with rubbish outside number 15, Honeyford Road, so the police car was parked at an angle, its rear end sticking out into the street. Already, within minutes of its arrival, a small crowd was gathering in the November late-afternoon gloom, peering out from under umbrellas as the drizzle thickened, swirling in the sodium-yellow streetlights. The neighbourhood was mainly West Indian, with a sprinkling of Asians, and rumour spread much faster here than it might have done in a white middle-class area. And ever since the Derrick Cameron case a few years ago, any police activity aroused curiosity and suspicion in equal measure; the presence of white cops didn't mean protection for the local community, it invariably spelled trouble.

The front door of number 15 was wide open, a uniformed policeman on the top step, his colleague in the hallway talking to the builder. Or trying to listen to him, which was difficult, what with Mr Viswandha, the house's owner, gabbling away ten-to-the-dozen in Urdu on the phone. His wife and their two children stood shivering and bewildered in the passage, the draught from the front door whipping through the house.

'One of my men found it.' The builder jerked a grimy thumb towards the rear. 'We're laying new drains. Seems to be wrapped in polythene . . .'

The crowd at the garden gate was growing by the minute. Several young black kids had climbed on the wall, trying to peer through the open door. One had propped his mountain bike against the gatepost and was jostling for position. The murmur and rumble of voices went on under the pattering of rain on the umbrellas and plastic hoods as the drizzle turned into a steady downpour. Then a real buzz went up. Two cars had pulled up, CID officers piling out, shouldering their way through the crowd. Rumour and speculation were rife now: the heavy mob didn't show unless a serious crime had been committed, and by the look of it this was shaping up to be the most serious of all.

As the officers came through, the young boy with the mountain bike piped up, 'Have the Pakis murdered someone?'

Detective Inspector Frank Burkin didn't break his stride. 'Shut up and move that bike!'

The kid's older brother, wearing a beaded cap with dreadlocks trailing down, wasn't too thrilled with Burkin's attitude. 'What makes you think you can talk to him like that?' he burst out angrily. 'We live here, man, not you . . . what is it with you?'

Impatiently, DI Tony Muddyman pushed past, leaving Burkin to argue with the youth. Diplomacy never was top priority on Frank's list, but why the hell did he have to alienate the local community the minute he planted his size elevens in Honeyford Road? Getting people's backs up was no way to start.

Mr Viswandha had finished on the phone and met Muddyman as he came through the front door. Eyes glittering, head jerking back and forth, the Indian watched the file of men troop past him down the passage.

'Are you in charge?'

'For the time being, sir,' Muddyman nodded.

'Then please . . .' Mr Viswandha's brown plump

hands paddled the air nervously. 'Just take it away.'

'We will, sir, as soon as possible —'

'Not as soon as possible.' He glanced at his wife hugging the two children to her, a boy of seven and a girl of five. 'Now. I pay my poll tax.'

'I'm afraid it's a suspicious death, sir, and as such, all this has to be done properly.' Muddyman beckoned DC Jones forward. 'Now, will you go with this officer and answer his questions, please.'

With a nod to Mrs Viswandha, Muddyman carried on; he always tried to be polite, especially with the ethnics, but why was it that he always felt he had to compensate for Burkin's crass, insensitive behaviour? As if the bloody job wasn't hard enough.

'So she consented to sex with you?'

Tennison kept her voice deliberately flat, unemotional. She wanted to feed him just enough rope to hang himself with.

Oswalde gave a lazy grin. 'What ya gwan an with? She was beggin' for it, man.'

'If she was a willing partner, why did you use violence?' Casually the Chief Inspector fed him a bit more rope. 'Why did you hit her?'

'You know these t'ings,' said Oswalde with a shrug, 'how them happen . . .'

'No, I don't know.'

'Some of them white t'ing like it rough.' Again the overt sexual insult in his eyes, teasing, taunting. Watching him, Tennison decided to draw the noose tighter. She glanced down at the sheet of paper in front of her.

'But the doctor reports "severe gripping contusions to

the upper arms".' She glanced up. 'Bruises where you'd held her down.'

Oswalde looked blank. Turning, he frowned at DCI Thorndike who was sitting to one side, arms folded across his double-breasted lapels, his narrow pale face and watery eyes just beyond the arc of lamplight. Thorndike dropped his eyes, as though embarrassed by the explicit nature of the interrogation. Unlike Tennison, who was not in the least put out. It seemed as if nothing could shock her, not even if Oswalde had stripped off and done a handstand on the table.

'All right, Robert, let me ask you this.' Tennison leaned forward, the curtain of honey-blonde hair slanting across her forehead. 'How did you know that this girl liked it "rough"?'

'I knew. The way she looked.'

'Well – how did she look?' Tennison pressed him.

'She had blonde hair.' Oswalde stared straight back. 'She was wearin' a red blouse . . .'

Tennison had on a red blouse.

'An' she had a tight, tight black skirt . . . like for you.'

'I see. So she didn't actually say anything to encourage you?'

Tennison let the silence hang for a moment, and then her voice had a harder edge to it. 'But then that's not surprising since you tore her tights off and rammed them down her throat.'

Oswalde stiffened. 'That's just her word against mine.' There was a faint sheen of perspiration on the smooth wide forehead.

'No, it's the doctor's report, the forensic evidence, and her word against yours,' Tennison corrected him. She pulled the rope a notch tighter. 'How many other

5

women have you attacked? How long before you kill someone, Robert?'

Oswalde's handsome face had gone sullen. Perhaps he could feel the chafing noose tightening, tightening around his neck.

By the time Superintendent Mike Kernan arrived at Honeyford Road, the Area Major Incident Team, known as AMIT, based at Southampton Row, was already in action. Kernan had been looking forward to a quiet evening at home, feet up, glass of Famous Grouse, something undemanding on the box. In fact, already hightailing it down the M4 in his BMW when the call had come through, he had debated whether to respond or let the AMIT boys get on with it. But he hadn't debated long; first reports from the Scene of Crime suggested that this was more than just a run-of-the-mill case of domestic violence, the cause of most murders. And with his interview coming up, the Super didn't want to be conspicuous by his absence in what might turn out to be a major homicide investigation on his patch. So he turned around at the next intersection and headed back, grimly reconciled to his duty, the telly and the Scotch already a fading mirage.

'Heh – policeman! Kernan!'

A small pudgy West Indian woman in a shapeless dark coat tried to grab his sleeve as he pushed his burly frame through the crowd on the slick-wet pavement. Kernan was annoyed – not so much with the woman, who he recognised as Nola Cameron – but that the area hadn't been cleared and cordoned off. Where were the uniformed lads? This could reach the level of public disorder if it wasn't nipped in the bud.

'What's happenin'? Heh, policeman, listen to me! If that's my Simone in there . . .'

Kernan appealed to her. 'Nola, you can see I've just arrived. Give me a chance to find out what's happening. We won't be issuing any statements tonight. Now go home.' He looked round, raising his voice. 'You should all just go home.'

'You never tried to find my daughter,' Nola accused him passionately, bitterly. 'If it's her in that garden . . .'

Halfway up the path, Kernan swung his head round, really angry now. 'You people *should go home*!' He went on, gritting his teeth as Nola's wailing voice pursued him. 'If that's my Simone . . . you won't be able to stop us getting to her . . .'

Kernan made a beeline for Muddyman, who seemed to be directing operations from the kitchen.

'Get the area cordoned off properly,' he snapped. 'If it turns out to be Simone Cameron we could have a real problem.'

Notepad in hand, looming over her from his muscular six-foot-three, DI Burkin was interviewing Mrs Viswandha, the two kids clutching their mother and peering out with large brown eyes, more curious than apprehensive. Burkin was having problems. She had to spell 'Viswandha' for him, and when he asked for her first name, she said 'Sakuntala.' Burkin sighed.

DC Jones and Mr Viswandha were just inside the front room, off the central passage. The constable's glasses had misted up, and he was peering over the top of them, looking like an eager boy scientist, with his fresh-faced looks and wavy brown hair.

'And the slabs were already in place when you bought the house?'

'Of course.'

'You've done no work yourself in the garden? Or had any work done?'

'I'm telling you, no,' said Mr Viswandha through tight lips, his patience wearing thin.

Superintendent Kernan took Muddyman by the arm, leading him to the back door which overlooked the garden. 'Are the Forensic boys here?' he asked, satisfied that inquiries with the family were proceeding smoothly, all the angles covered.

'Waiting for you, Guv.' Tony Muddyman opened the door. Kernan went first down the steps, the entire garden area as brightly lit as a film set, the steady downpour like a boiling mist under the arc lamps.

The back garden had been completely paved over when the Viswandhas moved in. Then there was trouble with the drains. A local building firm had been brought in to lay new soil pipes, to connect with the main sewage system which ran along the rear alleyway. Paving slabs had been lifted and digging commenced to remove the old pipework. About two feet down, the workmen had uncovered something far more grisly than broken soil pipes. Their spades had slashed through some polythene sheeting, exposing the pale gleam of bones.

Kernan, raincoat collar turned up, stood at the edge of the makeshift structure of plastic sheeting the Forensic people had erected to keep out the rain. There were three or four people down in the shallow trench, so it was difficult to make anything out. Water had seeped down anyway, and the bottom and sides had congealed into sticky, clinging mud. Peter Gold, Forensic's bright new boy, was there, Kernan saw, clad in white overalls and green wellington boots, down on his knees in the mire. Above him, crouched down on the paving slabs, Richards, the police photographer, was trying for the best position to get a clear shot.

Further along the trench, buttoned up to the neck in his waterproofs, the portly, balding figure of Oscar Bream, Chief Pathologist, was leaning forward, gloved hands gripping his knees. Bream's heavily-lidded eyes, as ever, revealed nothing. He had only one expression – inscrutable. Perhaps he really felt nothing, felt no real emotion, just another job of work; or perhaps the years of looking into the pit of horrors of what human beings were capable of doing to their fellow creatures had forced him to adopt this dead-eyed mask as a form of protective camouflage.

Gold was using a small trowel and paintbrush to clear away the mud. 'Over here, sir . . . see?'

'Right,' Bream grunted, bending lower. 'Let's take a dekko.'

Protruding from the wall of the trench, about eighteen inches from the surface, part of a rib-cage and pelvis gleamed under the arc lamps. Bream stepped back and gestured to Richards. The camera flashed three times. Bream bent forward, brushing away a smear of mud with his gloved hand. The remains of a human skull stared up, black sockets for eyes, with an expression almost as inscrutable as Oscar Bream's.

*

'So tell me what happened,' Tennison said, 'when you sodomised her.'

Oswalde was out of his chair. She had him on

9

the run now; she knew it, and he was catching on fast.

'I know what's gwan on . . .' He looked down on Tennison, and then his eyes flicked across to Thorndike, who was trying not to meet his gaze. Oswalde was nodding, dredging up a faint smile. '. . . with little pinktoes here.' His accent thickened. 'Look 'pon her nuh,' he sneered derisively, inviting the other male in the room to join forces against this sly female conspiracy.

'Sit down please, Robert,' Tennison said calmly.

'She love it.' Oswalde clicked his fingers. 'Cock-teaser, ennit? What she say I did to that bitch is just turnin' her on – '

'Sit down please, Robert,' Tennison repeated, and under the force of her level stare he slowly sank back into the chair. 'The thought of a woman being humiliated doesn't turn me on, Robert. Someone being frightened half to death. But that turns you on, doesn't it?'

Oswalde twitched his broad shoulders in a shrug.

'It must do. Why else would you need to force yourself on someone? You're a very attractive man. How tall are you?'

'Six foot four.'

Tennison raised one eyebrow. 'Really? I'm sure a lot of women do fall for you. But not this one.'

'Some women say "no" when they mean "yes".'

Tennison's head snapped up, eyes narrowed. 'So she said "no" to you?'

'I said "some" women.'

'But she said "no" to you?'

'I got nothin' to say . . .'

'She said "no" and that's not begging for it. That's not consent.'

10

'Bullshit.' Oswalde licked his lips. Getting rattled, he turned again to Thorndike, complaining, 'She puttin' words into my mouth.'

'She said no – that's rape.' Tennison pointed a finger. 'Okay, let me ask you this . . .'

'Good,' Thorndike interrupted, standing up. He cleared his throat, running his finger nervously inside his shirt collar. 'Yes, well, that seems a convenient place to stop.'

'Oh no – Mr Thorndike,' Tennison protested, 'I haven't finished yet.'

DCI Thorndike slid back his cuff to reveal his thin freckled wrist and tapped his watch. 'Unfortunately we're going to have to since it's well past six.' And with that he opened the door and went out.

Tennison brushed a hand through her hair and rolled her eyes towards the ceiling. 'Unbelievable,' she said through gritted teeth. 'Wanker.'

Oswalde stared at her, laughter bubbling in his chest. He smothered it with a cough. Tennison just shook her head.

As DCI Thorndike emerged through the door of the pre-fabricated 'Interview Room', built into one corner of the conference hall, he wondered what the grins and smirks were all about. Over ninety grins and smirks, lurking on the faces of the police officers seated at rows of tables who had been watching the interrogation on the banks of screens. They'd caught Jane Tennison's final words and seen her expression, but he hadn't, so he was never to know.

With his jerky, stiff-legged walk, Thorndike strode to the front of the hall and faced the assembly. This was the second session of a three-day seminar on interviewing techniques: lectures and study groups interspersed with simulated interview situations conducted by senior officers. The hall quietened as Thorndike raised his hand.

'Excellent . . . though I would just sound one word of warning. Some of DCI Tennison's more unconventional questions might get a less experienced officer into difficulties. Remember,' he went on pedantically, 'under PACE no attempt may be made to bully or threaten a suspect.' This was a reference to the rules and regulations for dealing with detainees as laid down by the Police and Criminal Evidence Act. 'Finally, well done to Detective Sergeant Oswalde for playing his part so convincingly.'

There were a few more snide grins at that. Convincing all right, because it seemed like he was damn well enjoying it, a lowly DS coming on strong to a female DCI – one of only four such senior officers in the country. And although Tennison had a reputation as a ball-breaker, there was hardly a man in the room who didn't fancy her.

She joined Thorndike at the front, shrugging into her tailored dark jacket. 'And finally, *finally*. Tomorrow's first session will be on interviewing the victims of rape. I'll see you all at ten o'clock.'

As the meeting broke up to the shuffling of papers and the scraping of chairs, Thorndike gave her a patronising pat on the shoulder, and she returned a brief, tight smile. God, she thought, he's like some prissy old maiden aunt. It was all theory with him, book-learning. If he encountered a real-life villain he'd have been totally clueless; probably have to skim through the PACE manual to find the right questions and in which order to ask them. He wasn't attached to the regular force, but a member of MS15, the Metropolitan body which investigated complaints by

12

the public on matters of police procedure and suspected rule-bending – in other words, digging the dirt on his fellow officers.

Going up to her room in the crowded lift, Tennison glanced behind her to DS Oswalde. 'You're too good at that, Detective Sergeant.'

'Thank you, ma'am.'

'Are you going for a drink later on?'

'Maybe. But I might just have an early night.'

The bell pinged for the second floor and the doors slid open.

'Oh well, might see you,' Tennison said, going out. 'Goodnight.'

'Quick as you can,' Bream urged Richards, standing aside as the photographer took another series of shots. When he was done, the pathologist had another look at the crumbling trench wall. 'I'm going to need all the bones if I'm to reassemble the bugger,' he told Gold. 'So make sure you collect all the earth from around the corpse as well.'

Gold was relishing this. It was his first really juicy forensic investigation, and working with Professor Oscar Bream was a bonus. He instructed his helpers with enthusiasm: 'We'll put the lot in these boxes and take it to the labs for sifting. We're after small bones, cloth fragments, jewellery, coins . . . well, absolutely anything, really.'

'The skull's been badly smashed, so collect those pieces with care,' Bream cautioned the two assistants.

Standing just inside the plastic canopy, Kernan said gloomily, 'Let's hope the rain gets people back inside.'

Gold was carefully scooping out dollops of mud and putting them in plastic boxes, his assistants sealing the lids and marking each one with a Chinagraph pencil to indicate the sequence in which the various fragments were excavated. Gradually, piece by painstaking piece, the corpse was disinterred, the larger bones being bagged and tagged in black plastic binliners.

'Looks like it is a female, Oscar . . .'

'Oh yes, and what makes you say that, Mr Gold?'

The young scientist looked up, positively beaming. 'It's wearing a bra.'

Kernan rubbed his chin and groaned. 'Oh God.'

'Don't worry, Mike,' said Bream, deadpan as usual. 'It could still turn out to be Danny La Rue.'

'Yeah, and if it is, Nola Cameron will claim him for a daughter.' Kernan had seen enough. He turned to Muddyman, whose brown curly hair was plastered down, his bald spot plainly visible. 'Tony, take over until Tennison gets here.'

Muddyman blinked at him. 'She's on that course, isn't she, Guv?'

'Not any more she's not,' Kernan said, trudging back over the muddy paving stones and mounting the steps.

Muddyman huddled deeper into his raincoat. 'Oh great . . .'

*

The kiss was long and deep, making her senses swirl. He had gorgeous skin, smooth enough for a woman's, but with the hard, sensual feel of solid muscle rippling underneath. Jane drew back, took a breath, and gazed into Bob Oswalde's dark brown eyes. He smiled as her fingers slid from his chest and probed under the towelled bathrobe to his shoulder.

14

'Already?' he teased.

'Mmmm . . .' Wrapped in his arms, she gave him a wicked little grin.

They had dined here, in her room, drunk the bottle of Chateauneuf-du-pape dry, and then made love. Secretly, she was amazed at how naturally it had come about, without, it seemed, any devious planning or premeditation on either part. She wasn't a promiscuous woman, had only had one brief fling since she broke up with Peter, with whom she'd lived for less than six months. The demands and pressures of her job had been the cause of that; taking charge of the Marlow case, her first murder investigation, had consumed every waking moment – and most sleeping ones too. Peter had been understanding, up to a point, though he was going through a rough patch himself, trying to get his building firm up and running, and the pair of them found themselves between a rock and a hard place. Something had to give, and something had. The relationship.

While her job still had priority, the attraction, the sexual chemistry, between her and Bob Oswalde had been just too great to resist. And she'd thought, why the hell not? All work and no play makes Jane a dull girl. She wasn't feeling dull and jaded now; her body felt vibrant and alive, and the night was still young.

Taking up his teasing mood, she said archly, 'Now what was it you were saying about white women liking it rough?'

The instant the words came out, she knew that it was the wrong thing to say. Bob Oswalde reared back a little, his arms slackening, and she cursed her own clumsiness.

'Hey, that wasn't me,' he protested, hurt. 'I don't think like that.'

'I know – I'm sorry.' She kissed his chest and then the side of his neck, snuggling up to him, cosy and warm in the fluffy white bathrobe, feeling the heat of his body. She had an idea. 'Know what I'd like to do now?'

'No, what?' Bob Oswalde said through a crooked half-grin.

'Let's drink the entire contents of the mini-bar.'

'Why?'

'Oh I don't know – I just feel like it.' Jane suddenly sat up and grinned at him. Her short, ruffled blonde hair and impish grin made her appear like a mischievous tomboy, a startling transformation from her conventional role as the cool, at times obsessive, professional policewoman with a daunting reputation.

Bob Oswalde swung his long legs around to sit on the edge of the bed. 'Okay, what would you like first?'

Jane clapped her hands. 'Champagne!'

'Right.'

As he went over to the mini-bar she flopped full-length on the bed, stretching out her arms luxuriously. She hadn't felt so content and totally relaxed in a long time. She hadn't been looking forward to this three-day conference at all, confined to airless, smoke-filled rooms and conference halls (especially as she was trying to give up the noxious weed), having her brains picked by male colleagues who, deep down, probably resented being lectured to by a woman. The Super had suggested she 'volunteer', which was his unsubtle way of giving a direct order by stealth. Well, the laugh was on him. She was enjoying herself, and at the expense of the ratepayer to boot.

The phone rang, a soft trilling tone. Bob Oswalde was stripping the foil from a half-bottle of champagne, and

Jane said quickly before she answered it, 'That's Dame Sybil. Don't make a sound.'

But it was Kernan, and Jane sat up straighter, holding her robe close to her neck, as if it made any difference.

'Oh, hello, Guv. About two hours ... why?' She listened, her eyes serious, nodding. 'Yeah, right ... okay. Oh yeah, absolutely. Okay, see you. 'Bye.'

She hung up, staring straight ahead at the built-in closet.

'What's wrong?'

'That was my Guv. He wants me back.'

'Oh.' The champagne dangled in his hand.

'Now.'

'What?'

'Yeah.' Jane slid off the bed, unfastening her bathrobe as she hopped round to open the closet door. 'He wants me to head a murder inquiry. I'll have to tell Thorndike.' She brushed her fingers through her hair. 'Damn, and it's my lecture tomorrow too ...'

'Look, sod Thorndike.' Oswalde glanced down at the bottle he was holding, then placed it on top of the mini-bar.

Burrowing in the closet, Jane said over her shoulder, 'I'm sorry, Bob, there's nothing I can do about it.'

'I know that.' The words were neutral enough, though he was looking at her from under his eyebrows. Jane paused in laying out her blouse and suit on the bed. She glanced up.

'So what's your problem then?'

'What about us?'

'What about us?' she asked, frowning slightly.

'Oh I see.'

Jane spread her hands. 'Bob, I'm not saying I don't want to see you again. Okay?'

17

'Aren't you?'

She watched him in silence as he whipped off his bathrobe and rapidly dressed, eyes downcast, handsome face empty of expression.

Jane sighed. 'C'mon, this is hard enough as it is . . .'

'Look, I hear you, okay?' He sat with his back to her, pulling on his socks and shoes. He stated flatly, 'The Detective Chief Inspector has given her orders.'

'What did you expect?' His attitude was annoying her, and she clenched her fists. 'You know that's really unfair. It's not as though the love of your life is walking out on you.'

Bob Oswalde snatched his sweater from the back of a chair and dragged it on over his T-shirt. His dark eyes flashed at her. 'I just don't like being treated like some black stud.'

Hands on hips, Jane said with faint disbelief, 'Is that what you think's been going on here?'

'Yes I do.'

'Well, that's in your head.'

'Is it?'

She could do without this. It was him who was hung up on racial stereotyping, not her. He was an attractive man, period, and she'd enjoyed tremendously having sex with him, but if he had difficulty accepting it simply for what it was, tough luck. His problem, not hers.

Jane said, 'I think you'd better go.'

'Don't worry,' Oswalde said, already on the move, 'I'm going.'

'I hope I can rely on you to be discreet.'

With his hand on the doorknob, Oswalde slowly turned his head and gave her a long, hard stare over his shoulder.

18

'You really are something else, aren't you?' he muttered softly, and with a little shake of the head went out.

Returning to his room after dinner, DCI David Thorndike was fumbling for his key when he heard a door slam, followed by the rapid thump of footsteps. Craning backwards, he spied DS Oswalde, head down, marching along the corridor towards the lift. He'd come out of the room two doors away from his, Thorndike noted. Well, well, well. Tennison . . . fraternising with the troops no less.

He turned the key in the lock and slipped into his room as Oswalde, muttering to himself, came up to the lift. Standing with his ear to the crack in the door, Thorndike heard Oswalde's low, angry 'Bitch!' as he punched the button.

Pursuing his lips prudishly, DCI Thorndike eased the door shut.

2

Within ten minutes Tennison was fully dressed, had applied a dab of make-up, run a brush through her hair, packed her case and was ready to go. She gave herself a final once-over in the dressing-table mirror and set off to beard Thorndike in his lair. He was the type, she knew very well, who never made life easy, always had to nit-pick. But she steeled herself to deal with him as quickly and calmly as possible and get the hell out. She had a job to do.

After she'd broken the news he paced up and down his room, rubbing the little cluster of blue veins at his temple, shaking his head distractedly. 'But I don't know anything about rape victims,' he complained, realising he would have to give the lecture at ten the next morning.

'Then it's time you did. It's attitudes like that that account for the fact that only eight per cent of rapes are ever reported.' Tennison took a sheaf of papers from her briefcase and held them out. 'I'll leave you my notes.'

'Well, that would be a help, but ...' Thorndike dropped the papers on a table, sighing. 'It's still bloody annoying.'

'What can I do, David?' She was fed up to the back teeth with his prissy whining, but she controlled her temper.

He glanced at her with a pained expression. 'Hasn't Mike Kernan got other DCIs available?'

'Yes, but he wants me to head it.'

'Why?'

'Maybe he thinks I'm a good detective,' Tennison said tightly.

Thorndike nagged on. 'But why this specific investigation?'

'The body's been found in Honeyford Road, where the Cameron family still live. Added to which, it looks like it could be Simone Cameron.'

'Politically sensitive, certainly,' Thorndike agreed. He gave her a sideways look. 'A word of advice. Charges may be brought against the officers involved in the Derrick Cameron case if it goes to the Court of Appeal . . .'

'Quite right too if that boy was fitted up.' She frowned at him. 'What are you getting at?'

'I'd be careful if I were you – this may not turn out to be such a prize for you.' And then turning away, not meeting her eye, he added, 'Obviously you're a liberated and enlightened woman.'

'Thank you, David,' said Tennison dryly. But she still didn't have a clue what, in his pussy-footing way, he was driving at. Of course it wasn't straightforward police work to him, it was bloody politics, dropping poison into people's ears, watching your back all the time in case there was a knife sticking in it. Tennison hadn't the time or patience for all that bullshit; life was too short.

Thorndike saw her to the door. 'Don't be too trusting of our Afro-Caribbean friends.'

'That's your advice, is it?' She tucked the briefcase under her arm, giving him a quick, formal smile. 'Good luck tomorrow.'

Thorndike waited by the open door, his weak watery eyes fixed on her as she entered the lift. 'Oh, and drive carefully if you've been drinking,' was his final word of warning.

Going down in the lift, Tennison cupped her hand to her mouth, trying to smell her own breath. Didn't seem that bad, and besides, she'd only had two glasses of red wine. Old Mother Thorndike must have a keen sense of smell if he'd got a whiff of alcohol fumes from that.

Honeyford Road was quiet again. The crowd had dispersed, returned to their homes, the stretch of pavement outside number 15 cordoned off with striped tape that had POLICE – NO ENTRY stamped on it in red letters. The rain had eased off, but there was a damp, chill breeze blowing as Tennison drove her Orion along the street, searching for a place to park. She slowed down, bending sideways to peer through the misted-up passenger window at a lone figure still standing vigil next to the flapping tape. Tennison recognised the short, dumpy woman in the woven cap, the long shapeless coat reaching almost to the ground; she pressed the button to lower the window.

'Nola – go home!'

Nola Cameron shook her head defiantly. 'Not if that's my Simone. I won't lose her a second time!' And turned back to stare at the house, chin set stubbornly, feet planted on the wet pavement.

Gold was enjoying himself. He didn't seem to notice, or to mind, that he had been kneeling at the bottom of a cold slimy trench since early evening, and it was now past ten-thirty. With the arrival of DCI Tennison, the officer appointed to take charge of the case, he had a new and receptive listener on whom to vent his expertise.

Crouched down on her haunches on the paving stones, muffled inside the hood of her weatherproofs, Tennison watched intently as the work of excavation went on; the skull and most of the upper part of the skeleton had been removed, and the team was now concentrating on the lower torso. For the moment she was content to listen to Gold, giving his impromptu lecture.

'. . . natural plant fibre such as cotton tends to disintegrate, form part of the diet of the early inhabitants of the corpse. But wool, like hair – they're made of the same stuff – can be remarkably resilient. Now, I've got some bits of pullover and Professor Bream has quite a lot of hair –'

'If only,' Bream said lugubriously, cleaning his spectacles with the end of his tie. It was meant to be a joke, but everyone was too tired and cold and pissed off to even raise a smile.

'With beads in it,' Gold continued, so intent that the pathologist's remark hadn't even registered with him.

'Did the Cameron girl wear her hair like this?' Tennison's question was addressed to the assembly at large.

'I'm told she did sometimes,' DI Muddyman put in.

Arms clasped around her knees, Tennison rubbed her gloved palms together, already feeling the cold night air creeping into her fingers and toes. 'How old do you think she is, Oscar?'

'She hadn't quite finished growing, so still in her teens, I'd say.'

'Well, how long do you think it would take for a corpse to get like this?'

'That I can't tell.' There was the suggestion of a weary sigh in Bream's voice. Always the same, the murder squad, expecting answers up front to impossible questions. They'd only ever be happy if he could look at the decaying remains of a corpse and give them its name, address and national insurance number.

Tennison was a terrier, not so easily put off. 'Come on, Oscar. Minimum time?'

'Two years? Don't quote me on that.'

'So it could be Simone . . .'

'You see, you're doing it already!'

Tennison eased herself up, stamping her feet to get the circulation going. She could have cheerfully murdered for a fag, but this was the real testing time, and she was determined to kick the habit. It had scared her badly when her consumption climbed to sixty a day, the dread spectre of the big C giving her the cold sweats. Now or never, shit or bust. Quelling the desire, she glanced round to her officers, Muddyman, Lillie and Jones, their tall figures silhouetted in the glare of the arc lamps.

'When were these garden slabs laid?'

'Before the Viswandhas came here,' Jones told her.

'Which was?'

'About eighteen months ago.'

'Do we know who they bought the house from?'

'All Mr Viswandha could tell me was the name of a property developer,' Jones said.

'So have these slabs been disturbed since then?'

DC Lillie shook his head. 'Not according to the workmen.'

Tennison gazed down into the shallow trench, trying to get the chronology straight in her own mind. 'So she must have been put there before the slabs were laid, which means our prime suspect has to be whoever was living here when she was buried. We need a definite date of death, Oscar.'

Bream gave her his fishy-eyed stare and called out to Lillie, 'Is there any of that soup left?'

'Oh – if there is,' Tennison said, 'can you get some to Nola Cameron, if she's still out there?' She looked at her watch. 'The rest of you might as well go home and get some sleep. I'll aim to brief the team at ten in the morning.'

'Right, Guv,' said Muddyman, not bothering to hide his heartfelt relief. Knowing Tennison, her obsessive tenacity with any case she took on, he'd been afraid she'd keep them there till the wee small hours, standing around watching Bream & Co digging up the rest of Simone Cameron – if that's who it was. The woman didn't seem to have a home to go to; any private life at all, come to that.

The officers dispersed, leaving through the back garden gate. Tennison stayed. She was glad she did, because a few moments later Gold made an important discovery. He beckoned the photographer over to take several close-up shots of the corpse's wrists, behind its back, beneath the pelvis.

Bream craned forward, speaking softly into a small pocket recorder. 'Hands tied together at the back with . . .'

Gingerly, Gold pulled something out and held it up.

'. . . a leather belt,' Bream intoned.

A movement caught Tennison's eye and she turned to see the little Viswandha boy standing on the top step, all agog.

'For God's sake . . . did no one think to get the

family moved?' She went up the steps, ushering him ahead of her. 'It'll be gone soon.'

He wasn't a bit frightened, just filled with curiosity. 'Is it a real person?'

'Let's get you inside, you'll catch cold. You should be in bed.'

'It should have been buried deeper, shouldn't it?' he said with a child's irrefutable logic. 'Then it wouldn't have come back.'

Mrs Viswandha was on her way downstairs, clearly distraught after trying to comfort her daughter. She clutched the boy to her, scolding and hugging him at the same time.

'Don't you have family or friends you could go to stay with?' Tennison asked sympathetically.

'My husband won't leave here ...' She was almost in tears.

'Do you want me to talk to him?'

The woman found a wan smile, nodding gratefully. 'Thank you.'

Tennison had hoped that the Forensic boys might have finished before daybreak, folded their tents and stolen silently away under cover of darkness. But it was not to be. In the grey light of dawn, with grey, haggard faces to match, they trudged along the alleyway carrying a bodybag and several large plastic containers. As they came between the tall Victorian houses into Honeyford Road where the dark blue police van was parked, rear doors open, the pathetic figure of Nola Cameron, shivering, eyes red-rimmed, let out a shrill cry and went stumbling towards them.

'Simone! Simone!'

Standing by her car, Tennison watched the uniformed policeman on duty at the front gate step forward, barring her way. The pitiful cries rang out in the quiet street – 'Simone, *Simone*!' – as the bodybag was hoisted into the van and the doors slammed shut.

Tennison drove away, averting her eyes from the rearview mirror, from the terrible pain of the grieving mother. If it really was Simone Cameron in that bodybag, she knew one thing for sure. All hell was about to break loose.

There wasn't time to return to the flat. She drove straight to Southampton Row, knowing that Mike Kernan would be hopping about like a scalded cat on broken glass. The canteen didn't open till eight-thirty. She had to make do with a styrofoam cup of disgusting machine coffee to wash down three paracetamol, in the hope that she could keep the dull, throbbing headache at bay for a few hours at least. Going without sleep was part of the job, but she was no spring chicken any more, couldn't handle it as she used to.

Kernan was at his desk, enveloped in a cloud of blue smoke, which wouldn't do his ulcer much good, Tennison thought. With his heavy-lidded eyes and pouchy cheeks, he put her in mind of a grumpy chipmunk with a hangover. He launched right in, telling her about the meeting, that same evening, which couldn't have come at a worse time. 'It was all arranged weeks ago. I'm going with the Community Liaison Officer, bloke named Patterson. I can't back out now, but it's going to be a nightmare. I want you to be there. Starts at eight.'

Kernan sucked in a lungful, pushed his packet of Embassy her way.

'No thanks.' Tennison shook her head firmly. 'I'm trying to give up.'

'Christ,' Kernan muttered, in a state of shock. 'Since when?'

'Five days, six hours and . . .' Tennison gazed at the ceiling '. . . 'bout fifteen minutes.'

Kernan was so impressed he stubbed out his cigarette and immediately lit another. 'The meeting's supposed to be to discuss community policing, but given what's happening just now we're sure to be dragged face-down through the shit about the Cameron family.' His heavy brows came together. 'And Phelps is coming down tonight, and he's bound to have the media in tow. That man can smell a vote-winner from fifty miles.'

'Let's face it, Guv — Nola may be jumping to conclusions but we can't claim to have done well by her family, can we? Not if it turns out that Derrick was fitted up.'

'Yeah, well . . .' Kernan was uncomfortable with the subject. 'Let's concentrate on the immediate problem. Is it the Cameron girl or not?'

'I don't know. And I won't find anything out from Oscar Bream till tomorrow at the earliest.'

The phone rang and Kernan snatched it up. His secretary informed him that Commander Trayner was on the line. 'Right, I'll hold.' He looked at Tennison through the wreaths of tobacco smoke. 'If we knew one way or another before tonight's meeting, our lives would be a whole lot easier.'

Tennison nodded. 'I'll see if the Forensic boys can shed some light. And I want the rest of the garden dug up in case there are other bodies . . .'

'Jesus, what do you want?' Kernan growled, aghast.

'Another Nilsen?' He stiffened slightly as the Commander came on. 'Sir?' He listened, nodding, his drooping eyes fixed on the desk blotter.

'That's right. I thought she was the very best person for the job. It requires tact and . . . well, I'm sure she'll be able to cope.'

Tennison pursed her mouth, giving a little rueful half-smile. The anti-women bias in the Force extended all the way from the ranks right to the upper echelons. Having a female DCI heading a murder inquiry still went against the grain, even though the official line was that there was no sexual discrimination; everyone rose by merit, experience, hard work. Which was a load of old cock.

'I will do. Bye, sir.' Thoughtfully, Kernan hung up. He took a long drag, letting the smoke plume from his nostrils, and stared across the desk with cloudy eyes. 'Now how in hell does the Commander know what happened on your course already?'

Tennison went very still. 'What do you mean?'

'That I brought you back to lead this inquiry?'

She breathed out. For a nasty moment there she had a dreadful, sinking sensation that her dalliance in the hotel room had spread like wildfire, sniggers and dirty jokes in the locker rooms . . . *Hey, heard the latest – that bitch Tennison likes her men big, rough and black!*

'I'll give you one guess,' she told Kernan. 'And it involves some funny handshakes.'

'Thorndike? The same Lodge?'

'I'd put money on it,' Tennison said, getting up, smoothing her skirt.

'Then you'd better make sure you vindicate my decision,' Kernan said, and he wasn't joking.

'I'll do my best, sir,' she said crisply, and went.

The cold water felt good. Leaning over the washbasin in the locker room, Tennison splashed a couple more palmfuls into her face, then dried herself and made a critical inspection in the mirror. Oh God. The Creature from the Black Lagoon. It seemed a world away now, though it was less than twelve hours since she'd been lying in Bob Oswalde's arms in the hotel room, drinking Chateauneuf-du-pape.

Two WPCs came in, chattering away, though Tennison seemed oblivious, intent on repairing the ravages of a night without sleep, giving her hair a vigorous brushing and applying fresh make-up. Usually sparing with perfume when on duty, this morning she put an extra dab on her wrists and behind her ears to perk herself up. Then, shrugging into her tailored jacket and straightening her shoulders, she was ready for the fray.

There was a fug of smoke in the Incident Room, the members of the team lounging around drinking coffee, laying bets on the identity of the collection of bones discovered in the back garden of Honeyford Road.

'Fiver says it's Simone . . .'

'You're on!'

'What odds you offering?'

'I'm starting a book.'

'Huh!' said DC Lillie with a scowl. 'Last time I ended up seventy-five quid out of pocket . . .'

Tennison came in, calling out to Muddyman as she strode briskly to the desk in front of the long white notice-board that took up one full wall. 'Tony, we need a name. Where we up to in the *A to Z*?'

'I think it's "N", Guv.'

'Look up the first "N" for us then, Tony.' She stood at the desk, waiting a moment or two for the chatter to die down. When there was complete silence, Tennison began.

'As some of you will be aware, workmen digging in the back garden of number 15, Honeyford Road, have uncovered skeletonised human remains. The arms have been tied behind the back and the body wrapped in polythene, so it's a suspicious death.'

Tennison pointed to the photographs of the corpse, which had been processed overnight and pinned up on the board by DC Jones.

'Those of you who've been down there will know that there's a lot of speculation that it could be the body of a local girl who went missing two years ago – Simone Cameron. Her mother, Nola, who still lives a few doors away from number 15, is completely convinced it's Simone. We'll get the Forensic boys and the Pathologist boys to give us an answer to that as soon as possible.'

Tennison paused, her eyes raking over the assembled officers, who were all, to a man, paying rapt attention.

'In the meantime, we have to treat Nola Cameron's fears seriously. The unfortunate thing is that the Cameron family have been the focus of attention in that area for some years now. The oldest boy, Derrick, was accused of stabbing a white youth to death. He was sent to prison on the basis of that confession, made here in this nick. Now there are doubts about the safety of that conviction.'

Dark glances were exchanged between the men. Tennison raised her voice to cut short the rumbling murmurs.

'A campaign led by Jonathan Phelps – Labour's candidate in the by-election – to have Derrick's case brought before the Court of Appeal is gaining a lot of support from all sorts of people. So . . . there's a lot of anger and bitterness, and resentment against the police. It looks like we can rule out the present owners, so our first priority is to locate all former occupants of number 15. Let's get down there straightaway and see what information we can gather.'

There was a general movement. Climbing to his feet, DI Burkin glanced round, a grin on his handsome, slightly battered face, the result of several bouts in the boxing ring, current holder of the south Thames Metropolitan title. 'Passports at the ready, lads . . .'

'Frank, you know that's out of order,' Tennison snapped, wiping away his grin. 'Have you been listening to anything I've said?'

Silence fell. Tennison's gaze swept round the room, her face stony. 'I don't want the Camerons — and that means aunts, uncles, the lot — interviewed at all. As far as the other residents go, remember this: if we go in there expecting aggro, start leaning on people, we'll get it. So it's easy does it.' She came round the desk, raising an eyebrow and softening her tone to take the sting out of her rebuke. 'You're all graduates of the Rank Charm School, right? I want a list of all former residents of the Honeyford Road area over the last ten years . . .'

Groans and muttered oaths. That kind of follow-up meant days of futile leg-work, endless hours tramping the streets, knocking on doors and getting blank stares and shaken heads. In short, a lot of hard graft for minimal return.

'I've asked DS Haskons to be Office Manager.' Tennison looked towards Muddyman, leafing through a dog-eared copy of the A to Z. 'Tony – a name for this operation.'

'The first "N" is Nadine Street, Guv.'

'Very nice. So it's Operation Nadine then.'

Somebody clicked his fingers and started to sing the old Buddy Holly number *Nadine, Honey, Is That You?* and the others took it up, joining in the chorus.

Already halfway to the door, Tennison rapped out, 'Right, let's go . . . Jonesy!'

While the team got on with the house-to-house, Tennison, with DC Jones trailing in her wake, went down two flights to the Forensic Science labs, situated in an annex at the rear of the station. Two white-coated technicians were scooping mud from the plastic containers, mixing it with water into a thin soup, and sieving it. Any resulting fragments, even the tiniest specks, were placed on sheets of white blotting paper for Gold to examine later.

Gold looked a bit pale and drawn, but his enthusiasm was undimmed, and so was his industry. He'd separated the various items of clothing and artefacts found with the body and lined them up in shallow trays on the bench. He went along, detailing his finds to Tennison, while Jones took notes.

'I'll get all this stuff bagged up for you as soon as possible if you want Mrs Cameron to look at it.' Gold lifted some woven material with a rubber-gloved hand. 'The pullover remains – pretty colour, don't you think?' He moved along. 'Bra, pants, labels, some studs from her Levis, Adidas trainers, and so on. Not very helpful, I'm afraid . . .'

One of his assistants came up, holding a small fragment in stainless steel tweezers. Gold squinted at it. 'Looks like a bit of skull. Get it sent over to Oscar Bream.'

He gestured Tennison forward to another bench. Here, laid out on separate sheets of blotting paper, were a number of smaller, tarnished items. They didn't look much to Tennison, though Gold seemed quite pleased. 'But we have found several coins! The most recent of which is 1986.'

Tennison frowned at him. 'So?'

'Have you got any change in your pocket?'

Jones fished out a handful and Gold plucked out a five-pence piece, which he held up with a conjurer's flourish. 'There. 1991. Which proves that you were walking around above ground until at least that year.'

'Thank God for that,' Jones muttered, pulling a face for Tennison's benefit behind the young scientist's back.

Gold was holding up a scabby piece of coiled leather, covered in green mildew. Evidently his prize specimen, from the way he was beaming. 'Perhaps most promising so far – the belt that secured her hands behind her back. Distinctive buckle.'

Distinctive, Tennison thought, but not all that rare, having seen the design before: a Red Indian chief with full feathered headdress, in profile, cast in silvery metal that was now dulled and pitted.

'Could have belonged to her, I suppose,' Gold conjectured.

Tennison nodded slowly, tugging her earlobe. 'Or the killer,' she said.

As the front door opened, Ken Lillie switched on his best smile, showing his warrant card to the middle-aged black woman in a floral print pinny and fluffy pink slippers.

'Good morning, madam. DC Lillie, local CID. We're investigating a suspicious death in the –'

He jerked his head round, distracted by one hell of a commotion coming from two doors along. He could hear a man's voice, yelling, and then a woman's, screaming blue murder. 'Excuse me . . .' Lillie muttered, retreating fast down the path. He caught sight of Frank Burkin dragging a black teenager through the garden gate into the street. Behind the pair, a woman in a brightly-patterned headscarf – the boy's mother, Lillie judged – was beating her fists at Burkin's broad back, screaming at him to leave the lad alone.

People from neighbouring houses were running into the street, shouting and shaking their fists as Burkin wrestled the black kid into the back of the Ford Sierra. Lillie ran up, waving both hands in an attempt to placate what had already the makings of an ugly mob. As he reached the spot, the Sierra's doors slammed and the car sped off with a squeal of tyres, leaving Lillie to confront a sea of angry black faces and the distraught mother, tears streaming down her cheeks.

Tennison sent DC Jones off to get her a mug of decent coffee instead of the pig-swill from the machine, and returned to the Incident Room to help Haskons collate whatever information was to hand. She was suffering the symptoms of nicotine withdrawal acutely, and desperately trying to concentrate whilst ignoring the craving itch at the back of her throat.

'What have we got on the property developer?' she asked, leaning over Haskons' shoulder.

'Has since gone bankrupt and disappeared off the face of the earth, boss . . .'

Mike Kernan pushed open the swing door and stuck his head in. 'Jane. A word.'

Tennison glanced round. 'I'll be there in a minute.'

'My office,' Kernan barked. 'Now.'

Tennison exchanged a look with Haskons, tugged her jacket straight, and went through the door, catching it on the second swing. Haskons' doom-laden voice floated after her. 'Kernan the Barbarian . . .'

Cigarette in hand, the Super was pacing his office, shoulders hunched, thunderclouds gathering overhead. He said, 'Burkin has just arrested a young black lad for possession.'

Tennison leaned against the door, eyes closed. 'Oh God.'

Kernan jabbed the air. 'He's doing his bloody house-to-house, there's the smell of spliff, and he barges in. Pulls the lad out by the scruff of the neck.'

'I don't believe it . . .'

'So now we've got bricks thrown into the garden of number 15 and a reception full of people bleating on about infringement of civil liberties and police harassment.' He kicked his desk. 'And with this bloody meeting tonight – I just don't believe it!'

'Do you want me to remove Burkin from this inquiry?' asked Tennison quietly. She didn't know what else to suggest.

Kernan shook his head, gave her a sideways glance. 'We can't do that, Jane.' He took a drag. 'I'm up for promotion.'

There was a slight pause as it sank in. 'Promotion?'

'Chief Super.' Kernan cleared his throat. He'd kept this under wraps till now, hadn't intended to tell anyone, least of all DCI Jane Tennison. 'Right now I can't afford to do my dirty washing in public,' he went on, a bit pathetically, she thought. 'My interview will be a nightmare if this keeps up.'

Tennison let a moment pass. The sly bastard wouldn't have breathed a word if this cock-up with Burkin hadn't happened. She stepped forward and said in a quiet, controlled voice, 'I hope you'll be recommending me for your post.'

'Oh do you?' Kernan said darkly, glowering at her from under his brows. 'Well don't take too much for granted.' More finger jabbing, as if he was trying to bore a hole through galvanised steel. 'Now make sure this boy is cautioned and released and tear bloody Burkin up for arse paper!'

Seething and trying not to show it, Tennison marched straight to her office and told her secretary, WPC Havers, to have DI Burkin report to her *pronto*. She wasn't sure who she was most pissed off with – Burkin for antagonising the local community and trying to wreck the murder inquiry before it had even got off the ground, or Mike Kernan and his devious little schemes to get shunted up the ladder without telling her. Bloody typical, and she was fed up with it. As the senior AMIT officer under his command, she was naturally next in line for his position, and what's more she deserved it. She'd paid her dues, eighteen months at the Reading Rape Centre, five years with the Flying Squad, and to top it all, cracking the Marlow serial killer case when the rest of the team had been flapping around like headless chickens. She was damn sure that if Kernan's most senior officer had been male, Kernan would have been grooming him for stardom, bringing him along, even putting in a good word for him with the 'board', the panel of senior Metropolitan officers who decided these matters. But of course she was a stupid weak woman, with half a brain, hysterical with PMT once a month, and what's more a dire threat to the macho image that even today prevailed throughout the police force. God, it made her feel like weeping, but she wouldn't, and didn't.

So she was in fine mood for Burkin, when he appeared, and she faced him standing, even though he was a clear twelve inches taller, his bruiser's mug showing not a trace of doubt or remorse.

'Look, he was blatant, Guv. Almost blowing the smoke in my face, as if to say, go on, nick me.'

'That's not the point. At the moment, what with the Cameron case –'

Burkin rudely interrupted. 'Derrick Cameron was a villain and he deserves to be banged up.'

'Frank . . .' Tennison said, holding on to her temper, but Burkin barged on, as set in his ways as quick-drying concrete.

'So we had to lean on him a little to get a confession – so what?'

Tennison bristled. 'So what? So our reputation goes down the toilet again!'

'What reputation?' Burkin's mouth twisted in a scathing sneer. 'They bloody hate us. Well – I'll tell you something, I ain't so keen on them. As far as I'm concerned, one less on the streets is no loss.'

'You're making a fool of yourself, Frank.'

'Look,' Burkin said stolidly, 'if they don't want to

be part of our country they should go home, sort this problem out.'

Tennison stared up at him, her eyes glacial. 'That's enough, Frank. Just shut it.'

Burkin's mouth tightened. He was near the edge and he knew it. It chafed him raw that he had to stand here, like a snotty-nosed kid in the headmaster's study, taking all this crap from a slag with a dried-up crack. Give him half a chance, he'd soon sort her out, give her what she was short of, wipe that holier-than-fucking-thou expression off her face. Make her into a real woman instead of this Miss Prim Little Bossy Boots act she tried to put on. Underneath she was like all the rest. A good juicy shag from a real man would sort her out.

'If I hear an outburst like that from you again, it'll be a disciplinary matter.'

'Yeah, then perhaps you better take me off the case,' Burkin said, looking straight past her to the opposite wall.

'You won't be off the case, Frank, you'll be off the Force.' Tennison's voice was lethal. 'If you think fitting someone up because they're black is okay, then you shouldn't be Old Bill at all. Simple as that.'

The intercom buzzed. Tennison reached over to press the button, and Maureen Havers announced that Nola Cameron was in reception, waiting to see her. Tennison said she'd be right there, and turned back to Burkin, shaking her head.

'Jesus, this is a murder investigation, Frank. A young girl ends up buried in someone's backyard like the family cat? Her skull smashed to pieces? What difference does it make what colour her skin used to be?' She said with quiet finality, 'I want the boy cautioned and released and then get back to work.'

Without a word, Burkin turned and left the office.

3

Nola Cameron was a pathetic sight, still wearing the woven cap and shapeless coat of the previous night. Tennison escorted her into the interview room, holding her arm. 'This way, Nola, my love . . .'

The clothing and other items were laid out on a table; stained with mud and partially decayed, they were sad mementos of a young life that had been brutally cut short, stopped in its tracks before it had time to flower into womanhood.

Tennison said gently, 'Now, Nola, I want you to look at these things and tell me if you recognise any of them as having belonged to Simone.' She kept her eyes on the woman's face, watching her closely as Nola Cameron fingered the pullover, then touched the other scraps of clothing. Almost at once she was nodding, a haunted expression straining her features.

'Yes.' She swallowed hard. 'These are her things.'

'Nola, please, look carefully, take your time.'

'These are all her things,' Nola Cameron insisted, nodding again, blinking back her tears.

'We found this belt buried with her.' Tennison showed her the large silver buckle in the shape of the Red Indian's head. 'Do you recognise that?'

'Yes, yes,' Nola Cameron said, hardly glancing at it. 'That is her belt. She always wore this belt.'

'I see.' Tennison slipped off her wristwatch and laid it next to the Adidas trainers. 'And what about this watch?'

'That is hers.' Nola Cameron started sobbing, head bowed, rocking back and forth. 'I bought her this watch . . .'

Tennison wrapped her arm around the shaking shoulders. 'Nola, would you like a cup of tea? Do you want to sit down?'

'No thank you.'

Tennison led her to the door. 'The experts will be able to give us a lot more information soon. Your dentist has provided Simone's dental records and we can compare those against those of the girl we found. That will tell us for sure.' She hesitated. 'And so until then – these things are all we have got to go on. Are you sure you recognise them?'

'Oh yes,' Nola Cameron whispered. 'Yes.'

'I see, all right. Well thank you very much.'

Thoughtfully, Tennison watched as the bowed figure shuffled off across the reception area. Then with a sigh she picked up her watch, slipped it back on, and returned to the Incident Room.

DC Jones was standing at the board. While most of the desk-bound team worked in shirtsleeves, Jones prided himself on keeping up appearances, jacket on, necktie neatly knotted; with his glasses firmly on his nose he looked like an earnest insurance salesman about to make a pitch. He held up a sheaf of typewritten sheets, claiming her attention.

'Report in from Gold, boss. He reckons "Nadine" was infested by maggots. Bluebottles.'

'So?'

'Bluebottles won't lay their eggs underground . . .'

Arms folded, Tennison studied the 10 × 8 glossy photographs pinned to the board, the whole grisly sequence as the corpse was disinterred.

'So that means she was above ground for a while before she was buried?'

Jones nodded eagerly. 'At least a few hours. The other thing is that she must have been killed in the summer, 'cos that's when bluebottles are active.'

'And Simone went missing in February.' Tennison subsided into a chair, rubbing her eyes, feeling suddenly very weary. 'Which means I go into tonight's meeting none the bloody wiser.'

The community centre was packed to overflowing. There would have been a reasonable turnout anyway, but what with the Derrick Cameron case back in the headlines, and now the discovery of the body in Honeyford Road, the local, mainly black residents had turned out in force. Community policing had always been a contentious issue, and here was a golden opportunity for them to air their grievances and put the senior police officers on the spot.

Tennison and Kernan arrived together, to be met by Don Patterson, who was to chair the meeting, a young West Indian casually dressed in T-shirt, jeans and leather sandals. He led them through the crowd milling around the entrance, skirting the television crew and knot of reporters clamouring for Jonathan Phelps to make a statement. Phelps, of mixed West Indian and Asian parentage, was a tall, balding, well-dressed man, rather good-looking in a severe way, keenly intelligent and a forceful presence. He had been educated at the London School of Economics, where he himself now lectured, and had been selected as Labour's candidate in the forthcoming by-election. Tonight's meeting was a gift on a silver platter, and he was making the most of the media exposure to pursue his political ambitions.

Tennison couldn't quite see him through the ruck of newsmen and photographers, but she could hear him all right: the firm, resonant voice, the incisive delivery, confidence in every phrase.

'. . . my concern is that Derrick Cameron's case reaches the Court of Appeal – and that someone who has been wrongly imprisoned for six years is released. The Police and Criminal Evidence Act brought in stricter safeguards for the interrogating of suspects, but that was not much help to Derrick Cameron, who along with an increasing number of individuals . . .' Here a pause for emphasis, while his voice took on a dry, mocking tone '. . . apparently wanted to confess to the police in the car on the way to the station.'

The media lapped it up. Passing inside, Tennison and Kernan exchanged gloomy looks. This was going to be as bad – worse perhaps – as they had feared. Phelps had set the tone and the agenda for the evening with his opening remarks, and any hope of a cool, reasonable discussion had flown out of the window. And that's how it turned out. Seated up on the platform with Phelps and Patterson, and Tennison beside him, Kernan was fighting a losing battle from the start, struggling to make himself heard above the rowdy, packed hall, constantly interrupted in mid-sentence by people leaping up, not so much to ask questions as to hurl abuse.

The TV crew had set up station at the back of the hall, the photographers crouching in the central aisle, getting lovely close-ups of Kernan's mounting frustration, and then swivelling to take in the crowd's angry reactions.

'If that means a no-go area,' Kernan was saying, palms raised, 'if that means a no-go area . . .'

'With respect,' Phelps chimed in.

'. . . I can make no such assurances. I am unable . . .' Kernan valiantly tried again, almost drowned out by the racket from the floor. '. . . I am unable to give any such assurances.'

'The idea is not to create no-go areas,' Phelps said, responding to the point but directly addressing the audience and the cameras. 'Quite the reverse. We've heard from your Community Liaison Officer – who is of course a white police officer –'

Kernan was stung. 'Surely that's a racist remark.'

Ignoring him, Phelps steamrollered on. '. . . heard about sensitive policing, so-called community policing. Yet once again local people are being treated as second-class citizens.'

A chorus of cheers at this, waving fists, the bottled-up antagonism and anger of the black crowd as potent as an invisible yet deadly nerve-gas.

It was obvious what Phelps was referring to, and for the first time Tennison spoke up, determined to get her six penn'orth in before Phelps turned the meeting into a one-man election address. 'If you are talking about the investigation that I am heading –'

'I am!'

'Then I believe it's being carried out in a –'

'In a hostile and intimidatory manner – exactly.' Phelps was nodding, and almost smiling, happy to have scored another point. 'With violent arrests being made by your officers . . . though of course, no charges were brought.'

It would be so easy, too easy, to get into a slanging

match with Phelps, but that would have been catastrophic. He held all the aces. The best she could do was to remain calm, state the facts as best she could, and trust that there were enough reasonable people out there to give her a fair hearing.

'One of my officers was provoked into making what in retrospect was seen as a hasty action . . .' The hall erupted in a storm of derisive laughter and catcalls. Tennison waited for the din to die down.

'Look – the most important thing is that we have a murderer who has been walking free for six years. We have to find that person. To do that we need the support and cooperation of this community. Now, myself and two of my colleagues are going to stay behind afterwards to see if you can help to give us some crucial information. For example, who lived at number 15 before the Viswandhas.'

'We know, we know that . . .' Midway down the hall, Nola Cameron was on her feet, waving her arms, appealing to those around her. 'He left at the same time as Simone went missing. What was his name? Someone here will remember . . .'

Before anyone could, however, Don Patterson had what he thought was a more pressing question. 'I'd like to ask Mr Kernan about the heavy police presence in the Honeyford Road area at the moment . . .'

About to reply, Kernan was cut short by a young guy in the audience, who leapt up, face livid, dreadlocks swinging, pointing an accusing finger. 'I wanna ask him how he's got the front to come here at all!' he shouted. 'When Derrick Cameron's banged up for somethin' he didn't do!'

Kernan held up his hands. 'Obviously, I am unable to discuss the details of that case . . . but I should have

46

thought my mere presence here this evening is an indication of good faith.'

Howls of laughter at that. More people were climbing to their feet, gesticulating, screaming their heads off, and the whole thing was fast sinking to the level of farce. Tight-lipped, Kernan glanced aside at Tennison, shaking his head. What was the use?

Phelps waited for a slight lull and seized the opportunity.

'The justifiable anger and unhappiness at what has happened to Derrick Cameron cannot be so easily dismissed by a police officer who was stationed at Southampton Row.'

'I'm not dismissing anything,' said Kernan heatedly. 'I'm just trying . . . I'm just . . .'

'When the boy,' Phelps went on, 'supposedly confessed. Because – just let me finish – the Cameron case focuses on a fundamental question: *is it possible to expect justice in this country if you are a person of colour?*'

Excluding Kernan and Tennison on the platform and DCs Rosper and Lillie at the back of the hall, the verdict was unanimous.

Afterwards, pencils sharpened, notepads at the ready, Rosper and Lillie manned two desks in the entrance hall. They felt like a couple of lepers. The crowd had streamed out, most not bothering to give them a second glance, one or two openly sniggering and dropping heavy hints about the officers' parentage.

Lillie was doodling clockfaces, when the man in the leather hat plonked himself down in the seat opposite and leaned his elbows on the desk. He was chewing the stub of an unlit cigar, and seemed to have a sunny disposition, judging by his permanent grin that revealed two front gold teeth.

'I don't like the police,' he began cheerfully.

Lillie nodded. 'Thank you.'

'But I'll tell you this, you should talk to the guy that Nola mentioned.' He removed the cigar stub, leaving the glinting grin intact. 'White guy about fifty. Worked as a builder.'

Lillie dutifully jotted this down. 'Can you tell me his name, sir?'

'We argued about parkin' space, you know. Then in the mornin' all my car is covered in brake fluid.'

'I see.'

'Don't worry, I got me own back.'

Lillie waited. 'Go on, then, tell me.'

The man in the leather hat started wheezing. 'I pissed in his petrol tank.' He let out a bellow of laughter, thumping the desk.

Lillie smiled, still waiting.

The man chewed on the dead stub, eyes roaming about. 'Dave Hardy? Harley? Somethin' like that. You talk to him.'

Lillie wrote it down.

When Tennison returned from seeing Kernan off, the haul was meagre. Lillie gave her what little information he had, though Rosper thought he might have got a lead.

'Word is that a family lived in number 17 called Allen. One or two people reckon they might have owned number 15 as well.' He tore off the sheet and handed it to her. 'Point is, Esme Allen still runs a West Indian takeaway nearby.'

Tennison looked at the address he'd jotted down, then at her watch. She was starting to see double.

'Give it another half an hour here, then call it a day.'

As far as she was concerned, DCI Jane Tennison was about to call it a day, a night, and a day.

She let herself into the empty flat and trailed through to the bedroom, carrying the small suitcase she'd had with her on the course. Dumping it on a chair, she switched on the bedside lamp, kicked off her shoes, and lay down on top of the pink duvet, fully-clothed. The instant her eyelids closed she was fast asleep, arms by her sides, snoring softly.

The hand-lettered sign in the window read 'Esme's Take-Away Fast Food.' The café was in the middle of a row of small shops which served the local West Indian community, cardboard boxes and wooden trays of exotic foodstuffs – breadfruit, mooli, okra and yams – laid out on the pavement.

Tennison lingered outside the open door. It was a few minutes after nine-thirty, the sky hazy overhead with the sun doing its best to break through. She was warm inside her Burberry raincoat, beginning to wish she'd put on something lighter, though it had looked like rain when she left the flat. Her hair, hastily dried after the shower while she wolfed down two pieces of toast and Marmite, was still damp at the roots.

Inside the café, behind the high counter, Esme Allen was chatting to a middle-aged woman with silvery hair coiled into a neat bun. Esme was a tall, graceful black woman, somewhere in her early forties, Tennison judged, noting the faint traces of grey in her curly, cropped hair. She wore a long plastic apron over a red sweater, the

49

elegant curve of her neck accentuated by a pair of dangling earrings that swung as she chattered away.

'Me small son study for his school exam, you know, an' me daughter Sarah, she study Law at the university . . .'

Tennison stepped inside. 'Mrs Allen?'

'. . . I tell you, them think the world is at them feet. They'll never have to scrub floors or take out rubbish!'

The silvery-haired woman nodded. 'Let's hope them don't come down to earth with a bump, ennit?'

'Mrs Allen? Mrs Esme Allen?'

Esme Allen turned to her with a bright smile. 'Yes, dear?'

'I'm Jane Tennison. I'm a police officer.'

The smile faltered and her large brown eyes clouded over. 'It's not bad news? Don't tell me someone's been hurt . . . Sarah? Not Tony?'

'No, no, it's nothing like that,' Tennison said promptly, shaking her head. 'I'm making some inquiries, that's all.'

'Oh my Lord, you gave me such a fright,' Esme Allen breathed, clutching the sweater above her heart. She patted her chest, regaining her composure. 'Is it about that poor Cameron girl?'

'In a way.' Tennison glanced round. The café was quite small, with just two tables for those customers who wanted to eat their food on the premises. 'Is there somewhere more private we could talk?'

The silvery-haired woman, a friend, it seemed, as well as a customer, put her shopping-bag down and made a shooing motion. 'You take the lady through to the back. I'll look after the shop.'

Esme Allen raised the counter-flap and Tennison

followed her into a narrow, cramped room with a single window, part office, part storeroom, shelves to the ceiling stacked with provisions. The air was pungent with the mingled odours of herbs and spices. Esme indicated a canvas-backed folding chair and invited Tennison to sit down. She herself took the chair next to the desk, pushing aside a bundle of invoices to rest her elbow. She smiled attentively, lacing together her long, slender fingers.

'Mrs Allen, I understand in the 1980s you and your husband owned number 15, Honeyford Road.'

'Yes, that's right.'

'While you lived at number 17 with your family.'

'Yes.'

Without a pause, Tennison said, 'I'm sorry to have to tell you that a body has been found buried in the back garden of number 15.'

Esme Allen sat back, her strong white teeth biting her lower lip. 'My God ... you think he killed poor Simone?' she asked in a small, shocked voice.

'We just want to eliminate him from our inquiries,' Tennison replied, giving the standard line. If Esme Allen had been friendly with the occupant of number 15, then it was possible that she might wish to protect him, or throw the police off the scent. 'What was his name, Esme?'

'David Harvey.' No hesitation. Straight out with it.

Tennison nodded, 'Right.' She unscrewed the cap off her gold pen and wrote down the name on her notepad. She glanced up. 'Do you know where he is now?'

'No.' Esme shook her head, blinking as she tried to think. 'My husband Vernon might know, but ... well, we tried not to have anything to do with the man. I would never let my daughter Sarah go near that house. We all knew what he was like. Particularly with young girls.'

Tennison leaned forward slightly but said nothing.

'He wasn't always like that, but after his wife died
. . . I thought they were a lovely couple, but after she'd
gone . . .' Esme lowered her voice. 'Drinking and cursing
and, you know, carrying on . . .'

Tennison put her fountain pen away and slipped
the notepad into her pocket. 'I'd like to speak to your
husband if it's possible – in fact to the whole family.'
She got up to leave. 'As soon as possible, please.'

'This evening,' Esme said, ushering Tennison through
to the shop. 'We'll all be there this evening.'

'Fine. Thank you.'

Tennison went directly to a phone booth and got
through to Muddyman in the Incident Room.

'It's Harvey, not Harley or Hardy – Harvey. H-A-R-
V-E-Y. So we've got to start again. I'm off to see Oscar
Bream. Bye.'

'It makes a pleasant change, not being up to the
armpits in someone's viscera,' Bream said, opening
the door to the Path Lab. He went in first, his considerable bulk swathed in a green plastic apron, rubber
gloves up to the elbows. Two of his assistants were
at work, assembling and measuring the skeleton on
a table in the centre of the lab. His senior assistant,
Paul, was busy at another bench, reconstructing the
smashed skull, piece by piece. It was largely complete, except for a jagged hole towards the back on
the right-hand side, and he was fiddling with several
fragments, puzzling how they might fit into the bone
jigsaw.

Bream gestured towards the skeleton. 'Though I must

admit this girlie is sorely taxing my memory of my student anatomy classes,' he admitted to Tennison. 'You know there are two hundred and six named bones of the body? Twenty-six to each foot alone. Luckily, most of those were still inside her plimsolls.'

'Fascinating, Oscar. But is it Simone Cameron?'

Bream had planted himself in front of the skeleton, arms folded across the green plastic apron. 'Absolutely not.'

Tennison, coming round to join him, stopped dead in her tracks, mouth dropping open. 'What?'

'As I said before, *like* Simone, in her teens – sixteen to seventeen. But taller – Simone was five-seven, this girl is five-eight, five-nine.' He bent his head, peering at Tennison over the top of his glasses. 'At the moment it looks as if she was all there, no mutilation. Good head of hair . . .'

And there it was, in a shallow tray, like a discarded wig, plaited and beaded. Bream moved over to the skull, which was raised up on a plinth, the beams of a spotlight shining eerily through the empty eye sockets. 'Luckily, Paul here likes jigsaws.' He examined a fragment and handed it to his assistant, muttering, 'Could be a bit of the zygomatic arch.'

Tennison was still grappling with this new revelation. Always unwise to jump to conclusions without any sort of proof, but it was easily done, and Simone's disappearance and the discovery of the body had seemed a neat fit. Too neat, as it now turned out. But she had to be absolutely certain that Oscar Bream was certain.

'You're sure it's not Simone?'

'Yeah.' He wandered over to the lightbox and stuck up X-rays of two skulls, side by side. One was Simone

Cameron's, taken from her medical records, the other 'Nadine's'. Bream turned to her. 'Do you want me to point out the differences?'

'Not particularly, no.'

'Well, what else?' Bream mused, scratching his chin with his gloved finger. He looked across at the skeleton. 'Fractured her wrist when she was younger ... playing netball? Perhaps she fell off her bike? That's for you to discover.'

Tennison sighed. 'Don't rub it in. Can you tell me if she was black or white?'

'No.'

'*Shit*. I've been going up a dead-end street.'

Bream was trying to be helpful. He had a good deal of respect for Jane Tennison, considered her a fine police officer with a keen intelligence and an intuitive grasp of the many complex strands that went to make up a homicide inquiry. And to top it all, he rather liked her. Not an opinion he would have extended to quite a few Chief Inspectors of his acquaintance. He said, 'Well, we've got a man here who does all kinds of jiggery-pokery with the skull to ascertain ethnic origins. Better still, a medical artist who could make you a clay head, at a price.'

'Is he good?'

'He's our very own Auguste Rodin,' Bream said, a glimmer of a smile lurking behind his usual deadpan façade.

'Yeah, but is he good?'

'*Naturellement*.'

'That's expensive, right?'

Bream nodded, looking down on her over his glasses. 'Do you want a word with Mike Kernan?'

Tennison nibbled her lip. Then she decided. 'No, sod it. Let's just do it.'

'Okay.'

'So how long before I can collect it?'

'Three weeks.'

'Fine,' Tennison said, moving back to watch Paul engaged in his painstaking assembly of the skull. 'I'll pick it up in three days.'

'I'll have a word with him.' Bream stood at her shoulder. 'Perhaps if you were prepared to model in the nude . . .?'

'That's sexual harassment.'

Bream slowly blinked, his expression sanguine. 'What isn't these days?'

Tennison folded her arms, stroking her chin as she gazed at the skull in the bright cone of light. 'How did she die, Oscar?'

'I've no idea,' Bream confessed. 'Her skull could've been smashed after death. For all I know she could've been buried alive.'

The Incident Room was buzzing with activity when Tennison walked in. Almost all the team was here, shirt-sleeves rolled up, ploughing through the Harveys in the telephone directories. It was tedious and frustrating, having to redial when the line was engaged, or waiting with drumming fingers for a phone that was never answered. When they did get through to someone, the drill was always the same.

'David Harvey? I'm a police officer carrying out routine inquiries. I wonder if you can help me. Can you tell me whether you were ever domiciled at number 15, Honeyford Road?'

The same drill, and up to now, the same response. Tick the name off and start again. What the hell, Rosper thought, tapping out the next number. It was better than digging up gas mains for a living.

Tennison draped her raincoat over the back of a chair and tucked her blouse into her straight black skirt. Covering her mouth, she belched softly, still digesting the egg and cottage cheese sandwich she'd eaten driving back in the car, washed down with a carton of pure orange juice. She did a quick scan of the board, checking if anything new had been pinned up.

'Got anything for me?'

'Nothing so far, boss,' Haskons said, glancing up, keeping his finger on the number he was about to dial. 'But we have got some more stuff that's been dug up in the garden of number 15. Jonesey's getting it from Gold.'

'Let's hope it's good.' Standing at the desk, Tennison raised her voice. 'Right, listen up. I've just come back from Oscar Bream at the Path Labs. It's definitely not Simone Cameron.' A wave of disgruntled mutters and sighs went through the room; dark looks were exchanged. As well as an unidentified murderer, they now had an unidentified victim too.

'So we need to operate on two fronts,' Tennison went on. 'Find David Harvey and identify "Nadine". It's a bottle of Scotch for David Harvey.'

The team went back to work. Tennison busied herself with the duty rotas, wondering if she needed to ask the Super for more manpower. Then she remembered the clay model head she'd requested, without first clearing it with him, and decided to let it hang for the time being.

Jones arrived with the new material from Forensic. Tennison shoved the papers aside to make space on the desk.

'They found a plastic bag buried as well, ma'am,

56

and Gold has linked it to the girl. Contained this.'

Tennison stared down at the roll of heavily-woven cloth, dark browns and greens with threads of gold. Next to it Jones had placed two large chunky bracelets, hand-carved with an intricate design.

'The cloth is West African,' Jones said, consulting his notebook. 'Several yards of it, in fact. And these ivory bracelets are Nigerian.'

Tennison picked them up, turning them round and round. She was surprised at their weight. She slipped one on to her own wrist. Worn smooth through long use, its internal circumference was large enough to slide up to her elbow.

'Yoruba amulets,' Jones informed her, 'supposed to ward off evil spirits. Obviously didn't work for our "Nadine". Apparently they're very old and very valuable.'

Tennison was shaking her head and frowning at the two bracelets she held in her hands. As if speaking to herself, she murmured under her breath, 'Who was this girl?'

4

Many of the houses on the quiet, tree-lined road were detached, others substantial semi-detached properties of the thirties' period. It was clear that the Allens had gone up in the world. Esme's café must be a little goldmine, Tennison thought, parking the Orion alongside a low stone wall bordered by neatly-trimmed shrubbery. She made a mental note, and walked up the driveway, brief-case in hand.

Lights glowed behind a vestibule door of stained glass. She rang the bell, and in a few moments a boy of about nine appeared, very smart in a white shirt and school tie, shorts with knife-edge creases in them, polished black shoes.

Tennison smiled. 'Can I see your Mummy, please?'

'Yes. Please wait here,' said the boy politely, and turned back indoors. She heard him call, 'Mum, someone to see you,' and then Esme Allen came through, smiling, holding the door wider.

'Hello, it's Jane Tennison.'

'Yes, come in.'

The lounge was warm and cosy, with a beige fitted car-pet and a three-piece suite in burgundy with embroidered backs. Wall lights with red tasselled shades and thick vel-vet curtains made for a restful atmosphere. Tennison had interrupted a dressmaking session. On the coffee table stood a pretty child of three, with pigtails, being fitted for a bridesmaid's dress. The hem of the pale yellow satin dress had been partly pinned. The little girl's chubby black fists dreamily smoothed the material as she waited patiently for it to be finished.

A young man in a grey sweater and jeans, early twenties, Tennison guessed, and rather good-looking, was sitting on the edge of the sofa, hands between his knees, rubbing his palms together. He gave her a brief sidelong glance as she came in, then looked away shyly. Still smiling, the elegant, graceful Esme introduced them.

'This is my son Tony. And this is his daughter, Cleo. Say hello, Cleo.'

'Hello,' Cleo said, dimples in her cheeks.

'Tony and his girlfriend are doing the decent thing – at long last,' Esme confided, casting a look at Tennison under her eyelashes. She spoke educated, standard English; no trace of the heavy West Indian patois she'd used in the shop that morning. 'Their daughter is to be a bridesmaid. Lord, how times have changed! You wanted to see my husband?'

'Yes please.'

Esme sat the little girl on the edge of the coffee table and went out. Tennison took the armchair opposite the sofa and placed her briefcase flat on her knees. There was a momentary awkward silence, filled with the ticking of a gilt carriage clock on the mantelpiece.

Tennison said, 'So when's the happy day, Tony?'

Nervously, Tony cleared his throat. 'Ummm . . .' He gazed off at something in the corner of the room.

'Do you like my dress?' Cleo asked, plucking at it, her legs in white ankle socks swinging under the table.

'Yes, I do. I think it's lovely – oh, Tony, just a minute.'

Tennison put her hand up as he half rose, about to leave. He sank back again.

Tennison opened her briefcase and handed him a typewritten sheet. 'Could you have a look at this, please? That's a description of the dead girl. Do you remember seeing anyone like her in the Honeyford Road area in the mid-eighties? She may have been at school with you.'

'I'm a Bride's Maid,' Cleo said importantly, pronouncing it very clearly as two distinct words.

'You are, aren't you?' Tennison agreed, touching the satiny material and smiling.

'Have you ever been a Bride's Maid?'

'Do you know, I have. But never the bride.'

Tony held out the sheet of paper. 'No,' he said shortly, and got up again to leave as Esme came in. She swung the child up. 'Come along, baby. Say bye-bye.'

Cleo waved her fingers at Tennison, mouthing, 'Bye-bye.'

'Bye.'

In the doorway, Vernon Allen stood aside to let Tony pass. 'Wedding boy,' he said jovially, adding a chuckle, his voice a deep rumbling bass. He turned then, a big bear of a man casually dressed in a check shirt and loose buttoned cardigan, and looked keenly at Tennison through horn-rimmed glasses. 'Chief Inspector . . . what can I do for you?'

*

In the tiny box room upstairs that Vernon Allen used as an office, Tennison sat at the desk, flicking through the pile of old rent books dating back ten years. Everything was neatly filled in: tenants, dates, amounts. It all seemed kosher.

She screwed the cap back on her pen. 'But you have no idea where David Aloysius Harvey lives now?'

'I'm afraid not.'

Tennison sat back in the swivel chair, tilting her head to look at him. In the light of the desk lamp her blonde hair shimmered like a fuzzy golden halo. Her first instinct, which she put great faith in, was that Vernon Allen was a decent, trustworthy man. He'd answered her questions simply and directly, speaking slowly in his deep rumbling voice. At all times his eyes met hers, slightly magnified through the lenses of his spectacles. She'd have laid bets he was as kosher as the rent books, but she had to probe deeper.

'So you bought the property in 1981, right?'

'Yes.'

'And Harvey moved in shortly after?'

Vernon Allen nodded. 'With his wife. After she died he let things go.'

'And you sold the property in . . .' Tennison checked her notes '. . . '89, with Mr Harvey as a sitting tenant?' Vernon Allen's nod confirmed this. 'Did that lead to much bad feeling between you and Mr Harvey?'

'Some. Not much.' He wagged his head from side to side, the light catching the flecks of grey in his thick dark hair. 'The problem we had was that he was very erratic in paying the rent. Sometimes he seemed to have money, sometimes not.'

'Mmm,' Tennison said, as if mulling this over, and then she said quickly, 'I presume you had a set of keys to the property?'

'Yes.'

61

'Mr Allen, did you do anything to the garden while you were the owner of the property?'

'No. Harvey laid the slabs. I didn't want him to, but he did very much as he pleased really.'

'When were those slabs laid?'

'I'd say 1986. 1987 . . .?'

The door was ajar a couple of inches. There was a movement outside on the landing, the creaking of a floorboard.

'Because, you know,' Tennison went on, 'it's almost certain that the body was buried before the slabs went down.'

'Yes, I can see that,' Vernon Allen said.

'Mr Allen, how is it you could afford two properties on your pay?'

He didn't seem surprised at this change of tack, or even mildly annoyed by the question.

'Esme's café has always done well.' He shrugged his broad shoulders in the rumpled cardigan. 'To tell you the truth, it was her money that paid for the second mortgage.'

'And your son's at public school?' Tennison said, having jotted down in her mental file the blue-and-green striped tie the polite schoolboy had been wearing.

At that moment the door was pushed roughly open and a tall, willowy girl barged in, an exact younger version of Esme Allen, hair cropped very short with tiny plaited dreadlocks trailing over her ears. Attractive and vivacious, with large flashing eyes, the effect was spoiled somewhat by the way she was twisting her mouth.

'When will you ever learn, Pop? Black people aren't supposed to own businesses, houses, get an education . . .'

She regarded Tennison with open hostility.

'This is my daughter, Sarah,' Vernon Allen said, standing up. 'There's no need to be rude,' he gently rebuked her.

'I agree,' Sarah snapped.

Tennison rose, glancing down at the notebook in her hand. 'Sarah ... you're the Law student. And you're twenty. So in the summer of, say, 1986, you would have been ... let me see ...'

There was a slight pause.

'Fourteen. Mathematics not your strong point?' the girl said sarcastically.

Tennison was unabashed. 'Not particularly, no.' She smiled. Sarah's rudeness didn't upset her one bit, but it embarrassed Vernon Allen.

'It's my son David who's the wizard at maths,' he said, trying to lighten up the atmosphere.

Tennison took the description of 'Nadine' from her briefcase and handed it to the girl. 'Do you recall seeing anyone like that in the vicinity of Honeyford Road?'

Sarah hardly glanced at it. 'Yes of course, Simone Cameron,' she said curtly.

'It's not Simone. We're quite sure about that,' Tennison stated evenly. 'Would you look at the description, please.'

Sarah blinked rapidly, obviously taken aback. Then the icy, scathing tone returned, this time with a touch of venom.

'Well then, if it's not Simone, you'll need to be a bit more specific, won't you? That's if you can be bothered!'

'And would that mean ...'

Sarah interrupted, 'The police aren't exactly noted for their enthusiasm in solving cases when the victim is black, are they?' Again the sneering twist to her mouth, her contemptuous summing up of all police officers, be they male or female.

Tennison raised her eyebrows. 'Was she black? It doesn't say so here.' Taking back the description, she gave Sarah a cool, level stare. 'Maybe it's you who's jumping to conclusions.'

Tony was in the hallway with Cleo in his arms when Vernon Allen showed Tennison to the front door. Tennison smiled at the little girl and asked, 'When's the happy day, Tony?'

He looked down at the carpet, throat working, too shy or too tongue-tied to give a coherent reply. Sarah had followed them downstairs. She came into the hallway, transformed into a beautiful young woman by a beaming smile as she looked fondly at her brother and his daughter, and Tennison noticed that she gripped Tony's hand and squeezed it reassuringly.

'Two weeks away now,' Sarah said, and even her voice was different, warm and affectionate, when speaking of Tony.

'Well, I'll see you again before that,' Tennison said, nodding to Vernon Allen as he held the door open for her. 'Thanks for your help. Goodbye.'

*

It was late when she returned to Southampton Row. The cleaners didn't start their assault on the disaster area of the Incident Room till the early hours. Everyone had gone, except for DS Haskons, who was tidying up his desk, getting ready for home. He looked frazzled after the long day, shirt collar wrinkled, tie undone, wavy brown hair tousled from continually brushing his fingers through it.

'Got anything on David Harvey?' Tennison asked, dumping her briefcase on the desk.

'Not yet, Guv,' Haskons said wearily. He wondered what Tennison did in her spare time. Traffic duty at Hyde Park Corner? 'We've tried the electoral rolls, NHS, DSS, rates.' He gestured at the piles of directories. 'I've just finished working my way through the phone book . . .'

'You know,' Tennison said, her brain still ticking over after twelve straight hours on the job, 'Vernon Allen said Harvey was erratic in paying his rent. Have we checked out the credit reference agencies?'

Haskons mumbled that they hadn't. Tossing her raincoat aside and pushing up her sleeves, Tennison got down to it. She pulled a chair up to the computer terminal, and slipped in a Nicorette lozenge while she studied the code manual. Haskons leaned over, watching as Tennison keyed in the letters 'SVR'. The computer clicked and whirred, and in a second or two the 'CREDIT REFERENCE AGENCIES' program flashed up on the VDU screen.

Tennison carefully typed 'DAVID ALOYSIUS HARVEY, 15 HONEYFORD ROAD, LONDON N1.' A few more clicks followed while the computer carried out its search. Then up came:

'CREDIT REF: DAH/18329
DATE: 12 2 86
SUM: £5000 × 60 FIN.'

Tennison leaned forward, rubbing her hands. 'Yes . . .'
The next line appeared.

'FORWARD 10 3 90 – 136 DWYFOR HOUSE, LLOYD GEORGE ESTATE, LONDON SW8.'

Tennison clicked her fingers for a pen. Haskons handed her his ballpoint. She noted down the details, then keyed in a new code, and the computer responded.

'LOAN REPAYMENTS TAKEN OVER BY MRS EILEEN REYNOLDS, 6 6 90.'

'Well done, boss,' Haskons murmured admiringly. You had to hand it to the woman. Like a bloody terrier with a bone.

Tennison was scribbling on the pad. 'Do you fancy a drink?' she asked, the Nicorette bulging in her cheek.

Haskons hesitated. 'I should get home really . . .'

Tennison glanced round. 'Yes, right — the twins.' She gave him a grin and a quick nod. 'Off you go.'

''Night,' Haskons said, on his way out.

''Night, Richard.'

The door swung shut, rocking to and fro on its hinges. The room was silent, except for the low hum of the computer. Alone, crouched over the keyboard, in a world of her own, Tennison clenched both fists and stared at the screen in triumph.

'Got you . . . got you!'

*

Muddyman drove along Wandsworth Road, heading for Clapham. Beside him, Tennison was doing her best to control her impatience. They were twenty minutes behind schedule, caused mainly by a traffic foul-up on Waterloo Bridge. The day couldn't be far off, Tennison fantasised, when they'd switch from cars to helicopters; given the paralysis of central London, it would soon be the only way of getting around.

The Lloyd George Estate was situated to the northeast of Clapham Common. It was easy to find, four twenty-storey concrete towers sticking up into the overcast sky, some of the balconies festooned with washing. Muddyman drove into the carpark of Dwyfor House and found a space. As he switched off the engine, Tennison hung up the handset in its cradle, having received a message from Lillie back at base.

She said, 'They've done the tests on "Nadine"'s skull. Seems she was of mixed race, West Indian and English.'

'That would explain the Nigerian bracelets,' Muddyman said.

Tennison climbed out and stared up at the tower block. 'Right,' she muttered, a gleam in her eye, 'let's see what David Harvey can tell us.'

The lift was out of order. Harvey lived in Flat 136, on the thirteenth floor. They began to climb the concrete stairs, trying to ignore the unidentifiable odour that permeated the place; the nearest Tennison could come to it was a mixture of greasy cooking, stale underwear and dead cat. She inhaled Givenchy *Mirage* from her silk scarf, and ploughed steadily onwards and upwards. Muddyman lit up, pausing on the half-landings for a swift drag.

Tennison said, 'You know, you ought to give up cigarettes. Make you feel a whole lot better.'

Leaning against a wall, taking a breather, Muddyman gave her a fishy-eyed stare. 'There's nothing worse than a born-again non-smoker,' he growled tetchily.

Tennison hadn't formed any preconceived idea of what David Harvey would be like, but even so she was taken aback by the appearance of the man when he opened the door of 136. It was a small miracle that he'd made it to the door at all. A slight, stopped figure in a grimy striped shirt and threadbare cardigan, he had a pale, rinsed-out face and bleary blue eyes, a ragged grey moustache adding to his mournful, hang-dog look. Just standing there, he seemed to be fighting for every breath, and Tennison could hear his chest whistling and wheezing. The hand holding the edge of the door was thin and veined, visibly trembling.

'Mr David Harvey?'

'Yes.'

'We're police officers. We'd like to have a few words with you.'

Harvey didn't seem surprised; but then he didn't seem anything. It was as though he'd lost interest in the business of living, or it had given up on him.

As he led them inside, Tennison glanced at Muddyman. He met her look, registering the same faint sense of shock she felt. They hadn't expected to be interviewing a semi-invalid.

Harvey shuffled across to an armchair, trousers hanging baggily at the seat, and using both arms, lowered himself into it. There was a lit cigarette in the ashtray, and Harvey picked it up and stuck it in the corner of his mouth, the smoke trailing past his eyes.

The flat was neat if spartan. There was the bare minimum of furniture: armchair, sofa, a couple of straight-backed chairs against the wall, a coffee table with circular heat rings and cigarette burns. Next to the window, the best piece of furniture in the room – a glass-fronted bureau – had arranged along the top a collection of framed photographs. A gas fire with an imitation coal effect hissed in the grate. Above it, in the centre of the chimney-breast, a luridly-coloured picture of the Virgin Mary gazed into eternity.

Tennison explained the purpose of their visit, sitting opposite Harvey on the sofa, while Muddyman stood near the window, open notebook in hand. She showed him the description of 'Nadine', which he read without expression or comment, squinting his eyes through the smoke. Now and then he had to remove the cigarette in order to cough. Something else Tennison hadn't expected was his pronounced Glaswegian accent. With his wheezing breath it made some of his answers hard to catch, and it took her a while to get accustomed to it. She was taking it very gently. Harvey was a seriously sick man, no question of that. And the way he was lighting one cigarette from the stub of the last one, it would be unwise of him to take out a subscription to a book club.

Having established that he had lived at number 15, Honeyford Road, Tennison was anxious to broach the main subject. But she was still soft-pedalling, keeping her tone casual and low-key as she asked him, 'So why did you move away, Mr Harvey?'

'I had my first heart attack. When I got out of hospital I came here to be closer to Eileen – my sister. I didna' want to live there anyway, not after the wife died. I only stayed on because that big darkie wanted me out so badly ...' He narrowed his bleary eyes and looked round with an expression of loathing, the first real emotion he'd shown. 'I should never have moved to this dump though. I'm a bloody prisoner. Lift's always on the blink, the place full of junkies and pimps ...'

He broke off to have another puff and a cough. Tennison waited for him to wipe his mouth with a bunched-up tissue. She was about to continue her questioning when Harvey pointed a quivering finger at one of the photographs on the sideboard.

'That's her. The wife. She was the gardener. Lovely garden when she was alive.'

Muddyman picked it up in its gilt frame to show Tennison a rather muddy black and white image of a plump, pleasant-looking woman in a floral print dress, sitting in a deckchair and smiling at the camera.

Harvey gave a wheezing sigh. 'I tried to keep it going after, but . . . d'ye know? In the end I paved it over. I can tell you exactly when as well.'

He dragged himself out of the chair and shuffled over to the sideboard and rummaged in the left-hand drawer, pushing aside bundles of old bills, leaflets and junk mail. Muddyman caught Tennison's eye, and she could tell by his slight frown that he was struggling to get a handle on David Harvey, but thus far the jury was out. She felt the same, bemused and disconcerted by the man.

'I hired some stone-cutting equipment . . . Ah!' Harvey found what he was searching for. 'There ye go. The last week of August,' he said, peering closely at a faded, creased invoice. On his slow stooping creep back to the armchair he handed it to Tennison. 'I did all the digging during that week. Took up the grass, levelled it all off. I suppose I'd laid about half the slabs by the Saturday. I went down to Eileen's first thing Sunday morning. Stayed till Monday.'

'And Eileen lives locally?' Tennison asked.

'She does now, but in those days she lived in Margate,' Harvey replied, puffing a new cigarette into life. 'Anyway, when I got back Monday I finished laying the rest. Cemented them in.'

Tennison slowly nodded. 'So the only time the house was left unattended was . . . that must have been Sunday the thirty-first of August?'

'That's right.'

'Did you notice anything unusual when you got back?'

Harvey scratched his chin with long, dirt-rimmed nails, his fingers brown with nicotine. 'Unusual . . .?'

'No signs that anyone had been digging in the garden? No extra earth anywhere?'

'No.'

Tennison allowed a small silence to gather. Hands clasped on her knees, she tilted her head a fraction, raising one eyebrow. 'I must say, Mr Harvey, if someone asked me what I was doing the last weekend in August in 1986 I don't think I'd be able to remember. How is it that you can recollect so clearly?'

Without hesitation, Harvey said drably, 'Because my wife died on that day the year before.'

'Oh, I see . . .'

'Eileen asked me down to stay with her – you know, so I'd not be on my own.' The front door opened and they heard someone enter. Harvey jerked his head. 'That'll be my lunch.' He took a drag and went on, 'I spend that weekend with her every year. Don't know how I'd manage without her. She always sends my food over.'

Tennison looked towards the door. 'Perhaps I can ask her a few questions while she's here . . .?'

'Oh no, that's not her,' Harvey said, and with an effort craned round in his chair as a young man carrying a tray covered with a clean white tea-towel came in. 'This is my nephew Jason.'

Jason paused in the doorway, pale blue eyes under

71

fair lashes flicking from one to the other. 'What's going on?' he asked sharply.

'We're police officers,' Muddyman said. He picked up the typewritten sheet from the coffee table and dangled it in Harvey's face. 'You're sure you don't recognise the girl from this description?'

Jason flushed, getting angry. 'What do you want with my uncle?' he demanded, hands gripping the tray tightly. He wore faded jeans and trainers, a dark windcheater over a white T-shirt, which he filled quite impressively. His blond hair was cut short and neatly brushed, though he favoured long sideburns.

In reply to Muddyman's question, Harvey said in a tired, undisturbed tone, 'Quite sure.' To his nephew he murmured, 'I'll tell you in a minute.'

Jason was glaring at Muddyman with ill-concealed distaste. 'You know he's very ill?'

'It's fine, don't worry,' Harvey said, waving a trembling hand placatingly. 'I'm fine . . .'

'No you're not! What's this about?'

'Your uncle will tell you later, Jason,' Tennison said, fastening her briefcase and getting up. 'Thank you very much, Mr Harvey. We'll see ourselves out.'

'Have a good dinner,' Muddyman said, and followed Tennison, Jason's stare burning holes in his back.

On the landing below, lighting up, Muddyman said, 'Lying bastard. Trotting out his alibi like a speech he'd learnt by heart.' He flung the match into the piss-stained corner.

'Yeah, right . . .'

'And he wasn't shuffling about like that six years ago! If he could lay those slabs he could smash a young girl's skull.'

'Well, we'd better get a move on,' Tennison said, giving him a hard sidelong look. 'Before David Aloysius Harvey dies on us.'

Superintendent Kernan pushed the swing door of the Incident Room and held it open for the tall, handsome, broad-shouldered figure who came after him. He looked round the busy room and approached Haskons at the duty desk. 'Where's DCI Tennison?'

'Following up a lead, Guv.'

The bustle ceased as Kernan called out, 'Can I have your attention please.' Heads turned. Kernan held out his hand. 'This is DS Bob Oswalde. Bob's joining us from West End Lane to assist on Operation Nadine.'

There were one or two puzzled, uncertain looks exchanged; this was the first they'd heard about drafting in new manpower. Never one to waste time on formalities, Kernan waved to them to get on with it, then beckoned Oswalde over. 'DS Haskons here is the Office Manager. He'll fill you in.'

'Hello Bob.'

Oswalde returned the nod. 'Richard.'

'You two know each other?' Kernan said.

'I used to be at West End Lane,' Haskons said.

'Of course you were. Good.' Job done, Kernan departed.

Haskons was as puzzled as some of the others. He said, 'Tennison didn't mention that you were joining us.'

Oswalde turned from sizing up the situation, seeing if there was anyone else he recognised. He looked down on Haskons' mere six feet from his six-foot-four. 'She doesn't know,' he said.

A hospital porter pointed the way to the medical artist's studio. Tennison walked along the echoing, white-tiled corridor and found the door with a piece of white card sellotaped to it, 'STUDIO' scrawled on the card in green felt-tip. It looked to her like a shoestring operation; this guy had better be good, the money they were shelling out.

It wasn't a studio at all, more a medical science laboratory. There were human organs immersed in fluid in giant test-tubes, which she didn't examine too closely in case they turned out to be real. A tall young man in a black polo-necked sweater and a grey apron was working on the far side of the room, next to a wide slanting window to gain the maximum natural daylight. Feeling as though she were at Madame Tussaud's, Tennison threaded through the exhibits, keeping her eyes to the front. She'd seen real human beings in gruesome conditions, and the sight of blood didn't bother her, but these mummified floating bits of internal plumbing gave her the creeps.

'I'm DCI Tennison. I think you're making a clay head for us?'

It was the clay head he was actually working on. He stood back, wiping brown clay on to his apron, allowing her to have a proper view.

'It may not look much at the moment, but I have high hopes.' He had a drawling, dreamlike voice, as if he spent much of his time on another plane of existence. Probably did, Tennison thought.

She moved closer. A plaster cast had been taken of 'Nadine's' skull into which he had hammered dozens of steel pins. These formed the scaffolding for the features he was building up in clay. At the moment the underlying structure could be seen, exposed muscles and ligatures, and the effect was macabre, a face stripped down to its component parts.

'She had the most beautiful skull I've ever seen,' the young man said.

'Really?'

'Yes. See this ...' He used a stainless steel scalpel as a pointer. 'The orbicularis oris. The muscle originates on the maxilla and mandible, near the mid-line, on the eminences due to the incisor and canine teeth. Its fibres surround the oral aperture. Function — closing of the mouth and pursing of lips. You see, I'm a scientist,' he added, giving her his shy, dreamy smile. 'Otherwise I'd have said it's the muscle that allows you to kiss someone.'

'When will she be ready?'

'By the end of the week.'

As Office Manager, Haskons was doing a bit of re-organising — much to Ken Lillie's displeasure, because he was the one being re-organised.

'But why?' Lillie asked, his arms piled up with document files.

'I'm moving you.'

'Why me?'

'Bob needs a desk.'

'No, no, that's not an answer ... why me?'

Haskons plonked a cardboard box of miscellaneous

stuff on top of the pile, so that Lillie had to raise his head to peer over it.

'Because you're only ever at your desk to drink coffee.'

'Yeah,' Lillie agreed vehemently. 'Normally I'm out there making sure the streets are safe to walk.'

Hoots of derision from all corners of the room. Catcalls and shouts of 'SuperLillie Strikes Again,' and 'Batman and Lillie.'

Oswalde was studying the photographs of 'Nadine' on the big notice-board, keeping well out of it. He was edgy enough as it was, nervously watching the door for Tennison's arrival. Kernan had arranged his transfer without consulting her, which put him, Oswalde, in a spot he shouldn't be in. Especially after what had occurred at the conference. Had he been paranoid, Oswalde reflected, he might have suspected that Kernan had deliberately thrown the two of them together, part of a gleeful, devious plot so he could sit back and watch the pair of them squirm.

No, Kernan would never stoop to that. Would he?

Oswalde had other eyes on him. Burkin was slumped in his chair, long legs splayed out, chewing a matchstick. He muttered to Rosper at the next desk, 'It's bad enough having to police the buggers, let alone work with them.'

'You're only saying that 'cos he's taller than you,' Rosper quipped, always the easy-going one.

Burkin was stung. 'No he ain't.'

The door swung open and Tennison breezed in, raincoat flapping around her. Halfway to her desk she caught sight of Oswalde and stopped dead in her tracks. Oswalde was attempting the impossible, hoping not to draw attention to them both by not looking at her, at the same time trying to convey to her by some mysterious telepathic process that he was as blameless as she was, just another innocent pawn in the game.

'Tony. Can I have a word, please?'

Tennison turned about-face and went out.

Muddyman left his desk and went into the corridor, where he found her pacing up and down, hands deep in her raincoat pockets.

'Guv?'

'What's Bob Oswalde doing here?'

'You know him?'

'Answer the question, Tony.'

'He's part of the team. Kernan brought him in.'

'Thank you.'

With that she marched off to Kernan's office, leaving Muddyman standing there, wondering what the fuck all this was about.

Kernan was dictating letters to a WPC when Tennison walked in. He seemed very pleased with himself about something, leaning back with a smug grin on his pouchy, pock-marked face. Tennison's mind was racing ten to the dozen. It was all a jumble; she wasn't sure which emotion came first, nor which one to trust. She knew she had to be careful how she handled this.

'Jane?' Kernan said, which showed he was in a good mood, because normally he would have said with a sigh, *Well, what is it?*

'I want a word with you, Guv. Now.'

'Thank you, Sharon.'

Immediately the WPC had gone and the door had closed, Tennison said, 'Why did you co-opt someone on to my team without telling me?' She was holding herself in check, her voice reasonably calm, her temper under control, for the moment.

Kernan lit a cigarette. 'It seemed to me that a black officer would be a – how can I put it? – a useful addition.'

'Why didn't you consult with me?'

'Actually, I consulted the Community Liaison Officer, who thought it was an excellent idea.' Kernan gestured with the cigarette. 'A black face prominent in this inquiry. An antidote to the Burkins of this world. You're saying you can't use an extra man?'

'No.'

'Well, what are you saying?'

'You've called in this officer as back-up,' Tennison said questioningly, making sure she understood, 'because he's black?'

Now Kernan did sigh, and rolled his eyes a little. 'Jane, I'm not looking for a political argument . . .'

'It would have been different if he'd been part of the team from the beginning, but now every time I ask him to do something, it's open to misinterpretation.'

Kernan gazed blankly up at her. 'I don't understand.'

Tennison came nearer the desk, her hands clutching the air. 'It smacks of tokenism. It's political manoeuvring.'

Kernan didn't want to listen to this claptrap, and didn't see why he should. But Tennison had pumped herself up and wasn't about to stop. She said heatedly, 'You should have asked me first. Pulling rank just undermines me.'

It was Kernan's turn to get annoyed. 'I wasn't pulling rank. I was trying to help you out . . .'

'Oh bollocks,' Tennison said. 'Sir.'

What could he do with the bloody woman? Against all the odds she'd made it to Chief Inspector of the Metropolitan Force, in charge of a murder squad – which was what she'd always wanted – and still she wasn't happy. He never had this problem with his male colleagues. If only she wasn't so good at her job, he'd have got shot of her double-quick.

Kernan rubbed his eyelids with his fingertips, feeling the ulcer start to nag. 'You can't work with the man?' he asked finally, doing his level best to get to the root of her objection.

'Yes, I can work with him.'

'Because all my sources reckon he's a good officer.'

'I'm sure he is.'

Kernan spread his hands, appealing to her. 'Then what have you got against him?'

'Nothing,' Tennison said, tight-lipped. 'Well . . .' She gave a half-shrug. 'We didn't hit it off particularly well on the course, but . . .'

'I don't want you to marry the man, for Chrissake!' Kernan practically shouted, squashing his cigarette in the overflowing ashtray.

Tennison's tangle of emotions nearly got the better of her. She almost blurted out the real reason why she objected to Bob Oswalde joining the squad – how could she possibly work with a man she was strongly attracted to, who had been her lover? It would set up all kinds of impossible conflicts, make normal, everyday working relations a knife-edge balancing act. And what if it came out? She'd become a laughing stock. Her credibility would pop like a toy balloon, her reputation plummet to zilch, lower than a snake's belly.

But in the end, sanity prevailed. She didn't make a fool of herself, and she didn't blurt anything out. She simply stated, as forcefully as she could, that she didn't want him on the team.

Kernan's patience had been worn to a fine point, and finally it snapped. 'He's on the team already. I've made my decision and I'm not going back on it. Get the man briefed and put him to work. We'll review the situation at the end of the week. I'll be watching the progress of this case very carefully from now on.'

Tennison left the office.

Ten minutes later, on the pretext of offically welcoming DS Oswalde to Southampton Row, Tennison summoned him to her office. She was still het up and dying for a smoke. She stood in front of her desk, arms folded, looking up at him, accusation in her eyes.

'Are you expecting me to believe this is a complete coincidence?'

Oswalde regarded her placidly. 'I don't know about coincidence – how many black detectives did he have to choose from? What I'm saying is that it had nothing to do with me. You know me well enough to know I wouldn't ask to be the token black on your team.'

He seemed quite sanguine about it.

Tennison said sharply, 'Just don't think that what happened on the course gives you any special privileges.'

'I don't.'

'And don't you dare tell anyone.'

'Jane, please . . . what do you take me for?'

'And don't call me Jane.'

Oswalde wore a pained expression. 'Look, give me some credit. What happened, happened. It's gone, long since forgotten about. Let's not give it another thought . . .'

'Yes. Right.' Tennison waved her hand, dismissing him. 'Go back to the Incident Room. I'll be along in a minute.'

When he'd gone she stared at the door for a long moment, then stuck a Nicorette in her mouth and chewed the hell out of it.

All the team was there, assembled for the four o'clock briefing. There was an odd, strained atmosphere, Tennison snapping out instructions, and the men were uneasy. They guessed it had something to do with Kernan and Oswalde, but beyond that they were completely in the dark.

Tennison stood in front of the board, her eyes raking over them. 'We could have the clay head by tomorrow with any luck. By the end of the week at the latest. After talking to Harvey, our best bet is to concentrate on Sunday, August the thirty-first, 1986.'

'Has Harvey got an alibi?' Burkin asked.

Tennison nodded. 'His sister, Eileen. I'm going to talk to her soon. We need a name. We need to build up "Nadine"'s life story, then we might be able to connect her to Harvey.'

'I've been wading through these statements,' Haskons said, sitting on the edge of his desk and indicating a pile of papers. 'One or two people talk about a young girl staying in the basement of number 15.'

'Really?' Tennison said.

'Conflicting reports, but it could have been '86.'

'Brilliant. I'd like to make a start on missing persons. Bob, perhaps you could handle that.'

Oswalde straightened up, his face stiffening, and then gave an abrupt nod. Some of the others exchanged looks. 'Mispers' wasn't normally a job for a Detective Sergeant, especially one as experienced as Oswalde.

'Tony, can you go and see if you can have a word

with Harvey's consultant, make sure he's not just a bloody good actor.'

'If he is, he should win an Oscar,' Muddyman said.

'Right. That's all for now.'

As she went out, Burkin turned to Haskons with a grin, muttering, 'Glad to see the boss is keeping our coloured friend in his place.' Haskons didn't agree, and he was less than happy with Tennison's duty allocation. He followed and caught up with her in the corridor.

'Guv . . . can I put someone else on Mispers?'

'Why?'

'With respect, ma'am, it's ridiculous having a man of his experience . . .'

'No.' Tennison was already striding off. 'He might pick up on something a more junior man might miss. Don't call me ma'am.'

Haskons watched her go, shaking his head. Of all the crap excuses . . .

*

Eileen Reynolds was a younger, much tougher version of her brother David Harvey. A hard-bitten Glaswegian woman with a shrewd, sharp-nosed face under a silvery cap of bleached hair, she sat in Tennison's office wearing a powder blue coat and a tartan scarf that clashed badly with everything. Her son Jason sat meekly by her side, as if cowed by her domineering presence.

Tennison was trying to establish the pattern of Harvey's visits to his sister, and whether he had been there on the weekend in question.

'I'm sure, of course I'm sure! Every year since his Jeanie died. He wouldn't have left till the Monday morning.' Eileen Reynolds suddenly bent forward, her workworn hands clutching the shiny black handbag in her lap. 'What you lot've got to remember is that he's a sick man. You shouldn't be hounding him.'

'Mum.' Jason tugged at her sleeve. He seemed embarrassed. 'They've got their job to do.'

'He's waiting for an operation, you know? You'll be the bloody death of him . . .'

'We're not hounding him, Mrs Reynolds. We're trying to eliminate him from our inquiries.'

Leaning forward again, beady eyes glittering, the woman said hoarsely, 'You wouldn't be hounding him like this if he was a black man.'

'Mum . . .!'

'Mrs Reynolds,' Tennison said patiently, 'I've questioned your brother once, that's all. Which is not surprising given that the body of a young girl was found buried in his garden.'

Eileen Reynolds snorted. 'Well that's a lot of rubbish. Simone Cameron this, Simone Cameron that. Was it Simone?'

'No.'

'Exactly. It's my brother you should be concerned about. He's the one that's dying.'

'Is that all for now?' Jason asked, standing up.

'Yes. Thank you very much for coming.'

'Come on, Mum . . .'

'Don't pull me about!' At the door she turned her sharp, angry face towards Tennison for a parting shot. 'He's at the hospital tomorrow thanks to you.'

'Come on,' Jason said, steering her out into the corridor.

Tennison went to the door and indicated to a passing

WPC that she should see them to reception. With his arm around the back of the powder blue coat, Jason guided his mother after the WPC, the dutiful, attentive son.

Tennison looked at her watch, debated for a moment, and grabbed her coat from the hook. If she hurried she'd just be in time to catch Vernon Allen before he left his office.

He wasn't as friendly and cooperative this time. Perhaps it was because he was in his management role, sitting at a mahogany desk, his broad frame inside a well-cut suit and matching waistcoat. Or perhaps he was just fed up with Tennison re-treading the same questions he thought he'd already answered.

Aware that he was fretting, impatient to get away, Tennison said, 'Just one last thing, Vernon. You said that you and Mr Harvey fell out because he wouldn't move.'

'Yes.'

'Nothing else?'

'What? No.'

'But didn't he sublet the basement? To a girl?'

'That had nothing to do with me.'

'What had nothing to do with you?'

'Whatever she was doing.'

'What was she doing?'

'Look – I don't know. It was none of my business.'

Vernon Allen sniffed and turned his head away, gazing through the venetian blinds at the London skyline in the gathering dusk. Far below, the rush-hour traffic was clogging up the Euston underpass.

'It was if she was a prostitute, Vernon,' Tennison said.

'Why?'

'Because as the landlord you could have been done for running a brothel.'

He was offended. 'How dare you use the word "brothel"?'

'What word would you use?'

He looked at her through his heavy, dark-framed glasses, a hint of uncertainty there, as if he wasn't sure of his ground any more. With a weary motion he pressed the palm of his hand to his forehead, and said, 'I was at work all hours, Esme was too. A neighbour told us men were calling there. I spoke to Harvey straight away but I had no proof. Then suddenly the . . . the girl . . . seemed to have gone.'

Tennison leaned forward. 'But did you see her?'

Vernon Allen gave a barely perceptible nod. 'Yes.'

'Was it the girl whose remains we've found? Is that why you won't cooperate?'

'Listen. My family are very upset.' He was making a great effort to speak slowly, holding his emotions in check. 'It's an important time for us. A wedding should be a time of joy. I have cooperated with you in every way so far . . .'

'Then please answer the question. Did she answer the description I've given you?'

'No.' He stared straight back. 'She was a white girl.'

'Not just light-skinned?'

'No. White.'

Tennison leaned back, pressing her lips together. 'Can you describe her, please?'

Vernon Allen thought for a moment. 'Small, perhaps five foot two. A tiny thing, really. Blonde hair – bleached, I would say.' Tennison nodded, making notes. 'Young, but not the girl you described.'

Tennison looked up from her pad. 'Did you have sexual relations with this girl?'

She saw in his eyes how disturbed he was by this question.

'I did not,' Vernon Allen replied gravely.

'What was the relationship between Harvey and this girl?'

'God knows. I wouldn't put anything past that man.'

'And when did all this happen, Vernon?'

He stared down at the desk, evading Tennison's gaze, but she was quite content to wait. He cleared his throat and swallowed, and reluctantly admitted, 'It could have been the summer you're talking about.'

Tennison replaced the cap on her pen and screwed it tight.

The medical artist had promised it by the end of the week, and the next day, shortly after three in the afternoon, he delivered the goods.

On her way back from the ladies' loo, Tennison nipped up to Kernan's office and invited him to come along to the Incident Room and take a gander at it. She thought it was the least she could do, seeing as how Kernan had been lumbered with finding the money from his budget to pay for it.

'The Viswandhas' brief has been bending my ear,' Kernan grumbled to her as they walked along the corridor. 'He tells me Forensic are still there, poking around inside the house, lifting carpets, floorboards, the lot.'

'So?'

'Let's get out of there as soon as possible.'

'Yes, of course.'

Kernan pushed open the door of the Incident Room, waving her to go first, and said with a distinct lack of enthusiasm, 'Let's see it then.'

There was an air of expectancy. All the team had gathered for the grand unveiling. Richards, the police photographer, had set up his tripod and lights. Tennison nodded to Haskons, who stepped forward and whisked off the cloth. There was a moment's stunned silence, and then a kind of collective gasp. The medical artist had been too modest, Tennison thought. He was as much artist as he was scientist, without doubt.

Modelled in brown clay, the head was astonishingly life-like. The girl was young and very beautiful, rather proud-looking, with braided hair swept back from a wide forehead. The artist had caught exactly the mixed-race caste of her features, high cheekbones and a generous mouth, and it reminded Tennison strongly of the sculpted head of an ancient goddess.

Everyone was impressed, even the hardened long-time pro's who thought they'd seen everything . . .

Everyone except Kernan, cynical old bugger, who was seeing a hole in his budget rather than an expertly-crafted clay head.

His only comment was a surly, 'Very nice,' and then the swing door was wafting the air as he disappeared through it.

Richards was popping off photographs, moving his camera around to cover all the angles. Tennison turned to the men.

'Right . . . I want these photographs to appear everywhere they can, local and national press. From now on you'll show them to anyone who might be able to help. Let's get the Allens in to see this –' She gestured towards the head. 'Vernon Allen has confirmed that there was a tom working from the basement of number 15 that summer. From his description it wasn't "Nadine" but it's possible that "Nadine" was a tom as well . . . perhaps Harvey was a small-time pimp? Harvey is at the hospital all day tomorrow,' she added, 'so I won't be able to see him till the evening to tackle him about it.'

'She doesn't look like a prostitute,' DC Lillie said.

'Start asking around anyway.' Tennison moved to the board. 'Vernon Allen has accounted for his family's whereabouts on the thirty-first. For the last ten years there's been a Reggae Sunsplash concert in Honeyford Park on the last Sunday in August. Vernon says Esme was at that concert – she's there every year running a stall selling West Indian food.

The men were silent, paying close attention. Glancing down at her notes now and then to refresh her memory, Tennison continued.

'Apparently Tony, the son, attended the concert, which is an all-day affair – ten to ten. Vernon says he spent the day at home with Sarah and David. Tony returned at about 9.00 p.m. to look after his brother and sister so Vernon could go to work. I've checked Vernon's work record. He did a double shift through Sunday night and late into Monday. By the time Esme had packed up, returned things to the café and got back home, it was about 10.45 p.m. She says by then all three children were asleep in bed. Obviously, wherever possible, I'd like these accounts verified.'

She looked round, and was about to call the briefing over when Oswalde, leaning back nonchalantly against a desk, arms folded, said casually, 'Perhaps that's the link between "Nadine" and Honeyford Road.'

'What?'

'The Reggae Sunsplash.'

Tennison's eyes narrowed. 'Go on.'

'Harvey could have met her there, or Tony Allen. Perhaps the victim's bag of African cloth was a costume of some sort. She might even have been performing at the concert.'

Nobody said anything. Oswalde's first contribution, after being on the team less than twenty-four hours, was a good one, and everybody knew it.

Tennison looked away from him, tapping her fingers on the desk. 'It's an interesting thought. Worth following up. Frank, Gary, I'd like you to visit the Sunsplash organisers first thing tomorrow – see if they can point you towards any bands using backing singers or musicians in African gear.'

Oswalde slowly unfolded his arms. He couldn't believe this. He'd just single-handedly come up with a promising lead and she'd tossed the juicy bone to someone else! Knowing what he must be feeling, the rest of the team couldn't meet his dark, angry eyes. Something was going down here, but they were damned if they knew what it was.

'Anything else?' said Tennison briskly. 'Right. That's it for now.' She strode out.

Oswalde went after her. He caught up with her in the corridor and made her stop. 'Why are you doing this to me?' he demanded, his voice low and furious.

'What?'

'Treating me like the office boy?'

'I don't know what you're talking about,' Tennison said, braving it out. Her eyes shifted away; people were passing, and it was a bit public for this exchange.

'Why didn't you send me to see the concert organisers?'

'You're busy already,' Tennison said, another convenient crap excuse. 'Besides, I thought that you didn't want to be given special tasks because of the colour of your skin.'

'I don't,' Oswalde said curtly. 'I want to be given a task commensurate with my abilities and experience.'

He was right to be pissed off, and right to make this request, they both knew it. Tennison was anxious to end this public confrontation lest tongues started to wag. She said, 'I want you to carry on overseeing Mispers –' Oswalde was about to protest, and she cut him short. 'But I'd also like you to arrange for the Allens to see the clay head. Watch their reactions.'

'Thank you,' Oswalde said stiffly, and went back to work.

While he was still sore at Tennison, Oswalde was chuffed to be more centrally involved in the investigation; combing through the endless Missing Persons files on the computer was brain-numbing, soul-destroying graft. He'd done his stint at it as a young DC, and thought those days were behind him.

He contacted the Allens and arranged for Vernon and Esme, and their son Tony, to come into Southampton Row to view the clay head. He went down to reception to meet them, and before taking them through to the interview room, explained to the three of them what was involved. They were being asked to say if they recognised the girl, and if possible, to identify her.

As they filed in, Oswalde kept a close eye on them, noting their reactions at the first sight of the head on the small wooden plinth. They studied it in silence. Oswalde glanced at Vernon Allen, who shook his head.

'Are you sure, Vernon?'

'Absolutely.'

'Esme?'

'Yes?' Her brows were drawn forward, gazing at the head with a harrowed expression. 'No, dear. I'd remember if I had.' She let out a pitiful sigh. 'What a beautiful child . . .'

There was a strange gasping, choking sound. Oswalde swung round to find Tony Allen on the verge of collapse. The boy was shuddering violently and clutching his throat, the awful noises issuing from his quivering mouth. He seemed unable to properly draw a breath.

'Tony – what's wrong?' Oswalde said, alarmed.

Esme took charge. 'Come, Tony, sit down.' She led the boy to a chair and sat beside him, her arm around his shoulders. 'Now don't make a fuss, you're all right,' his mother comforted him. 'It's very hot in here. He suffers from asthma,' she explained to Oswalde.

'I see.'

Oswalde watched him. He seemed calmer now, though there was a mist of sweat on his forehead. He kept staring at the clay head, then down at the floor, and then back again, as if the sight mesmerised him.

'Have you seen her before, Tony?'

'No.' He gulped air. 'I've never seen her.'

'You're certain?'

'I'm certain,' Tony Allen said.

6

'He's our prime suspect and he's dying. I'm not going to sit back and watch.'

'I don't know why you're so bothered,' Muddyman panted. 'Just another runaway, another dead prostitute . . .'

Tennison halted on the ninth floor of Dwyfor House and turned to him, her chest heaving. 'You don't mean that.'

'I do if it means climbing these poxy stairs again,' Muddyman said, staring up with deep loathing.

'She's someone's daughter, Tony.'

'Yeah, yeah, yeah . . .' Muddyman set off again. He said bitterly, 'Anything we get from the old sod will be thrown out of court anyway. "He didn't know what he was saying,"' Muddyman mimicked a light brown voice. '"Oppresive conduct by the police . . ."'

If when they'd seen him the previous time Harvey was on his last legs, he was at death's door now. He looked even more haggard, and kept swallowing tablets – ten different shapes, sizes and colours – as if they were Smarties. Tennison, seated opposite him on the sofa, treated him as gently as she knew how. She spread the photographs of 'Nadine' on the coffee table and gave him plenty of time to mull them over. Finally, chest wheezing and rattling, he shook his head.

'No, I've never seen her before. I did let the basement room that summer, I admit it. There's nothing wrong with that.' He fixed Tennison with his rheumy eyes. 'The big darkie complained about everything I did. He just wanted me out.'

'Why did you let the room, David? Did you know the girl already?'

'No, I'd never seen her before. It seemed such a big house for just me and I needed the money. I put a card in the newsagent's window.'

'What was her name?' Muddyman asked, leaning against the back of the sofa.

'Tracey? Sharon? I don't remember,' Harvey said wearily.

'How long did she stay?' Tennison asked.

'Couple of months.'

'What months?'

'June, July . . .'

'Not August?'

'No, she'd gone by then.'

'Did you know that she was a prostitute?' Muddyman said, his tone nowhere near as gentle as Tennison's.

'No.'

'Could she have been friends with that girl?' Tennison indicated the photographs.

'It's possible.'

'Could she have had a set of keys to the flat?'

Harvey's narrow shoulders twitched. 'Possible I suppose . . .'

'Could she and some friends have used the flat that Sunday you were at your sisters?' Tennison pressed him.

'How should I know?' His eyes were upon her, but

unfocused, as if he couldn't quite make her out. 'As you say, I wasn't there . . .'

His shoulders started heaving as he went into a coughing fit. Muddyman hesitated when Tennison pointed to the kitchen, but then went off and came back with a glass of water, which Harvey gulped down with four more assorted pills.

'Just one last thing, David.' Tennison smiled at him encouragingly. 'Could we have a photograph of you, please?'

Harvey wiped his mouth. Beads of water clung to the ragged fringes of his moustache. 'Why?'

'It'll help us eliminate you from our inquiries.'

'Will I get it back?'

'Of course.' Tennison watched him on his snail's progress to the glass-fronted bureau. 'One from the mid-eighties if you've got it.'

Harvey took a tattered red album from the drawer and leafed through it. Tennison went over to stand beside him. She picked up one of the framed photographs, a moody sunset over a grey, restless ocean, which to her inexpert eye looked to be of a professional quality.

'Are you the photographer?' Muddyman asked, taking an interest.

'No. My nephew Jason.'

'They're very good,' Tennison said, putting it back.

'Here.' Harvey gave her a snapshot of himself, a darker-haired, stronger-looking Harvey with a brown moustache. 'Younger and fitter, eh?' he said with a wan smile.

'Thank you. I'll get this copied and get it back to you as soon as possible.' She put it in her briefcase along with her notebook and snapped the catches.

They went through into the tiny hallway. Harvey leaned on the jamb of the living-room door, resting. Tennison reached out to release the yale lock when she noticed the front door key hanging down from the letterbox on a piece of string. 'I'd remove that if I were you, David. Not very safe.'

'It's so someone can get in if I collapse.' Harvey stated it matter-of-factly; no self-pitying appeal for sympathy.

Tennison gave him a look over her shoulder as she went out. 'Even so.'

As they were going down the stairs, Muddyman said mockingly, 'You'd make a wonderful Crime Prevention Officer.'

'Oh yeah?' Tennison drawled, punching him.

DS Oswalde lingered by the frozen food cabinets, not even bothering to put up a thin pretence that he was wondering what to buy. The supermarket wasn't all that busy at this late hour, and Oswalde had an uninterrupted view along the aisles of Tony Allen, neat and dapper in his short dark-blue coat and spotted bow-tie, the plastic badge on his left lapel engraved in black letters: 'A. ALLEN. TRAINEE MANAGER.'

Tony was aware of the scrutiny. Oswalde had made sure of that. The more rattled the young man became, the better he liked it. Esme Allen had called it an asthma attack. A load of old baloney. Tony had been scared shitless the minute he laid eyes on 'Nadine''s clay head. He'd recognised her instantly, of that Oswalde hadn't the slightest doubt.

Oswalde stalked him around the store for another ten minutes, watching him openly, noting with satisfaction the jerky body language, the fumbling with the clipboard when he tried to make an entry. At last, deciding that Tony had stewed long enough, Oswalde moved in. He cornered him next to cooked meats and stuck the description, the one Vernon Allen had given of the girl living in the basement, under his nose.

'Your father remembers her,' Oswalde said, looking down on Tony, a good eight or nine inches shorter. 'Bleached blonde, slim, about five foot two . . .'

'Well I don't.' Tony dodged around him and strode off.

'Do you like reggae, Tony?' Oswalde asked, matching stride for stride.

'What?'

'I do. Reggae, soul, jazz. Do you like jazz?'

Tony whirled around. 'What are you talking about?'

'I'm just talkin', man,' Oswalde shrugged, all sweetness and light.

'Well don't, just leave me alone . . .'

'All right, Tony,' Oswalde said with a glimmer of a smile, 'don't jump the rails.'

Tony started off, turned back, his face twitching. 'I don't remember any girl,' he said, grinding it between his teeth.

Oswalde stood watching him stump off. Nearly done, but not quite. Tony Allen needed to stew just a little while longer.

'This'll do,' Tennison said, and Muddyman pulled over on the corner of Glasshouse Street and Brewer Street. She tucked her briefcase under her arm and opened the door. 'I'll get a cab home.'

Muddyman raised his hand. 'Night, Guv. Hope you get something.'

Tennison strolled along through Soho, past the strip

joints with their garish neon signs and life-size colour photographs of semi-naked women contorting themselves to entice the punters downstairs. Separating the strip clubs were shadowy booths peddling racks of soft porn, and at the back, behind a curtain of fluttering plastic trailers, the hard Swedish and German stuff wrapped in cellophane. There was plenty of trade about, and groups of working girls in mini skirts and fishnet stockings, clustered round the concrete lamp-posts, their faces anaemic in the harsh sodium glare, black slashes for mouths.

Tennison glanced across the street. A tall girl with a mass of dark hair piled on top of her head, wearing a lime-green shortie plastic raincoat, registered who it was and gave a nod. Tennison strolled on. She stopped in a darkened doorway, waiting for Rachel, and hadn't been there more than a few seconds when a man approached and leaned towards her. She smelled whisky on his breath.

'Oh, I wouldn't if I were you,' Tennison said, and the man moved on, bewildered. A minute later Rachel appeared, and Tennison gave her a smile. 'You look like you could use something to eat, darling.'

In the café on the corner they sat at a plastic-topped table while Rachel did justice to a hot salt beef sandwich and Tennison sipped an espresso.

'If he's a pimp, I've never seen him before,' Rachel said, handing back the snapshot of David Harvey. She took another bite of her sandwich. 'I'll ask around about the bleached blonde, but it's not much to go on.'

'You're telling me,' Tennison said with feeling.

Rachel chewed while she had another think. 'Maybe she was one of those that tried it for five minutes and decided it was no kind of life. One of the sensible ones,' she said, the corner of her mouth curling up in a bleak, sardonic smile. 'I suppose someone might remember, since most of the girls who worked that area are black.'

Tennison held up the picture of 'Nadine.'

'Look. This is the likeness of the dead girl . . .'

Rachel bent forward to peer at the clay head, staring sightlessly into the camera. She pulled away with a little shudder. 'Spooky. No.' She shook her head of tousled curls. 'Never seen her before either.'

Tennison folded a twenty-pound note and slipped it under Rachel's saucer. 'Do your best, darling,' she said with a smile, and got up to leave.

'I always do,' Rachel said.

'Ask around. I must go . . . bye.'

Jane poured herself a treble of neat Bushmills and on her way back to the sofa pressed the playback button on the answering machine. She kicked off her shoes and curled up on the sofa, closed her eyes and rested her head on the cushions. She felt bone-weary, yet her brain was ticking like an unexploded bomb. She couldn't turn off her thoughts, they crowded in, swamping everything. When she was working on a case, she gave it every ounce of her concentration and emotional energy. No wonder Peter hadn't been able to stick it. Would any man? If it wasn't an empty-headed bimbo they wanted, it was a wife and homemaker, and she didn't fit either category.

She was DCI Jane Tennison, and having said that you'd said the lot.

The machine clicked on. It was her mother.

Jane, remember, this Friday is Emma's first birthday, so don't forget to send a card, will you?

Emma was her sister Pam's little girl. Pam was happily married to Tony, a company accountant, with three children, the perfect nuclear family. While Jane was the black sheep of her own family, the mad, obsessive career woman doing a job no woman should do – so Jane's mother thought. She had learnt to live with, if not fully accept, her family's total lack of understanding about the kind of work she did; it never ceased to puzzle them why she didn't find herself a steady bloke and settle down, have a couple of kids before it was too late, forget all this career nonsense.

'I haven't forgotten, Mum ...' Eyes closed, both hands round the glass, she took a sip of whisky.

... if you're in before ten-thirty you can telephone me. Daddy sends his love.

There was a click, a hissing pause, followed by the next message.

Mike Kernan at nine thirty-five. I was hoping for an update, Jane. Any results from your clay head? A slight hesitation then, throat-clearing. *Er ... it's my interview tomorrow and they're, um, bound to ask me about Operation Nadine. Particularly whether my DCI's come in on budget. Anyway, ring me tonight if you can – or drop by my office first thing.*

Jane stretched out and took another sip, feeling the Bushmills burn a molten path all the way down. She had no intention of calling a living soul.

Tennison was at the station bright and early the next morning. After dumping her coat and briefcase in her office, she went to the Incident Room and checked on the duty rota for the day, who was doing what. It was a few minutes after nine-thirty when she hurried along to Kernan's office and found him primping in front of the mirror, getting ready for his interview.

She reported, 'We've spoken to the Sunsplash concert organisers. They've given us the names of the bands using backing singers. We're talking to them now.'

'Tread carefully there, Jane. We're under the microscope.' Kernan adjusted the knot in his silk tie, glancing at her in the mirror. 'How's Oswalde getting on?'

'Fine.'

He turned and caught her smiling. 'What?' Tennison edged up his breast-pocket handkerchief a fraction and smoothed it flat. 'How do I look?' he asked anxiously.

'Like a Chief Superintendent.'

'Good,' Kernan said, and she could almost see his chest swell.

As she entered the Incident Room, DC Jones called her over.

'Guv!' He was elated, his eyes bright behind his rimless glasses. 'I thought you'd like to know – Forensic have found a fragment of our girl's tooth between the floorboards of the front room of number 15 . . .'

Tennison punched the air with her fist. 'Yes!'

News was coming in thick and fast. Next it was Oswalde's turn. He came over waving a page of computer print-out, the result of all those hours crouched over the VDU screen.

'I think I might've found her.'

'Yeah?' Tennison barely glanced at him, her tone neutral.

'Joanne Fagunwa, mixed parentage, went missing in early '85 from Birmingham.'

'Is there a photograph?'

'Yes, well, I suppose that's with the file in Birmingham.'

Tennison nodded brusquely. 'Let's get it faxed through. If it looks promising, then go . . .'

Oswalde perked up. 'To Birmingham?'

'Yes.' She turned away. 'Richard, have we checked when Mrs Harvey died?'

'August '85, wasn't it?' Haskons said.

'Let's check.'

''Course.'

Muddyman put his head in and said to Tennison, 'Let's go.'

She was gone, leaving Oswalde with the computer print-out in his hand and an expression of pent-up frustration on his face.

'Nice one, Bob,' Haskons said sincerely, a small token in lieu of Tennison's lukewarm appreciation for his efforts. Oswalde went back to his desk; he was getting more than a mite pissed off with being given the brush-off. As if he was here on sufferance, not really part of the team at all. Well. We'd see about that.

*

DI Burkin didn't like this detail, and he took no great pains to disguise the fact. The recording studio was in a prefabricated building, provided by the council, two streets away from Honeyford Road. A sheer criminal waste of Poll Tax, in Burkin's view, most of which had been coughed up by white people to give these jungle bunnies somewhere to hang out all day, amusing themselves at the tax-payer's expense.

In respect to his seniority, Rosper let Burkin carry out the questioning, though he was uncomfortable about it.

101

There was a recording session in progress. Through the large glass panel they could see, but couldn't hear, a group of musicians banging away at guitars and drums, with three guys in the brass section. The band they were interviewing had played at the Sunsplash festival, but they were none too cooperative, mainly, Rosper suspected, because of the hostile vibes coming off Burkin like a bad smell.

One of them, the bass player, lounging back in an old armchair with the stuffing spilling out, was more interested in the recording session than the photographs of 'Nadine' Burkin was showing him. He gave them a cursory glance. 'Don't know nothin' about it . . .'

'Do you wanna look at them, Sir, before you answer?' Burkin said, making the 'Sir' sound like he was having a tooth extracted without anaesthetic.

The bassman plucked one out, looked, flipped it back. 'I tell you I don't know her.'

Burkin's lips thinned. 'Okay. I'm going to ask you one more time. Will you please look at the photograph before you answer –'

The drummer, a thin wiry bloke wearing a Bob Marley T-shirt and a black velvet Zari hat, interrupted. 'You can't make a man look at a photograph if he doesn't want to.'

'Oh can't I?' Burkin bared his teeth in a nasty grin. 'I can nick him for obstructing police inquiries . . .'

Rosper put his hand over his eyes.

The drummer said, 'He wasn't even in the band then!'

Burkin's eyes flashed. He opened his mouth, and Rosper said quickly, 'Can I have a word, Frank? Guv?'

'Let me have a look,' the drummer said, reaching out.

'Your battyman wants a word with you, Frank,' the

bassman said to Burkin, pinching his nose, but keeping a straight face.

Rosper handed the sheaf of photographs to the drummer and got Burkin outside before he exploded. They stood on the piece of waste ground adjacent to the studio. Burkin was physically shaking.

'What did he call me?'

'I dunno,' Rosper muttered.

'Yes you do –' Burkin couldn't get over it, being referred to as a 'battyman', West Indian slang for homosexual. His face was livid. 'I'm going to nick him . . .'

Rosper sighed. He wasn't sure how to handle this. He thought Burkin was making a prize dickhead of himself. He said, 'That'll be a big help . . . look, perhaps the Guv gave you this lead to see if you could manage to talk to a black guy without arresting him.'

Burkin flexed his broad shoulders, breathing hard, but it had given him something to think about. He calmed down.

'And listen,' Rosper said, 'I think the drummer might know something. Can I go back and have a word on my own?'

'Go on then.' Burkin lit up and walked towards the car. 'You're wasting your time.'

'Where's Dirty Harry?' the drummer asked when Rosper returned.

'Eh?'

'Your partner.'

'Clint Eastwood, ennit?' the bassman said.

'Oh yeah,' Rosper said, cottoning on. He scratched the back of his head. 'Sorry about that.'

They regarded him with amusement.

'Do you like reggae?' the drummer said.

'Yeah, solid guy,' Rosper said, who thought he did, thrilled to be talking the jive.

They all laughed, even more amused.

'Then peruse these at your leisure,' the drummer said.

Rosper accepted the four videos, nodding enthusiastically, and gave them the thumbs-up. 'Wicked.'

When he got back to the car, Burkin was slumped in the passenger seat, sullenly blowing smoke-rings. Rosper slid behind the wheel, proudly showing the indifferent Burkin the fruits of his labours.

'Vids from '86. Apparently two bands used girl backing singers,' he said, well-pleased with himself, his pug-nosed face split in a broad grin. 'Do I have what it takes or do I have what it takes?'

Staring through the windscreen, Burkin blew another smoke-ring.

*

Tennison chose her words carefully. 'I'm not saying you killed her, David, but I am saying she was killed in your house.'

The same vague expression came into Harvey's eyes as if he wasn't really seeing her. He opened his mouth wide, closed it, and opened it again, wide; he looked to be doing an impression of a goldfish. Then he leaned to his right and kept on leaning.

'Are you all right, sir?' Muddyman said.

Stupid question. The man was hanging over the arm of the chair, doing his goldfish act.

'Shit.' Tennison was on her feet. 'Call an ambulance. Quick.'

Before she could get to him, Harvey was struggling

to stand up, one hand clawing the air. He made a lunge forward and fell across the coffee table, upsetting it and sending the ashtray, cigarettes and other bits and pieces flying. He lay on his side, face white as a sheet, staring sightlessly at the coal-effect gas-fire.

Muddyman was through to the emergency services, requesting an ambulance. It took nine minutes to arrive, which wasn't bad for central London, and Harvey was still alive when the paramedics got him downstairs and into the ambulance.

Tennison and Muddyman watched them close the doors and drive off. They would follow on in their own car. As the ambulance pulled out of Lloyd George Estate, siren wailing, Tennison said grimly, 'We could lose this one if Harvey croaks.'

Muddyman thought, That's all she cares about. All the cold-blooded bitch really fucking cares about.

*

Oswalde drove up the M1 to Birmingham. It was a relief to get away from Southampton Row, out of London in fact, if only for a few hours.

Mrs Fagunwa lived on the southern outskirts of the city, not many miles distant from Stratford-upon-Avon. It was a well-heeled, white, middle-class area with neat hedges and well-tended gardens. Some of the houses had double garages.

Oswalde had made an appointment, and Mrs Fagunwa was expecting him. Just like the neighbourhood, she was white and rather genteel, younger-looking than her forty-seven years, with thick black hair parted in the middle;

she still possessed the good bone structure and fine complexion that must have made her something of a beauty as a young woman.

She led him through the parquet-floored hallway, polished like an ice-rink, into a large, comfortably-furnished lounge which had patio doors looking out on to a lawn and flowerbeds. From the records Oswalde knew that she was a widow, and there was a stillness to the house, an unlived-in feel, that told him she had no companion and lived here alone. She had been married to a Nigerian businessman, and there was a large framed photograph of him on top of the bookcase, along with several more of a dark-skinned girl, showing her at every stage from cheeky pig-tailed toddler up to vivaciously attractive teenager.

Oswalde felt a flutter in his chest. Instantly, he hadn't the slightest doubt. The resemblance to the clay head was as close as it could be. Part of him was elated – *they'd found Nadine!* – but then he had to prepare himself for what he knew was not going to be a pleasant duty. He started gently.

'May I show you these photographs?'

'Yes . . .'

They were of the carved ivory bracelets, and she nodded as she looked at them. 'Do you recognise these amulets, Mrs Fagunwa?'

'Yes. They belonged to my husband's family. He gave them to Joanne.'

'Then I'm sorry to tell you that they were found with the remains of a young girl. May I show you a picture of a clay head that we've had made.'

Oswalde waited while she studied it. Her dark eyes in her pale face remained expressionless. He said quietly, 'Does that look like your daughter?'

She nodded. 'Oh yes. It's very like her. How clever.'

'I'm sorry,' Oswalde said. This was horrible, he felt like he had a knife in his guts.

Mrs Fagunwa gazed at him. 'How did she die?'

'We're not certain, but the circumstances are suspicious.'

'Don't tell me she suffered.' And now there was a shadow of pain in her dark eyes, and her voice was husky. 'Please don't tell me that.'

Riding in the car seemed to have loosened her tongue; it was like watching a dam slowly crumbling, the unstoppable surge of water pouring out. Oswalde drove back down the M1, Mrs Fagunwa, now she'd started, unable to stop.

'... her father died that year, you see. I still don't know why she left home. She had everything. She even had her own pony, she had everything ...'

'Did Joanne ever have any accidents as a child?'

'Oh no, the usual cuts and bruises, you know.' Then she bethought herself. 'Oh yes – once she did. She broke her wrist. She fell off her bike.'

Mrs Fagunwa looked across at him. For him to have asked that specific question meant that he knew, that he was certain. She refused to make herself believe it, but it did no good. She knew now that it was her daughter that had been found, but she couldn't bring herself to ask.

Swallowing hard, she plunged on. 'Well, anyway, then she rejected it all. She started having bits woven in her hair. You know, beads and things. Her hair isn't even black really, more a dark brown, with threads of gold in it. She was almost blonde when she was little. Her skin looks more tanned than anything else. She was such a pretty little girl – we have so many photographs. I keep meaning to sort them out.'

She made a sound in her throat and her voice stuck. Oswalde gripped the wheel tightly, doing seventy-five in the centre lane. Driving was about the best he could manage at the moment.

Mrs Fagunwa took a deep breath, rallying herself.

'I don't think the local police treated her disappearance seriously. Just another young girl leaving home, going to London. Loads of them do that, don't they? I saw a documentary. It's not just Joanne . . .'

Oswalde saw a sign for the motorway services, one mile ahead. His throat was parched and aching, and besides he needed to call base.

'She always thought the best of people. Perhaps we protected her too much. I don't know. Do you have children?'

'No, I don't. Would you like a cup of coffee?'

'Oh, that would be lovely.' Mrs Fagunwa smiled at him. Oswalde indicated and pulled over to the inside lane. 'Perhaps if ours hadn't been a mixed marriage. Do you think that could have been the problem? Made her run off like that?'

Hands behind his head, Rosper leaned back in his chair, watching the videos on the TV in a corner of the Incident Room. He was enjoying himself, tapping his foot to the reggae beat. The band was on a makeshift stage out in the street, bathed in sunshine, a real carnival atmosphere. Many of the performers wore colourful African costumes, as did the crowd, packed close to the stage, clapping their hands above their heads. Rosper hummed along and tapped his foot.

Haskons came over and leaned on his shoulder. 'How's it going, Gary?'

Rosper looked up with a beaming grin. 'I'm having a skanking good time, Skip.'

'Are you indeed.'

The incessant reggae beat was getting on people's nerves; some of them complained, so Rosper turned the sound low, but kept his eyes glued to the screen as one band followed another, studying the faces of the backing singers and the women in the crowd. His perseverence paid off. Leaping to his feet, he peered closely at the screen, and just at that moment the camera obligingly moved in on one of three girl backing singers to the left of the stage.

'Yes,' Rosper breathed, and then louder, 'Yes, Yes!'

It was her, no mistake, dressed in African costume, happily smiling in the sunshine, swaying and clapping, having one hell of a good time. So full of vibrant energy and youthful joy, her whole life ahead of her, a life that had less than twenty-four hours to run its course.

Standing in the busy hospital corridor, Tennison held one hand flat to her ear while she tried to concentrate on what Haskons was telling her over the phone. He was having to shout too, trying to be heard over the babble of noise as the men clustered round the TV. Not helped by the thumping reggae beat, which Rosper had turned back up.

'That's right,' Haskons was saying. 'And Bob Oswalde called in. He's got a positive ID. Joanne . . . Fagunwa? Not sure of the pronounciation. He's bringing Mum in now.' He shouted away from the phone, 'Look, turn it down, please.'

'Brilliant,' Tennison said. 'All right, thanks, Richard.'

She hung up and joined Muddyman, who was using his powers of persuasion on the Chinese female doctor, Dr Lim, in the hope that they would be allowed in to see David Harvey. He wasn't having much success.

'He's a very ill man, you've seen that for yourself,' Dr Lim said. 'You've also seen how he has great difficulty breathing when lying flat. He needs complete rest.'

Tennison laid it on the line. 'Dr Lim. We have reason to believe that Mr Harvey was involved in the murder of a seventeen-year-old girl. Now, I don't mind what conditions you make, but we have to talk to the man.'

Dr Lim didn't say anything, because the discussion was at an end; the look in the eyes of the Chief Inspector told her that.

Mrs Fagunwa was turning over Joanne's things in interview room C3 off reception. She was bearing up well, Oswalde thought. Not a tear, not a quiver, just quietly picking things up – muddy Wrangler jeans, wrinkled Adidas trainers – until she came to the blue pullover, and her hand shook as she held it up.

'This I recognise. My one and only attempt at knitting . . .'

She crumpled it in her hand, head bowed low over the table, her shoulders heaving. Oswalde did what he could to comfort her, uttering some soothing platitudes, his arm around her.

'Why her?' Mrs Fagunwa moaned, tears dripping off the end of her nose. 'Why her . . .?'

When she had dried her eyes, Oswalde asked if she would like a cup of tea in the canteen, but she said no, she'd prefer to start back. He walked her out to the car he had ordered, waiting in the car park.

Mrs Fagunwa faced him. She had regained her composure, though her chin kept quivering. She said, 'Thank you for your kindness. Do you think you'll find out how it happened? You know . . . find the person who did it?'

'I'm sure we will,' Oswalde replied, and this wasn't a platitude.

'I wonder, this may seem . . .' She hesitated. 'Could I buy the clay head when your inquiries are over? It's just . . . does that seem strange?' she asked anxiously, as if seeking his approval.

'No. I'll find out for you.'

'Only there's nothing else is there?' Mrs Fagunwa plucked at a loose thread on her scarf, her eyes a million light-years away. 'Nothing to remind me of my baby.'

Harvey was sleeping, breathing through his mouth. Tennison sat by the bed, back straight, hands clasped in her lap, watching him sleep and breathe, her eyes never leaving his face.

7

After seeing Mrs Fagunwa off, Oswalde went back up to
the Incident Room and sat at his desk. It was twenty past
four. He should have been famished, having missed lunch,
existing since breakfast on cups of coffee and a Toblerone,
but he wasn't hungry. It was the hours spent with the dead
girl's mother, he reckoned, and seeing her grief, that had
killed his appetite. Not good. After nearly nine years on
the Force he ought to be able to shut his own emotions
away, not get personally involved. You had to be cold
and dispassionate or you couldn't do the job. Doctors and
nurses and paramedics and firemen had to handle it, deal
unflinchingly with things that would have turned most
people's stomachs, and then go home and sleep nights.
He wished he could do it too, learn the trick. Cultivate a
heart like a swinging brick, as one of the tutors in training
college was fond of saying.

Get your brain back on the case, Oswalde advised
himself, that was the best way. He looked round. 'Did
the Allens have keys to Harvey's place?' he asked of no
one in particular. 'I suppose they must have. Where did
Tony Allen go to school?'

Lillie chucked a file over. Oswalde spent a few minutes going through it until Rosper wandered over and
interrupted him.

'Have you seen this?' Rosper asked, parking his arse

on the corner of the desk. He was holding a video tape.

'Is that the tape of Joanne?'

'You should watch it, Bob.' Rosper made a flicking motion with his tongue. 'I think I'm in love.'

Haskons had sent over a PC to relieve her. He came in and removed his helmet, holding it under his arm.

Tennison stood up and stretched. She bent over to peer closely at Harvey, his face lined and grey in the shaded strip light above the bed. He was out for the count, asleep or unconscious, it was hard to tell. She put on her coat, tucked in her scarf, and picked up her briefcase.

'Call me if he comes round.'

'I will.'

Mr Dugdale taught History, which possibly explained why he had such a good memory for dates. He wasn't bad on names either, and had no problem whatsoever with Tony Allen, as soon as Oswalde mentioned him.

'I was his head of year. I remember it very well.' They were walking towards Dugdale's office, the corridor deserted except for a cleaner with a bucket and mop. Oswalde had turned up on the off-chance that some of the teachers might have stayed behind to mark papers or something, and had struck lucky.

'He was a bright lad, done very well in the fifth form, good results, going on to A-Levels, sights set on a college place.' Dugdale shook his head of shaggy greying hair, depositing more flakes of dandruff on the collar of his tweed jacket. 'Then when he came back in September he'd changed. He was surly, introverted, a loner.'

They arrived at his office and Dugdale went straight

to the filing cabinet and started delving. Oswalde looked at the timetables pinned to the notice-board, at the silver trophies gathering dust on the shelf next to the wilting potted plant, but he was taking in every word.

'I spoke to him, the head mistress spoke to him. I got Dad up here. Nothing seemed to work.' Dugdale slipped on his glasses and opened the buff folder. 'There, you see . . . September '86. I'm usually right. Educational psychologist's report. Help yourself.'

Oswalde scanned through it and made a few notes while Dugdale pottered around.

'I see Tony played in a band . . .'

'Did he? I didn't know that. We did our best but there was really no point in him staying on. The only person he seemed to relate to was his Sarah. He'd gone by Christmas. I see him in the supermarket from time to time,' Dugdale said absently, polishing his glasses with the end of his tie. 'Waste really, he was a bright lad.'

Tennison was on her knees, scrubbing the bathtub, when the intercom buzzer sounded. She dried her hands on her loose cotton top and went to answer it, frowning as she lifted the entryphone receiver from its wall cradle. She hadn't a clue who it could be; she wasn't expecting anyone.

'Hello?'

'Jane?'

A man's voice, deep and resonant, one she couldn't put a name to. 'Who's this?' she asked guardedly.

'Bob Oswalde.'

She leaned her outstretched arm against the door frame, wondering what the hell was going on, and more specifically just what game he thought he was playing.

'Jane . . .? Look, I know this is a bit, er, unexpected . . . but I really do need to talk to you.'

'Well, can't it wait? I'm waiting for a call from the hospital.'

'No.'

Sighing, she pressed the button to release the street door and dropped the receiver back in its cradle. She started towards the living-room, only just realising in the nick of time that she was practically on display, wearing only the loose top with nothing underneath. She nipped back into the bathroom and pulled on a floppy sweater, then walked through the living-room, brushing her fingers through her hair.

Oswalde knocked and she opened the door. He was carrying a video tape. She said crisply, 'This'd better be good,' already walking off, leaving him to close the door.

She stood with her arms folded, watching him insert the video into the machine and turn on the set. He sat down on the sofa, still in his raincoat, and operated the remote. The image flickered and steadied: a reggae group blowing up a storm, a host of black faces smiling in the sunshine, women swaying to and fro in their multicoloured robes and turbans.

Tennison knelt on the carpet in front of the TV, chin propped on her fist. 'I've seen this,' she told him in a voice flat as a pancake.

Oswalde suddenly leaned forward and touched the screen, indicating a tiny figure on the far right. 'There.'

'Your finger, very interesting.'

'There's a better shot in a moment,' he said, on the defensive, hurt by her flippancy. The camera cut to a close-up of the bass player. Oswalde pressed the pause button and jabbed at the screen. 'There!'

Squinting, Tennison slowly leaned forward. 'Is that Tony Allen?'

Oswalde gave a grim smile. 'Tony Allen. He's concealed the fact that he was playing at the Sunsplash concert and evidently knew Joanne.'

'Jesus!'

'The Allens had keys to the house. I've been to the school –'

'Yes. Okay.' Tennison cut him short with a raised hand. She sat back on her heels. 'Let's think this through. Just because he was on the bandstand with her doesn't mean . . .' Her bleeper went. 'Shit, this could be it.' She dived for her shoulder-bag, found the bleeper and killed it. 'I'm waiting for Harvey to come round,' she told him, already reaching for the phone and dialling.

Oswalde discovered he'd been sitting on a plate of half-eaten congealed food. He removed it, mouth curling in distaste. 'What's this?'

'Last night's dinner – one of those frozen chilli con carne things.'

'What have you got for tonight?'

Clicking her fingers impatiently, waiting for the connection to be made, she glanced over at him. 'One of those frozen chilli con carne things . . . DCI Tennison,' she said into the phone.

Oswalde draped his raincoat over the back of the sofa, picked up the disgusting plate between outstretched fingertips, and wandered off with it. Tennison was momentarily distracted.

'Where d'you think you're going?' Then she was nodding, talking fast. 'Right. Did she leave a number? A callbox?' She scribbled it down. 'Okay . . . right . . . thanks.' She hung up and started to redial. Oswalde had

116

disappeared. 'It's not the hospital,' she called out to him. 'It's a snout of mine trying to get through to me.'

'Right . . .' Oswalde's voice floated in from the kitchen.

'What are you up to?' she wondered aloud. 'Rachel? It's me, Jane Tennison, darling. What've you got for me, darling?'

When she came through into the kitchen there was water on the boil, a packet of pasta waiting to go in. Bob Oswalde had raided her meagre shelves and come up with tinned tomatoes, a tin of tuna, one onion, and a few dried herbs, the last in the jar. He'd found a clean pan and had made a start on the sauce. Shirt-sleeves rolled up, he was standing at the counter-top, expertly chopping garlic and crushing it into a saucer.

Tennison leaned in the doorway, watching him. 'What the hell do you think you're doing?'

Oswalde wiped his hands and opened the fridge door. He rooted inside and picked something up. 'What's this?' he asked, holding up what appeared to be a mouldy brown tennis ball.

'It's a lettuce,' Tennison said. 'Well, it was once.'

Oswalde chucked it in the bin, tutting. 'You need to eat some decent food. What was the call about? Anything interesting?'

'No, not really,' she said, deciding to humour him, and besides, the smell was making her ravenous. 'Apparently it seems the girl that was at number 15 jacked it in afterwards and went legit. No one seems to know where she is now, but they're all sure she's not on the game.'

'Right,' Oswalde said, busy now forking tuna into a bowl. 'I took a look at Tony's school record. Everything was fine until 1986. When Tony came back from the summer holidays, he was a different person.' He glanced round at her, eyebrows raised. 'Educational psychologist's report talks of depression, anxiety attacks, low self-esteem.'

Tennison studied him for a moment, lips pursed. 'What is it with you?'

'What?' Oswalde said, blinking.

'What are you trying to prove?'

He emptied the tomatoes and stirred them in with a wooden spoon. 'Do you have any tomato purée?'

'No.'

'How can I work in these conditions?' he complained to the cupboard door, his brow furrowed.

'It's as if you're taking some kind of test all the time . . .'

'You should know,' he retorted, and that made her stand up straight. 'I watched you on the course. You know they're all lined up, wanting to see you fall flat on your face. Thorndike, all the Senior Shits. You always want to be the best, come out on top.'

This was straight from the shoulder, and Tennison wasn't sure she liked it. She certainly wasn't used to being spoken to so directly, least of all by a subordinate.

'I'm the same as you,' Oswalde went on imperturbably. He tasted the sauce, added black pepper. 'Which is why – when I calmed down and thought about it – I understood why you'd been treating me like the office boy.'

He was one cool customer, had it all sussed.

'And why you've gone off and done a number on your own?' Tennison accused him sharply. He had the gall to laugh – a confident, unforced laugh at that. 'I mean it, Bob. You are a member of a team,' she reminded him.

'Am I?' Oswalde said, instantly serious, his stern dark eyes coming round to meet hers.

'Well,' Tennison said, wishing to high heaven he wasn't such a big, broad-shouldered, handsome bastard. 'From now on you are.'

'Okay,' Oswalde said, back to his cheery self. He tipped the pasta into the boiling water and ladled the tuna into the sauce. 'I don't suppose you've got anything to drink?'

That she had, and she went off to open a bottle of Bulgarian red.

Tennison was confused, and annoyed with herself for letting him get the upper hand. Was Bob Oswalde taking liberties or just trying to be friendly? She knew she was paying the penalty for that one hour of passion in the hotel room. The demarcation lines had been blurred; no other officer under her command would have waltzed into her flat and made himself at home by cooking dinner, without so much as a by-your-leave. Damn Kernan for drafting him on to her team! It was all his bloody fault! But she was as angry with herself for getting into this pickle in the first place. Being ruled by her libido instead of her brain.

They ate off the coffee table in the living-room. Tasting freshly-prepared food and drinking three glasses of wine worked a minor miracle. It took the sting out of her anger and made her almost mellow. It even crossed her mind to wonder what might happen later, and instantly slammed the door shut on *that* speculation. Hadn't she made enough of a fool of herself already, for Chrissakes?

They didn't talk about work until the end of the meal, when Oswalde again brought up the subject of Tony Allen. He seemed to have almost a personal vendetta against the boy. Tennison was wary, not wanting to rush their fences. Oswalde couldn't see why. The fact that he'd known Joanne Fagunwa was sufficient in itself to have him picked up.

Tennison drained her glass and set it down. 'Not yet.'

'The boy was involved in that murder,' Oswalde insisted. 'I'm sure of it . . .'

'We have no evidence of that.'

'You didn't see his response to the clay head,' Oswalde told her bluntly.

'All we know is that he was on the same bandstand as Joanne –'

'So he's been lying.'

'– and we'll question him about that at the right time.'

'What does that mean?' asked Oswalde rudely, his face becoming stiff and surly. He detested all this fannying around. Get in there and get it done with.

'It means not yet.' Tennison's voice was firm. Three glasses of wine didn't make her a pushover. She held up a finger. 'I can crack Harvey. He holds the key – except the bastard might croak on us any minute. I'll talk to Tony when we've got more on him.'

'More?' Oswalde was both pained and puzzled. 'I thought you'd really go for this.'

'Look, Bob, I don't want to argue about it.' In other words, the Chief Inspector was saying, subject closed.

Oswalde got the message, or thought he did. He stared across at Jane Tennison, a muscle twitching in his cheek. 'But the real point,' he said stonily, 'is that I shouldn't have come here, should I?'

'No, you shouldn't – we said that in the hotel room. But that's not the point, actually. Look, all I'm trying to say is . . .'

'Don't bother.'

Ten seconds later he was gone, raincoat over his

shoulder, door slammed. Tennison piled the dirty dishes in the sink and went to bed.

The Incident Room was quiet when she arrived the next morning, shortly after eight-twenty. She went to her office to catch up on some paperwork before the rush started.

WPC Havers eventually turned up, looking a bit worse for wear, and Tennison sent her off to the canteen to get a coffee and bring one back for her. She was sipping this and fighting the desperate urge for a fag when word came from the hospital. Tennison slurped the rest of her coffee, spilt some on her best chiffon blouse, and made the air blue and Maureen Havers' ears turn red as she grabbed her coat from the hatstand and hurried out.

'Hello, Guv,' she greeted Kernan, who was about to enter his office, and kept on going.

'Yes, it went very well since you ask.'

Tennison halted. 'Sorry?'

'My interview.'

'Oh good . . . right . . .'

'Any news on Harvey?'

'He's regained consciousness. I'm going down there to see him right now.'

Kernan nodded, gave her a look. 'Well, gently does it, Jane.'

'Yes, I . . .'

'Get him everything he wants – solicitors, nurses, doctors, geisha girls – anything. Just so long as his brief can't say you got a statement from him unfairly.'

Tennison tightened her belt, knuckles showing white. 'Of course.' What did he think her intention was – throttle the truth out of a dying man?

Lillie emerged from the Incident Room, looking for her. 'Excuse me, Guv. Apparently Harvey's wife died in October '85. Not August.'

'So his sister's been telling fibs.'

'So it would seem.'

'Well, let's see what Harvey's got to say about that.'

Lillie went off, and Tennison was about to leave, when Kernan said, apropos of nothing, 'By-election today.'

Then she twigged it. Jonathan Phelps, Labour's firebrand, was up for election. There was a chance, a slim chance, that he might get in, and if he did there could be one or two ructions. Phelps was riding on the ticket of community policing in black areas, on newsworthy items such as the case of Derrick Cameron. And now Tennison was investigating a murder in the Honeyford Road area involving a girl of black-white parentage. A highly sensitive, highly potent mixture. Like most policemen, Kernan was a staunch Tory, and the last thing he desired was to give the opposition the ammunition to fire a broadside.

With a ghost of a smile, Tennison said, 'Well, why aren't you wearing your blue rosette?'

It wasn't a joke to Kernan; it was deadly serious.

'Senior policemen are politicians first and foremost, Jane. Remember that if you're up for Super.'

It was bad enough that he believed it, Tennison thought, even worse to realise that he was right.

The teenager in the black leather jacket, baseball cap worn back to front, stood at the counter of Esme's café, dithering. He pointed to a large bowl of mashed yams with cinnamon and nutmeg, topped with grated orange rind.

'How much is that?'

'One seventy-five,' Esme said.

'How much?' the boy said, goggling.

Esme switched her attention to the tall, good-looking man waiting patiently to be served. From her bright smile and cheerful, 'Yes, dear?' Oswalde knew that she hadn't recognised him.

'Let me have a medium fried chicken, rice and peas.'

While she dished it up, the boy in the baseball cap carried on moaning. He obviously had a sweet tooth, because he next pointed to a portion of plantain fritters, fried in butter and apple sauce. 'How much is that?'

'Seventy-five pence.'

'You're jokin', man . . . yeah, all right, then.'

Esme served him and he mooched off, the flaps of his trainers protruding like white tongues. She handed Oswalde his meal in a polystyrene tray and gave him change from a fiver. Oswalde ate it at the counter, watching Esme ice a large cake; Tony's wedding cake, Oswalde thought, the wedding a week on Saturday.

'How is it?' Esme asked him.

'Very good. It's been a long time.'

'Your mother doesn't cook for you?'

'No.'

She flashed him her bright smile. 'Then you come to Esme's. I'll cook for you.'

Oswalde moved along the counter, nearer to where she was working. 'You don't recognise me, Esme?' She straightened up, frowning, a slight shake of the head. 'I'm a police officer. I'm investigating the murder of Joanne Fagunwa. That was her name, Esme. The girl who was buried in Harvey's garden . . .'

Esme stared at him, surprise and shock mingled

123

on her face. But she was in for an even bigger shock when Oswalde said softly, 'Did you know that she was a member of Tony's band? That she was with Tony on the day she died?'

'No,' Esme said in a whisper. No longer smiling, her eyes were scared now.

Oswalde pushed the chicken aside, leaning his elbows on the counter. 'Are you sure Tony was there that night when you arrived home?'

'Yes. I'm sure.'

'He couldn't have been with Joanne?'

'No.'

Oswalde was convinced she was telling the truth – as much of the truth as she knew, anyway. He said, 'Why did you think he changed so much that summer, Esme? He's never been the same since, has he? What happened to change him like that?'

She didn't answer, though from her expression Oswalde knew he had scored a bull's-eye.

Muddyman was waiting for her outside Harvey's room. 'Are we in?' Tennison asked tersely.

'Dr Lim is still a bit jumpy, but yeah, I think so.'

At that moment Dr Lim arrived. As they were about to enter, she held up a cautioning hand. 'I don't want him upset. Any extra pressure on his heart could be fatal.'

No more fatal than what happened to Joanne Fagunwa, Tennison reckoned, though she merely nodded, following the small, round-shouldered doctor inside.

Harvey's breathing filled the room. He was looking up at the ceiling with his dull, bleary eyes. Tennison eased the chair up to the bed and leaned over, her mouth close to his ear. She held his hand.

'Don't you think it'd be a good idea to talk to me, David?' she said very softly. 'Get it off your chest?'

Harvey's tongue came out to lick his dry lips. He stared straight up, his voice a horrible croak. 'What . . .?'

'David, we know that Joanne – that was her name – we found that Joanne was killed in your home. A fragment of her tooth was found inside the house.'

Harvey swallowed. 'Doesn't mean I killed her,' he gasped.

Tennison went on steadily, 'Your wife didn't die in August, did she, David? Jeanie died in October 1985. What's the point of lying, David? Carrying all that guilt?' From the corner of her eye she saw a blur of white coat as Dr Lim, concerned for her patient, moved nearer, but Tennison kept on.

'You're a very ill man. If you do tell me, nothing will happen to you – it'll never come to that. We'll be able to clear all this up and . . .' She paused. 'Most important of all, you'll feel so much better.'

Harvey closed his eyes and then opened them again, as if he might be thinking about it. Tennison waited, the hoarse, ragged breathing loud in her ears, the smell of it foul in her nostrils.

Oswalde stalked his prey, biding his time until Tony Allen had moved on from chatting to one of the checkout girls, and then he closed in behind him, reaching inside his jacket pocket for the colour photograph of Joanne Fagunwa.

'Hello, Tony.'

Tony Allen jumped. 'Sorry?'

'You don't remember me? Detective Sergeant Oswalde. I was just doing a bit of shopping.' Tony Allen retreated a pace as Oswalde loomed over him. 'While I'm here, perhaps you could have a look at this. Recognise her?'

Tony barely glanced at the photograph. 'Why don't you people leave me alone?' he said, a tremor in his voice.

'Because you're telling us lies. You knew Joanne.'

'No . . .'

'You were both at the Sunsplash together. Better than that,' Oswalde said, quiet and lethal, 'you played in the same band.'

Tony's mouth dropped open. He wasn't expecting that. Another bull's-eye.

'Remember her African costume . . . her bracelets?'

'I don't know what you're talking about.'

'Oh yes you do.'

'I don't.' Tony backed into a freezer cabinet. '*I don't.*'

Oswalde watched him scoot off. There was no need to pursue him. Tony Allen wasn't going anywhere.

'I'm a Catholic too, David, and it's been a long time since my last Confession, but one thing I do remember is that feeling of relief. That weight being lifted off your shoulders.' Harvey's drab eyes stared up, and Tennison wasn't sure how much of this was getting through. But she kept at it, soft and remorseless.

'I think we all want to have faith in something, don't we? We'd like to think we can repent and it'll be all right . . . if only we could turn the clock back, make it all right. You're dying, David. Best get it off your chest. Tell me what happened, David. No more lies. It's too late for lies.'

Harvey blinked, and tears ran down from the corners of his eyes into his grey hair. Tennison leaned nearer, stroking his hand, her voice like velvet.

'You can talk to me . . .'

'Can I?' Harvey croaked.

'Of course you can. You can have a doctor present, a solicitor, your sister, Jason, anyone.'

Harvey's chin quivered. He said huskily, 'You know, I'm only fifty-five years old. It's a fucking joke.'

'I'm sure the doctors will do all they can,' Tennison said.

'I'm so frightened,' Harvey said. His face suddenly crumpled, and he wept.

The streetlights were just flickering into life as Tony Allen came out of the supermarket and walked to his car. He unlocked the door and was about to climb in when he noticed a tall figure leaning against the bonnet of a black Ford Sierra three cars along.

'Yo', Tony,' Oswalde greeted him. 'All right?'

Fists bunched, Tony stormed round his car and went up to him. 'What's wrong with you? Why're you doing this to me?'

Oswalde spread his hands, eyebrows raised. 'Hey, doin' what, man? I've been shopping, that's all . . .'

'Leave me alone,' Tony ground out, his eyes bulging furiously. *'Just leave me alone!'*

Oswalde grinned at him. Tony swung round and marched back to his car. In his haste and rage he nearly smashed into the car behind by putting it in reverse, then shot out across the car park and into the street. All the way home he kept glancing in his rearview mirror, and every time he looked the black Sierra was there, openly, blatantly, following him.

Tony gripped the wheel so tightly his arms ached. Over and over, almost choking on the words, he kept repeating, 'Leave me alone, leave me alone, leave me alone . . .'

Tennison and Muddyman were having a quiet confab outside Harvey's room when his nephew arrived. The young, fair-haired man came up to them, slightly out of breath, and asked straight out, 'How is he?'

'He's a little better,' Tennison replied, aware that she was being economical with the truth. Looking into the pale blue eyes, and seeing in them a family resemblance, she said quietly, 'Jason, your uncle wants to talk to me.'

'Yeah, so I was told.'

'And he's asked for you to be there.'

Jason nodded. 'Right.'

'But I would just ask for you to remain quiet, not to interrupt while I'm talking to him.'

'Right,' Jason said again, as if mentally preparing himself for an ordeal, which indeed it would be.

Tennison glanced at Muddyman and gave a slight nod. He opened the door and the three of them went in.

*

Oswalde rang the bell of the second-floor flat. From within he heard the murmur of voices, and a moment later the door was opened by Esta, Tony's wife-to-be. She glared up at him, chewing her lip.

'Is Tony in?'

Before she could answer, Tony appeared in the narrow hallway. He grabbed the edge of the door. 'You know I am, you followed me home.'

'Can I come in, Tony?'

'No, you can't.'

'I'd like to ask you a few questions,' Oswalde said.

'You heard him, he said no,' Esta snapped.

Tony pointed a finger, which was quivering with pent-up rage. He said hoarsely, 'I don't have to answer your questions.'

'Who told you that?' Oswalde said. His face wore a twisted grin. 'Sarah the Law Student?'

Cleo, dressed in her pyjamas, holding a teddy bear by its ears, was standing in the lounge doorway. Esta waved to her distractedly. 'Go back inside, love . . .'

Pumping himself up, convinced he was in the right, Tony was jabbing his finger in Oswalde's chest. 'She says you either arrest me or stop harassing me.'

That did it. If Oswalde's mind hadn't been made up already, that made it up for him. He lunged forward and grabbed Tony's arm, dragging him through the door on to the landing. 'Tony Allen, I am arresting you for the murder of Joanne Fagunwa.'

'No!' Esta shouted. But she was too late. Oswalde had Tony in an arm-lock and was frog-marching him to the stairs.

'You can't . . .' Esta wailed. 'Where are you . . .'

Bent double, Tony yelled back. 'Esta, phone my Dad . . . phone my Dad!'

Oswalde bundled him down the stairs. Seeing her father snatched away in front of her eyes, Cleo had burst into tears; but the child's crying didn't deter DS Oswalde, who knew what had to be done, and did it.

Harvey had been miked up. Tennison sat close to the bed, leaning over, while Muddyman kept an eye on the tape-recorder's winking red light. Jason stood behind Muddyman, his face and cap of blond hair a shadowy blur.

'Do you wish to consult a solicitor or have a solicitor present during the interview?'

'No.' The lost, bleary eyes stared up at the ceiling. 'Water.'

Tennison poured water into a glass and helped him to a couple of sips. Her entire job, it seemed, consisted of waiting, and she waited now, very patiently, for Harvey to compose himself.

Custody Sergeant Calder and an Asian PC were having one hell of a struggle, trying to get Tony Allen from the charge room into the cells. The boy was close to hysteria, his eyes wide and terrified in his sweating face. He was babbling, 'No, don't lock me up, don't lock me up, please don't lock me up . . .'

Eventually, after much straining and heaving, they managed to get him inside cell 7 and slammed the door. Calder walked back to the charge room, wiping his bald head, and tugging his uniform straight. He was an experienced officer and he didn't like the look of it; the kid was half-demented, and even now his moaning voice echoed down the corridor, pleading, 'Let me out . . . don't leave me alone, please . . . please let me out!'

Calder entered the charge room, shaking his head worriedly. 'I'd better get the doctor to take a look at him. I don't think he's fit to be detained.'

Oswalde thought this was overdoing it. 'He's all right,' he said dismissively. 'Just let him stew for a bit . . .'

'Look, I'm the Custody Sergeant,' Calder blazed at him. 'Don't try to tell me my job. Right?'

Oswalde gave him a look. Then he shrugged and went out. Calder reached for the phone but he didn't pick it up. He stood there for a moment, undecided, cracking his knuckles, and then barked, 'Yes?' at the Asian PC, who was holding out a docket to be signed. Calder scrawled his signature, which reminded him he had a mountain of paperwork to shift.

He made a noise that was half snort, half sigh. That's all they were these days, a legion of bloody pencil-pushers.

When he was ready, she began:

'You do not have to say anything unless you wish to do so, but what you say may be given in evidence. Do you understand, David?'

'Yes.' His breathing rasped in his throat. Slowly he turned his head on the pillow and looked straight at her.

8

Tennison had to steel herself not to show repugnance as his breath wafted over her. It seemed to her she had been sitting by his bedside for an eternity, breathing in the foul miasma of death. She herself felt soiled by it, as if it had entered her pores, and she had to use every ounce of willpower to repress the shudder at the touch of his cold, damp hand.

Her face betrayed none of this. And her voice stayed quiet and calm, almost soothing.

'All right, David . . . let me take you back to what you said originally. That you were with your sister in Margate on Sunday and Monday, and not at Honeyford Road.'

'Lies,' Harvey said drably. 'I didn't stay the night. I came back Sunday. Sunday afternoon. Not Monday like I said.'

'So – did you ask Eileen to provide you with an alibi?'

Harvey shook his head weakly. 'No. She knows nothing of this . . .'

Tennison frowned. 'But she must do, David, because she confirmed your story. She said that weekend was the anniversary of your wife's death. It wasn't. She said you spent it with her. You didn't.'

'I don't want my sister dragged into this,' Harvey

insisted, his voice thickening. He was staring at Tennison, blinking rapidly.

'I'm afraid she already is, David . . .'

'Leave her out of it.' Suddenly angry, he levered himself up on one elbow, the effort making him gasp. His eyes were wild, rolling. 'I'll tell you nothing if you drag her into it!'

Tennison put her hand on his shoulder, and he slowly subsided, flecks of spittle on his moustache. He lay flat, his chest heaving. The vehemence of his reaction puzzled her. She had seen real fear in his eyes . . . but fear of what? Involving his sister? His emotion had been too fierce and panic-stricken for that alone, Tennison thought. Unless he was trying to shield Eileen, divert suspicion from her possible complicity in what had taken place that weekend.

Harvey went on, almost in a drone, as if talking to himself. 'I hated it down there anyway. Godforsaken cold bastard of a place. Thought I might as well go home – do something useful, get some work done in the garden . . .'

'So what time did you get back to London?' Tennison asked.

'About five. I did some more work, then I went inside. I was watching the telly in the front room when I saw her.'

Tennison leaned forward, her eyes narrowing a fraction. 'Who did you see, David?'

'I saw the girl. Joanne.' Harvey stared into the shadows, as if seeing her now. 'She was standing at a bus stop. Waiting for a bus that didn't run on a Sunday.'

'What time was this?'

''Bout half-past eight, nine. It was just getting dark. I watched her . . .' His voice took on a dreamy, faraway tone. 'She stood with one leg behind the other, sort of swinging herself. I thought I'd better tell her. I went out to

133

her. I told her the bus didn't run. I said she should phone for a taxi. Told her she could use my phone.'

He paused, his dry lips parted. 'She came into the house,' he said in his drab, dreamy voice, and then, as if the recollection had exhausted him, he closed his eyes.

DI Burkin wasn't at all happy about this. Calder, the Custody Sergeant, had already voiced his doubts to him, and Burkin could see why. The kid was practically gibbering with fear. Sweat was trickling from the roots of his short black hair, making his face a shiny, petrified mask. Oswalde didn't seem to notice – or if he did, didn't appear to care.

Arms folded, Burkin leant against the wall of the interview room, watching with hooded eyes as Oswalde set up the tape-recorder. He didn't know what grounds Oswalde had for arresting Tony Allen, but they'd better be bloody good, or there'd be hell to pay.

Oswalde placed the mike on the table in front of Tony Allen, who stared at it like a rabbit hypnotised by a snake. Oswalde stretched out and pressed the Record button. Still standing, he began: 'This interview is being tape recorded. I am Detective Sergeant Robert Oswalde, attached to Southampton Row. The other officer present is . . .'

'Detective Inspector Frank Burkin,' Burkin said.

Oswalde sat down opposite Tony Allen. 'You are?'

Nothing. Not a flicker. The young man looked to be in some sort of trance. Oswalde leant his elbows on the table and laced his fingers together. 'State your full name and date of birth.'

Tony's lips moved. In a mumble that was almost

inaudible, he said, 'Anthony Allen. Fifth of May . . .'

'Louder for the tape, please.'

The command galvanised Tony into life. His head came up, eyes bulging, and he started gabbling like somebody on speed, '*Anthony Allen. Anthony Allen. Fifth of May. Nineteen sixty-nine. Nineteen sixty . . .*'

Jesus Wept, Burkin thought gloomily, rolling his eyes towards the ceiling. A jungle bunny off his trolley. That's all they fucking needed.

Vernon Allen and his wife had been in the waiting-room over an hour. Esme was frantic, out of her mind with worry, and it was all he could do to pacify her. The call from Esta, telling them that Tony had been arrested, had left them both shocked and scared. Vernon kept telling himself that it was a mistake, it would soon be sorted out, but as the minutes dragged by and they were told nothing, a hollow feeling of sick apprehension rose up inside, nearly choking him. But he had to keep a grip, not let it show, otherwise Esme would go completely to pieces.

She was back on her feet again, unable to sit still for more than a minute. The Asian PC behind the reception desk could only shrug and offer a bland, 'I'm sorry,' as Esme leaned against the counter, fists clenched, her eyes large and moist.

'We must be allowed to see our son!' she demanded for the umpteenth time.

'The officer in charge will be out to see you shortly, madam.'

Esme turned away, shaking her head, not knowing where to put herself. In a small, lost voice she said faintly, 'I don't believe this is happening . . .'

'Well it is,' Vernon said. He sighed and gave a weary gesture. 'Now come and sit down.'

'The officer won't be long,' the PC assured them.

Esme slumped down on the bench beside her husband. What was happening to her boy, her Tony? Why wouldn't they let them see him? What were they doing to him in there?

'I tried to touch her,' Harvey said, his voice harsh and rasping. 'Touch her tits.'

He returned Tennison's calm gaze with a challenging stare, as if hoping she might be offended by his crudity. But he was disappointed; she wasn't.

'Do you remember what she was wearing, David?' Tennison asked in the same quiet, even tone.

'No.'

'Was she wearing a bra?'

'I don't think so, no,' Harvey said after a slight hesitation.

Tennison paused a moment to consider this before asking, 'Then what happened?'

Harvey turned his head away. Under the shaded strip light on the wall above the bed his lined face and sunken cheeks had the appearance of a death's-head. 'I hit her,' he said.

*

He was going to break him; it was just a matter of going at him, unrelentingly, until he tripped himself up. But it wasn't quite working out that way. The more Oswalde pressed him, the angrier and more defiant Tony became. Burkin was surprised by the lad's guts. He'd have laid

136

odds that Tony Allen was the type to crumple as soon as the heat was turned on. It gave him a sly sense of amusement to watch Oswalde banging away and getting nowhere fast. Teach the cocky bastard a lesson.

'What did I just say?' Tony threw up his hands. '. . . I admit it, I admit I knew her!'

'She was your girlfriend, Tony,' Oswalde repeated for the third time, making it sound like a statement of established fact.

'No, she wasn't. I told you. She was going out with the lead singer. I asked her out but she said no –'

Oswalde pounced. 'So how come she ended up back at Honeyford Road with you?'

Tony closed his eyes and rested his forehead in the palm of his hand. He sighed and said wearily, 'I had some tapes there she wanted. Songs for her to learn.' He looked up at the man sitting opposite him, as taut and intense as a coiled spring. 'She came in after my dad went to work. Stayed for an hour or so, that's all.'

'And then you took her into Harvey's house.'

'No.'

'Because you knew he was away for the weekend. Used your father's keys and went next door with her.' More statements of fact, according to Oswalde. 'What happened then, Tony?'

Tony Allen shook his head. He went on shaking it as he said, slowly and distinctly, 'I – didn't – kill – her.'

Oswalde knew in his bones that the boy was lying through his teeth, but Burkin wasn't so sure.

'I tied her up. Hands behind her back.'

'What with?'

137

'I don't remember. I gagged her. Had sex with her. Afterwards I left her lying there.'

'Where was this?'

Harvey frowned. 'What do you mean?'

'Which room were you in?'

'The kitchen.' His eyelids flickered. 'A belt. I tied her with my belt . . .'

Without moving her head, Tennison turned her eyes to meet Muddyman's. He was leaning forward, elbows on his knees, a frown of concentration on his face. Behind him, in the darkened corner of the room, Jason was nothing more than a vague blur, his black T-shirt and dark windcheater merging into the background. Tennison turned her attention back to Harvey, to the drab, droning voice.

'. . . I left her lying there. Went and watched the telly. I don't know why. It was like a dream. As if it hadn't happened.'

Tennison pursed her lips, remained silent.

Tony twisted his lips in disgust. 'What kind of a brother are you?' he demanded contemptuously. 'To say things like that to me?'

'I'm not your brother, I'm a police officer,' Oswalde said stolidly. The guy was trying to play the black power card, and he wasn't having any. Burkin would just love that, all dem black folks jess one big happy family crap. Well stuff that.

With utter loathing in his voice, Tony practically spat in his face, 'Because you want to be white! You hate your black brothers and sisters. You're *black*!'

Oswalde was getting more irritated by the second. But he wasn't going to be drawn down that road. No chance. To show how calm he was, unaffected by Tony's outburst, he studied his fingernails and asked casually, 'Why did you give up playing the bass after that concert, Tony?'

'You're a sell-out, you wouldn't understand.'

'Try me.'

Tony's whole face seemed to be moving, as if he was trying to say something he didn't know how to express. There was a strange light in his eyes. Then it burst out of him in a flood.

'Bass notes are the pulse, they come up at you through the soles of your feet . . . they sound inside you, here. They beat with your heart. From beneath. A heartbeat. From beneath the earth.' He was like a mechanical doll, the words jerking out of him. His eyes suddenly focused on Oswalde, his voice filled with scathing contempt. 'You see, you don't understand. I couldn't play anymore . . . how could I play anymore?' Head straining forward, he yelled in Oswalde's impassive face, '*Why ask questions when you don't understand?*'

Burkin was staring at Tony, fascinated. Maybe Oswalde didn't understand, but he sure did; the kid was a loony tune. End of story.

*

The feel of the clammy hand clutching hers made Tennison feel nauseous. She swallowed hard, telling herself it would soon be over. Harvey was tiring fast, his voice becoming weaker, the gasping pauses more prolonged; but she nearly had it all now, down on tape, in his own words. The repulsion she felt was a small price to pay.

139

'. . . she must have choked on the gag. There was sick all round her mouth, her nose . . . I didn't mean to kill her.'

The door opened and a nurse came in bearing a small tray. Standing at the foot of the bed, she said quietly, 'I must give Mr Harvey his medication.'

Tennison nodded. She indicated to Muddyman and Jason that they should leave, then turned back to Harvey.

'I'll be back soon, David.' For the benefit of the tape, she said, 'I am concluding this interview. The time is eight-ten.'

Muddyman was standing with Jason in the corridor. The young man's hands hung limply by his sides, and the ordeal he was going through showed plainly on his face.

Tennison squeezed his shoulder. 'I'm sorry, this must be awful for you.'

Jason was staring at the floor, ashen to the lips. 'I've known him all my life,' he said in a stunned whisper. 'And I don't . . . I don't know him at all.'

'Will you be all right to go back in?' Tennison asked gently, and received a brief nod.

Muddyman stirred himself. 'I'll get us a coffee,' he said, and went off to find a machine.

Tennison felt soiled and grubby. What she really wanted was a hot cleansing shower and a large brandy. Wash away the stink from her body and deaden the memory of that gaunt, wasted face gasping out its last confession.

'If I had buried her,' Tony Allen told Oswalde, his eyes dangerously bright, 'I'd have buried her so deep you'd never have found her again. She'd never have come back . . .'

140

'Has she come back?' Oswalde asked, watching him closely.

Tony gave a pitying half-smile, the smile of someone trying to communicate an ultimate truth to an ignoramus. 'She's inside you,' he hissed. 'I can see her looking out at me. Looking at me through your eyes. Reaching out to me.' He tapped his chest. 'I'm her friend. She wants to get away from you. You're a coffin. You suffocate her. *You're her coffin.* Your eyes are little windows. I can see inside you. Through your eyes. See Joanne. She hates you . . .'

He wiped his mouth with the back of his hand. When it came away he was grinning at Oswalde with a strange mixture of triumph and the deepest loathing.

Harvey seemed to have regained a little strength. The pill, or injection – whatever it was – had brought him back into the world, banished for a short while the shades closing in around him.

Tennison pressed on, anxious to get it over and done with. 'What did you do with Joanne's body?'

'I kept it in the cupboard under the stairs. Till the following night. I dug a hole. I put the earth in bags. I had a lot of plastic sheeting. I wrapped her in the sheeting.' His voice broke. He stared sightlessly upwards. 'Buried her.'

Muddyman leaned forward into Tennison's eye-line, stroking his chin. She nodded slowly. Harvey was coming out with crucial details – the belt, the plastic sheeting – that hadn't been released to the media. Harvey couldn't possibly have known about them unless he was personally involved with the disposal of Joanne's body. It was the kind of clinching evidence they required to make the case stand up in court.

She was about to ask a further question when Harvey suddenly, and with great effort, raised himself up. His eyes probed the darkness, his slack mouth working desperately.

'I'm sorry, Jason, I'm sorry you have to hear all this. I just needed you to be here ...' Exhausted, he fell back, and Tennison waited for calm.

'Did you bury anything else with her, David?'

'Yes.'

'What?'

'A plastic bag.'

That hadn't been mentioned in the press either.

'What did it contain?'

Tennison had to crane forward to catch his mumbled, 'I don't know,' and it seemed to her that, having confessed to the murder, he was losing interest in the more mundane details of the crime.

Again she glanced towards Muddyman, who was looking like the cat that got the cream. Harvey was a goner, in more senses than one. He'd given them chapter and bloody verse on the whole sordid saga, committed it to tape, with three witnesses in attendance. Game, set and match.

Harvey continued to mumble. Tennison strained to hear, hoping the tape was picking it up.

'... I banged the earth flat. Laid the rest of the slabs, cemented them in. There was a smell. The darkie next door complained. I told him it was ... the drains ...'

His eyes closed.

The wheezing breath fluttered from his lips, emphasising the silence.

Tennison straightened her shoulders, sat back in her chair. 'Thank you, David,' she said, and indicated to

Muddyman that he could turn off the machine. Thank God that was over. Her flesh crawled at the memory of his clammy grip.

They went out into the corridor. Muddyman sealed the tape and asked Jason to countersign and date it. The young man did so, the pen shaking in his hand. He was still deathly pale, and looked sick to his stomach.

'Would you like a car to take you home?' Tennison asked, concerned about him.

'It's all right, thanks.' He raised his head and took a deep breath. 'I'd rather walk.'

They watched him trail off down the corridor, looking lost and aimless, but he turned the corner heading for reception, so that seemed okay. Muddyman stuffed the tape in his raincoat pocket and turned to Tennison with a fat grin.

'Well done! Nailed the bastard's bollocks to the floor.'

'You think so?'

Muddyman lit up and hungrily sucked in smoke. 'Know so.'

Tennison nodded, as if in agreement. She'd have given a month's pay for Muddyman's complete, unwavering certainty, but she couldn't make it gel. Something nagged at her. Some of the details Harvey had spilled she kept returning to, worrying at like a loose tooth.

But it had been a long, gruelling pig of a day and she was knackered. And somehow depressed on top of it. All her mind could focus on right this minute were the hot shower and the large brandy.

As they went down the stairs to the car park, Tennison said dully, 'God, hospitals depress me.'

Having finally got someone to babysit for her, Esta

flew down to Southampton Row and barged into the waiting-room. 'Have you seen him?' she asked them, huddled there on the bench. '*Have you seen him?*'

Esme shook her head tearfully. 'They won't . . . let me see my boy,' she wailed. 'My Tony . . .'

Esta stormed up to the counter. She banged on it with both fists. Through the glass panel she could see two or three uniformed officers sitting at desks in the back room. Beating on the counter, she yelled at them, 'I want to see somebody now! I want to see the person in charge! Come here – where is he?'

Vernon waved to her. 'They say somebody is just coming.'

Esta banged again, harder, louder.

'Come and sit down,' Vernon pleaded. 'Take it easy . . .'

Esta ignored him. She had no intention of taking it easy.

Tony was leaning his elbows on the table, his head in his hands. His voice was muffled.

'I'm a black bastard, I deserve all I get . . . I'm a black bastard, I deserve all I get . . .'

Standing opposite him, Oswalde thumped the table. 'Tony, just stop it, man!'

'I'm a black bastard, I deserve all I get . . . I'm a black bastard, I deserve all I get . . .'

'Tony, stop it! Just stop it, man . . .'

'That's enough,' Burkin said curtly. He strode to the door. 'Can I have a word, Sergeant Oswalde?'

'In a minute.'

'Now, Sergeant Oswalde!' Burkin went out.

Oswalde looked at his watch. 'I'm concluding this

interview at 11.25 p.m.' He switched off the machine and followed Burkin out.

Tony's hands came away from his face and clenched into fists.

'No, don't leave me alone! *Don't leave me alone in here!*'

In the corridor Burkin faced Oswalde. He had to raise his voice to be heard above Tony Allen's terrified, near-hysterical cries.

'What's all this about?'

'What?' Oswalde said. He was an inch or two taller than DI Burkin, and he stared into his eyes, knowing the man for the racist he was.

Burkin held up a warning finger. 'I don't know what's going on between you two . . .'

'What do you mean?'

'What do I mean?' Burkin's eyes bulged. He jerked his thumb at the pitiful, wavering sobs coming from the room – *Don't leave me alone . . . please don't leave me alone, please* . . . 'He's off his head!'

Oswalde looked down his nose at Burkin with narrowed eyes. 'That's your considered psychological opinion, is it?' he sneered.

'You're one arrogant bastard, do you know that?'

Oswalde dropped his voice to a low growl. 'Don't look at me like that, Frank. You've been wanting to have a go at me ever since I arrived at this poxy nick.' He squared up, flexing his shoulders. 'Well, go on then,' he challenged.

Eyeball to eyeball, the two men glowered at one another. Both well over six feet tall, both strongly built, both fired up with mutual hatred: Burkin the area boxing champion, Oswalde top of his class in unarmed combat,

145

they could have knocked seven kinds of shit out of one another. Both of them on a hair trigger, ready and raring to have a go.

'What the hell's going on?' Alerted by Tony's racket, Custody Sergeant Calder bustled into the corridor from the charge room, on his way to investigate.

'Butt out, Mike,' Oswalde said, tight-lipped.

Calder sized up the situation and acted at once to defuse it. He pushed the two men apart. 'I'm in charge of this area. Prisoners are my responsibility, right?'

Burkin turned his fury on him. 'So where's his brief?' he demanded.

'He said he didn't want one.'

'Look,' Burkin exploded, pointing his finger. 'That boy's climbing the fucking walls in there! Has he been seen by the doc?'

'Not yet,' Calder said defensively. He cleared his throat. 'It's all in hand . . .'

Burkin shot a fierce look at Oswalde. He said disparagingly, 'The arresting officer hasn't even got credible evidence.'

Calder was nettled. 'Look, don't tell me my job –'

'How do you know, anyway?' Oswalde said, glaring at Burkin.

'You've got nothing from him that would stick in court. He should go back into the cells until the boss has been informed.'

Calder tried to peer past them to the half-open door. 'Have you left him alone in there?'

Oswalde was really riled up now. He knew what Burkin's game was, and he told him straight. 'Hands off, Frank, this is my kill. You're just pissed off because the token black is going to have this case signed, sealed and on the guv'nor's desk by morning!'

Burkin said quietly, 'Bollocks you are.' And went striding off down the corridor to phone Tennison.

Oswalde returned to the interview room and slammed the door.

Calder, gnawing his thumbnail, was left standing, knowing he should have done as Burkin said and called the doc. He'd better do it. Right now.

Tennison, freshly showered and talced, wearing silk pyjamas, was on her way to bed when the phone rang. Passing by the little table, through sheer force of habit, she reached out to answer it. Her hand hovered, and then the answering machine clicked on. That's what answering machines were for, she reminded herself. For when you were out or too bloody tired or not in the mood to answer it. Score two out of three.

A voice was burbling. She turned the sound right down, switched off the lamp, and went through into the bedroom, shutting the door firmly behind her.

Whatever anger, whatever defiance, had been in Tony, it had left him as swiftly as the air leaves a punctured balloon. He sat with head bowed, shoulders hunched, his hands resting limply in his lap. Tears rolled down his cheeks. He made hardly any sound, just sat there weeping softly. Behind him, Oswalde paced, turned about, paced again, turned about. Burkin had got through to him, right to the quick. He'd nearly lost his temper, blown it completely. When above everything else he prided himself on his control, on not giving in to provocation. *That* close, and saved by the bell – or rather by Calder.

Oswalde saw it all too clearly. Burkin couldn't stomach an outside officer – a black one at that – coming in and solving the case and taking the credit. That's what this was about. That's why he'd blown a fuse. Well, sunshine, you're going to have to like it or lump it, Oswalde thought with grim satisfaction. He alone had collared Tony Allen and he intended to sweat it out of him. He didn't care if it took all night. From the minute he saw Tony's reaction to the clay head, he knew the boy was implicated in the girl's murder. All he had to do now was prove it.

Oswalde gripped the back of the chair and leaned over him.

'This is a waste of time. You're just wasting my time. Come on, Tony. You're as guilty as hell. I've known it from the first time I saw you.' He dug his fingers into Tony's hunched shoulder and hauled him back. 'Your guilty secret is written all over your face.'

Tony nodded feebly, his cheeks wet with tears. 'I am guilty . . .'

Oswalde quickly moved round and bent down, his face close to the boy's. 'Then tell me what happened that night.'

'We're all guilty . . .' Tony opened his mouth wide, fighting for breath. He clutched his throat. 'I'm choking . . .'

'No you're not.'

'I'm choking,' he gasped, clawing at his open-necked shirt with both hands.

'No you're *not*,' Oswalde barked at him. He turned away, fists clenching with frustration as Tony's face crumpled, tears squeezing out from under his eyelids. This was bloody hopeless. They'd been here for hours and he was getting nowhere. He had to make the boy crack. *Had* to.

He shook his head in disgust. 'All you've done is cry like a baby. Well, I'm sick of listening to you. You're pathetic. A bloody claat mummy's boy. Come on.' Oswalde waggled his thumb. 'You're going back in the cells.'

'No . . . I can't breathe in there,' Tony pleaded, gazing up at Oswalde with his pitiful, tear-streaked face. 'Don't, please . . .'

He half rose out of the chair, tugging at Oswalde's sleeve. Oswalde shook him off. 'Fuck you. You tell me how Joanne met her death or you go back in the bin and you *sweat*.'

Tony's head wobbled. 'No . . . no . . .'

Enough was enough. Oswalde turned away. He didn't see the change come over Tony's face. The eyes go suddenly wide and mad. The lips draw back in a snarl of rage. Tony leapt out of the chair. He went for Oswalde's throat, charging into him so that Oswalde was sent crashing against the wall. He was a head taller than Tony and over forty pounds heavier, but what a moment ago had been a pathetic cringing wreck was now transformed into a raving maniac with blood-lust in his eyes, attempting to throttle the life out of him.

Winded, Oswalde struggled to get a grip on the boy's wrists. He grabbed hold of the left, pivoted on one foot, and wrenched Tony's arm halfway up his back. He caught the other one and pinned both Tony's hands behind his back and slammed him head-first against the wall.

Calder was yelling, 'Number 7, right in, right in!' as the five officers ran with Tony Allen spreadeagled horizontally between them along the corridor and into the cell block. He was kicking and screaming blue murder. They got him inside, face down on the floor, arms pinioned behind him, ankles trapped under two heavy boots.

'Out!' Calder yelled. 'Out! Out!'

He was the last to leave, heaving the door shut and turning the key. Tony was up on his feet, battering the steel door with his fists. His terrified screams pierced the air. Calder wiped his face and blew out a sigh. That bloody racket was enough to wake the dead. He slid back the bolt and dropped the metal trap, peering in through the bars at the sweating black face and crazy rolling eyes.

'I'll leave the flap open – all right!'

Tony's screams sank to a whimpering moan. Calder turned away. Thank Christ for that. He jerked his head round at a drunken voice shouting from the cell next door. It was the crusty they'd picked up on a D and D. 'Fascist pigs!' the slurred voice raved on. 'Fucking police brutality! Kicking the shit out of innocent victims!'

Calder banged on the door, told him to shut it, and went off to find Burkin. He was in the corridor outside the charge room, waiting by the wall phone for Tennison to return his call.

'Tony Allen is back in his cell,' Calder reported. Burkin nodded, looking decidedly uneasy. He moved aside as Calder unhooked the phone, fretting, 'What's happened to that doctor? I'll give him another bell.'

'Right.' Burkin moodily watched him dial. 'Are Mr and Mrs Allen still in reception?' he asked.

'They won't budge.' Calder gave him a look. 'You should have gone hours ago.' He nodded back towards the cells. 'Let the lad sleep it off. Tennison can deal with it in the morning.'

Burkin was about to say something, and gave it

up as a bad job. He slouched off. Calder listened to the ringing tone, shifting impatiently from foot to foot. 'Come on . . . come on . . .!'

Oswalde took the lift up to the canteen. It was almost empty at this late hour, a few small groups dotted about, officers taking a break during night patrols. He didn't know any of the faces, and he was glad about that; he wanted to be alone. In the far corner a TV was burbling to itself, the sound turned low.

Oswalde carried his black coffee to an empty table and sat down. His official duty shift had finished three hours ago. He should have been home in bed now, getting a reasonably early night, because he was due on again at eight-thirty the next morning. He was in a curious mood, couldn't unwind. He felt tired and yet jumpy and keyed-up at the same time; his mind was racing, and he knew he was keeping alert on nervous energy alone.

The late-night news round-up was showing voters coming out of a polling station. It was the by-election, Oswalde remembered. Though not much interested, he switched his mind over to what the announcer was saying. Anything to sidetrack his thoughts away from Tony Allen's wild, staring eyes and slobbering mouth.

'. . . pollsters keeping a record at the door suggest that Conservative Ken Bagnall may have held his seat but with a greatly-reduced majority. There were angry scenes earlier when members of the Free Derrick Cameron Campaign clashed with Bagnall, who is a self-confessed supporter of capital punishment. Labour's candidate, Jonathan Phelps, has issued a statement . . .'

Whatever the statement was, Oswalde never learned. Somebody got up to switch channels, and boxing took its place. Oswalde sipped his coffee and watched with dull eyes as two black middleweights slugged it out.

Three floors below, in cell number 7, Tony Allen had stripped down to his boxer shorts. He was standing at the door, staring out through the square grille. Slowly and very methodically he was tearing his shirt into strips. In the cell next door the crusty was snoring off his skinful. The two prisoners in adjoining cells were sleeping more quietly. Tony stared out, tearing at the cloth, and he didn't stop until the shirt had been ripped apart.

9

Calder looked up at the wall clock. He took a last drag, stubbed his cigarette in the ashtray and heaved himself up from the desk. On his way out he lifted the heavy bunch of keys from the hook and walked along the corridor, humming under his breath.

Sliding back the greased bolt, he lowered the flap and took a peek at the old guy in number 5. Sleeping it off. Chances were they'd let him go in the morning with a caution. Silly old bugger, taking a slash in the street. Calder checked on the crusty in 6. A disgusting spectacle of matted hair, earrings and tattoos. The smell of booze and stale sweat coming through the grille made Calder step back, wafting the air. He slammed it shut, operated the bolt.

The next flap was open, as Calder had left it. He took a pace forward and then froze. Something was very wrong. A rope of white cloth was looped around one of the bars, hanging down inside. Calder's heart dropped into his bowels. Whatever the worst was, he feared it had happened. Breathing hard, he jammed his head against the bars and squinted down. At first he saw only a heap of clothing, a pair of brown shoes. He strained further, his heart trip-hammering in his chest, and made out the top of Tony's head, a few inches below the open flap.

'*Shit!*' Calder dived for the panic button and the alarm

bell drilled through the cell block. 'Dave, John,' he bellowed, 'get here quick!'

Back at the cell door, he fumbled for the right key, cursing through gritted teeth. Boots pounded along the corridor. Suddenly there were four or five uniformed bodies crowding round the cell door as Calder turned the key in the lock. The door was pulled open, dragging Tony's body with it, bare legs splayed out. It was very ingenious and very simple. He'd made a rope out of the torn strips of his shirt, looped it around the bars, and hanged himself from a sitting position. His bloodshot eyes bulged out, his tongue lolled between blue lips. Calder had seen his share of dead people, and he was looking at one now.

'Get me a knife,' he said, and kneeling down, took the clasp knife and cut through the rope of knotted shirt strips. The others grabbed Tony's body as it slumped forward, a dead weight, and laid it on the floor of the cell. Calder stood up, his hands shaking, a mist of sweat on his bald head.

'Oh Jesus Christ Almighty!' Oswalde arrived, pushing through the men crowding in the doorway. He dropped to his knees at Tony's side. He cupped the boy's slack jaw in his hand, bringing the head back, preparing to give mouth-to-mouth. 'Get a mask.'

Calder shook his head weakly. 'It's too late . . .'

'*Now.*'

'Mask!' Calder snapped.

Oswalde was leaning over, both hands spread flat on Tony's chest, using his weight to massage the heart. A hand thrust a resuscitation mask at him. Making sure the bloated tongue was clear, Oswalde fitted the mask over Tony's mouth. He filled his lungs and blew into the plastic mouthpiece. It whooshed back at him, forced out under the pressure of the surrounding air. He did it again, and again, and he was still doing it, watched in silence by the men in the doorway, when Burkin shouldered his way through.

He glanced at Calder, who shook his head. Then he watched Oswalde straighten up and thump Tony's chest with the heels of his palms, do a silent count, and thump it again. Everyone knew it was hopeless, a lost cause, everyone but him.

Burkin had seen enough. He said gently, 'Bob, it's no good . . .'

Oswalde thumped, did a silent count, thumped.

'It's no good, Bob . . .'

Thump, count, thump.

Burkin couldn't stand it. He leapt in, pulling Oswalde away. 'Listen to me. *Look at me!*'

Oswalde went stiff. He stopped counting. He felt Burkin's firm grip on his shoulder and heard Burkin's voice, quiet, in his ear.

'The boy's dead . . . he's dead.'

Oswalde slowly sat back on his heels, his arms flopping to his sides. Tony lay on the floor of the cell, the mask around his mouth, staring sightlessly up. Silence. Nobody said anything. There was nothing to say.

Tennison switched on the bedside lamp. Blinking painfully against the light, she reached for the phone, a wave of blonde hair falling over her eyes. 'Oh shit,' she mumbled, and then into the receiver, 'Yes?' and listened with her eyes half shut to Burkin's voice. 'Can't it wait till morning?'

Burkin told her it couldn't and told her why.

Tennison said faintly, 'What was he doing in the cells?' Burkin told her. 'Jesus Christ. I'm on my way.'

She hung up but for a minute she didn't move. The horror of what Burkin had told her was still sinking in. It still hadn't fully sunk in as she padded through into the living-room. She switched on the lamp and pressed the playback button on the answering machine. Burkin's message to her earlier that evening came on. She turned up the volume and his voice filled the room.

'Ma'am, it's DI Burkin. I'm a bit worried . . . well, not exactly worried, but, well . . . the thing is, Oswalde's arrested Tony Allen on suspicion of murder. He's got him in the interview room now, and, well, the kid's climbing the walls. I mean freaking out, and I'm . . . worried. Could you call me back?'

The line clicked off. Supporting herself on the table's edge, Tennison stared into space. This wasn't happening. It wasn't real. She'd wake up in a minute. It had to be a dream. A fucking nightmare.

Superintendent Kernan had been hauled out of a rugby club bash. Wearing his blazer and club tie, wreathed in whisky fumes, he arrived at Southampton Row and stumped inside with the ferocious look of a drunken man sobering up fast to an ugly reality.

Calder, puffing on a surreptitious fag behind the duty desk, was the first to get Kernan's glowering stare as he marched through like a thundercloud. Calder gazed hopelessly at the ceiling, as if seeking divine deliverance or a swift and painless death.

The thundercloud passed on through the station.

Oswalde was sitting in one of the interview rooms, trying to compose himself, when the door was shoved open and Kernan glared in at him. Then the door was slammed shut, leaving Oswalde alone like a penitent monk in a cell, with only purgatory to look forward to.

Kernan moved on. The Allens were still in reception, patiently waiting for news of their son, but Kernan couldn't bring himself to face them. Going up in the lift to his office, reeking of Johnnie Walker's Black Label, he had only one thing in mind. The mirage of Chief Superintendent Kernan fading further and further away in the distance. By God, he'd have someone's balls for this. And if Tennison was in any way to blame, he'd have her balls too.

The police photographer had just finished taking shots when Tennison entered the cell block. She had taken some time, and a few pains, to make herself smart and presentable, even at this ungodly hour. Freshly made-up, wearing a dark red suit with a flared jacket, she came in and took a long look at Tony Allen's body on the floor of cell number 7. The resuscitation mask had been removed. The boy's face still bore the expression of frozen terror that had been his last emotion. Tennison turned away. Through tight lips she said to Burkin, 'Cover him up, Frank.'

She stood aside as two uniformed officers escorted the crusty from the cells. They were hustling him along, trying to prevent him getting even a glimpse of what had happened in the cell next door. The crusty knew though – or had guessed from all the commotion – and nobody was going to shut him up.

'You've killed him, you bastards!' he started shouting, straining his unshaven face around to get a look. He kept it up, his angry voice floating back as they dragged him out into the corridor. 'You bastards have killed him, you bastards . . .'

Tennison brushed a hand through her hair. 'Oh brilliant,' she said.

Ten yards away from his office, Tennison could plainly hear Kernan's bellowing voice giving somebody a bollocking. She came up to the door, wincing a little. She felt sorry for whoever was on the receiving end, whether they deserved it or not.

'It's just not good enough, not bloody good enough!' Kernan raged. 'The prisoner is your sole responsibility!'

It was Calder, the Custody Sergeant, Tennison realised. She listened to the quiet, abject mumble of his reply, which was cut short by Kernan's, 'Don't tell me – put it in your report! Now!'

Calder emerged, looking white and shaken, and walked straight past without acknowledging her. He was close to tears. Tennison went in. She was glad she'd put a dab of perfume on because the office reeked of whisky. Kernan's tie was loose and his shirt collar was crumpled. He looked a bit of a mess, his eyes more heavily-lidded than usual, and his hands were none too steady as he lit a cigarette.

'Well, that's my promotion down the toilet,' was how he greeted her, blowing out smoke in a disgruntled sigh.

Tennison was shocked. 'A boy's lying dead in the cells and you're worried about your promotion?' she said, not bothering to hide her disapproval.

'Just don't start, all right?' Kernan said, flapping his hand. He gave her a baleful look. 'The Custody Sergeant told me Burkin was trying to call you, worried by what Oswalde was up to . . .'

The knives were out already, Tennison thought. But she wasn't about to be dumped on from a great height. She said with venom, 'Burkin's supposed to be a Detective Inspector, not a limp-dick. He should have sorted it. Calder should have sorted it.' And to think that two minutes ago she'd felt sorry for the man!

'But they bloody didn't, did they?' Kernan said, a veiled accusation in his voice.

Tennison paced in front of the desk, clenching her fists. 'Christ Almighty, do I have to do everything myself?'

Kernan said wearily, 'All right, all right . . .'

'I mean, what's Burkin being paid to do? For Christ's sake –'

'All right! I hear you.'

Tennison ceased pacing but she was still fuming. If Kernan wanted a scapegoat, he could damn well look elsewhere. She glared at him and he shifted his eyes. He said, 'How did it go with Harvey?'

'He confessed to murder.'

'Thank Christ for that,' Kernan said, relieved.

No point in hanging back; she was an experienced officer, paid to exercise her judgement. She said evenly, 'But I've got my doubts about it . . .'

'What?' Kernan gazed at her. 'We're being handed it gift-wrapped and you have your doubts?'

'Yes I do. And I have good reason.' Tennison appealed to him, 'Look, Guv, right now I need to know what went on in that interview room. I mean – what made Tony kill himself, for chrissake . . .?'

Kernan stubbed out his cigarette and stood up. 'All hell's gonna break loose when this gets out,' he said gloomily. 'Riots, the lot.'

'Oh don't be ridiculous,' Tennison said shortly.

Kernan slowly turned his head and gave her a hard stare. 'You remember who you're talking to.'

Now it was Tennison's turn to look away. She lifted her chin and said stiffly, 'I'll listen to those interviews and report back as soon as I can. Sir.'

'You do that.'

The cigarette was still smouldering in the ashtray. What with that and the whisky fumes, the place smelled like a saloon bar. 'By the way,' Tennison said, 'you know Tony's mum and dad are still in reception, don't you?'

'Well, they can't be told.' Kernan rubbed the side of his face and stifled a yawn. 'Not until we've got things sorted.'

'*What*?' Tennison said, aghast.

'Send them home. Tell them tomorrow.' It was starting, he could feel it now, a beaut of a headache working its way up from the back of his neck to the base of his skull. Terrific. 'For their own sakes it'll be better to be told in the morning,' he said.

'We can't do that.'

'Yes we can,' Kernan said irritably.

Tennison blinked rapidly. 'How would we explain that in court? It'd reek of a cover-up ... besides, think of the way they'd feel.'

'I've made my decision.'

'Yes, and it's a bad one.'

'Well, that's what I'm paid for!' Kernan snapped at her. His patience, threadbare at the best of times, was wearing dangerously thin. When he was in this frame of mind he sometimes blurted out things better left unsaid. And the icing on the cake was that his headache had just changed up into second gear.

But the bloody woman wouldn't let it rest. She said

tartly, 'You're paid to make bad decisions, are you?'

To stop himself from landing one on her, Kernan went over to the little bar and picked up the whisky bottle. 'You know what I mean,' he growled under his breath.

Tennison watched him pour, at least three fingers' worth. She said quietly, 'Mike, how much have you had to drink?'

Kernan shot a fierce glance over his shoulder. 'Now you bloody watch it,' he warned her, mottled patches appearing in his cheeks. 'None of this would have happened if you'd kept Oswalde on a tighter rein . . .'

That was rich, and Tennison flared up. 'You brought him in, not me,' she reminded the Superintendent. 'I didn't ask for him. He's a loner, a one-man-band, he's not my type.'

'That's not what I've heard.'

There was dead silence. Tennison wasn't sure he'd said what she'd heard, and then with a sickly feeling she knew that he had. She controlled the sudden panic fluttering in her chest and said coolly, 'I beg your pardon?'

'Nothing,' Kernan said. He took a gulp.

'No,' Tennison said, and her cool tone now had icicles hanging from it. 'You explain that comment.'

Kernan came back to the desk, swirling his whisky. 'I'm merely suggesting that you might have let your personal feelings for him cloud your judgement.'

'My personal feelings?' Tennison said carefully, and regretted saying it before the words were out of her mouth. She was right to, because Kernan put his glass down, and placing both hands flat on the desk, leaned towards her, looking her squarely in the face.

'Do I have to spell it out for you?' He paused. 'You

had an affair on that course! There. Now. I didn't want to mention it. But . . .' He shrugged and picked up his glass.

Tennison stared him out. 'Nothing happened on that course,' she said, her face stiff as a wooden mask.

'You will bloody argue, won't you?' Kernan closed his eyes, unutterably weary and pissed off with the woman.

'You've been misinformed . . .'

'I hope so,' Kernan said with a small sigh. 'For your sake.'

Tennison left the room. She needed to go to the lavatory, quick.

Downstairs, on the main floor, Tennison stopped a WPC in the corridor. 'Show Mr and Mrs Allen up to my office, will you, please? Not a word about what's happened, understood?'

'Yes, ma'am.'

'Thank you.'

Oswalde came through the swing doors, summoned by Kernan, on his way to the lift. Tennison glanced round, making sure the corridor was deserted. 'Bob . . .'

He stared past her with dull eyes. 'Look, I'm sorry, I can't talk about it right now,' he muttered. 'I've got to see Kernan.'

From the set of his mouth she could tell he was holding himself as tight as a coiled spring. But she couldn't let him step into the lion's den without warning him. As he moved to go round her, she said, 'Kernan knows about us on the course.'

Oswalde halted. Now he did look at her, his handsome face creasing in a bewildered frown. 'I don't know what . . .' he started to mumble.

'Listen.' Tennison cut him short. She was holding judgement on whether she ought to be absolutely furious or not. She said, 'If you've been bragging about laying the Guv'nor . . .'

'What do you take me for?' Oswalde was plainly hurt by this. 'Do you think I'd say anything? You think I'd . . .' He swallowed and looked away.

Tennison kneaded her palms anxiously. 'Well, all I can think about right now is that I've got to tell that boy's parents that their son is dead.'

'And that boy is dead because of me . . .' Oswalde choked on the words. He was very near the edge. He said emptily, 'Do you really think it matters that Kernan knows about us . . .'

Tennison's look was stony. 'Yes, it matters,' she said, and turned on her heel, leaving him to face Kernan's music.

*

The Allens were sitting in her office. Tennison would rather have walked barefoot on white-hot coals than go through with this, but that was the price she paid for being in charge of a murder investigation: the hard end of the stick.

Ever the gentleman, Vernon Allen rose to his feet as she came in. 'About time, Chief Inspector. We've been waiting out there for an eternity.' Even so, he sounded more reproachful than angry, blinking at her through his horn-rimmed spectacles. The man had the patience of a saint, Tennison thought; she quailed at the duty before her, almost turned and fled.

'Please . . . can you give my son this?'

Esme had risen and was holding out a thick woollen pullover, neatly folded. Tennison accepted it. She didn't know what else to do.

Esme wore a strained smile, her eyes large and moist. 'Esta said he didn't even have time to get a coat. I hate to think of him spending the night in a cell. I don't want him to catch cold . . .'

Tennison placed the pullover on the corner of the desk, next to Vernon's hat. She held out her hand. 'Please sit down. I have some bad news for you.'

'I just want my son!' Esme blurted out plaintively. Vernon patted her shoulder. The three of them were still standing. Tennison went round the desk, turned and faced them. 'Esme – Esme, please sit down.'

She waited then, hands clasped in front of her, until they were seated. She raised her eyes and looked at them. 'I'm afraid that after Tony was returned to his cell, after questioning, he took his own life.'

Vernon leaned forward slightly. He seemed puzzled. 'Is he hurt?'

Tennison said quietly, 'Vernon, your son is dead. I'm very sorry.'

The Allens just sat and looked at her with blank expressions. Was any of this getting through? 'Do you understand?' she asked them. She hesitated, then said wretchedly, 'I'm so sorry . . .'

Vernon had removed his glasses. In slow motion he reached out and put them on top of his hat. He looked up at Tennison, shaking his head almost imperceptibly. 'How?'

'He used strips of his own clothes to –'

Esme came up out of her chair. Her eyes gleamed. Spitting and scratching, she launched herself at Tennison, screeching at the top of her voice, 'You killed him! You killed my boy! You killed him! You killed him! You killed him . . .!'

Making no attempt to retaliate, defending herself as best she could by holding up her arms, Tennison retreated into a corner. She felt the bony fists and sharp nails striking at her head and face. There was a panic button under her desk. She could have tried to get to it and summoned help, but she didn't. She huddled in the corner, arms crossed to ward off the blows Esme was raining down on her with berserk, mindless rage.

'*You killed him, killed my boy, killed him, you killed him . . .*'

When finally Vernon managed to haul her off, Esme turned her fury on him, lashing out in a frenzy and pounding her fists into his chest. Vernon held her shoulders, taking the blows, letting her punch herself out. Esme sagged against him, sobbing into his chest, and the sight of this pitiful, distraught woman meant it took a lot of will-power for Tennison to hold on to herself. She felt so helpless in the face of this naked human pain and misery that she felt like sobbing too.

Vernon's arms were wrapped around his wife, holding and comforting her; without their support she would have collapsed.

Over her head, and calling upon some deep reserve of calmness and dignity, he said to Tennison, 'How did it happen?'

'He hanged himself.'

'When?' It seemed very important. 'I mean when exactly?'

Tennison pushed back her tangled hair. Her left cheek was stinging, and she touched it lightly with her fingertips, feeling a bruise starting to form. 'Between midnight and twelve-thirty,' she said.

Vernon stared at her, his wife huddled against him; muffled, broken sobs shuddered out of her. It was all Tennison could manage not to look away. 'While we were waiting in reception?' Vernon said.

'Yes.'

Vernon closed his eyes, his throat working above his collar and tie. He opened his eyes, and a spasm passed over his face. He said huskily, 'Lady. May you rot in hell for that.'

With a stiff, jerky movement he turned away, and half carrying her, steered his wife to the door. Tennison came forward, holding his hat and glasses. He slipped the glasses into his overcoat pocket and took his hat. 'Thank you,' he said politely.

Tennison stood in the doorway watching as they wandered off aimlessly, two lost souls numb with anguish.

'Where are they going?' Burkin asked, appearing at Tennison's side.

'I don't think they know. Organise a car for them,' she said. 'I think Mrs Allen may well need to see a doctor. Probably they both do.'

Burkin nodded, about to do her bidding, when he noticed her face. 'Are you okay, Guv?'

'Straight away, please, Frank.'

Burkin went after them, leading them out.

Tennison leaned weakly in the doorway for a moment. She felt nauseous, as though she'd been kicked in the stomach. She went back into her office.

Kernan had taken off his jacket and shoes and was lying on the leather sofa in his office, listening on the phone to Commander Trayner. He'd crunched three aspirin and swilled the mush down with neat whisky. He shaded his eyes, waiting for it to take effect, as he half-watched the television picture, the sound turned low. The by-election count was still going on. It was going to be a close-run thing.

At one time, Kernan reflected, in the dim and distant past, he'd been a copper on the beat. A real policeman. Doing real police work. Now he was trapped and tangled up in bleeding internal politics and PR and career moves, like a fly in a sticky web. On top of which he had a murder investigation that threatened to go off the rails, a dead black boy in the cells, and a stroppy DCI who'd been caught shagging a junior officer. He shut his eyes, and through the dull pounding in his head, tried to concentrate on what the Commander was saying.

'Have the family been informed? Good . . .'

Immaculate in a dark-blue suit, pale cream shirt and polka-dot tie, Trayner stood in the hallway, keeping one eye on the TV in the living-room. He'd invited the Thorndikes round to dinner, and they were sitting with his wife Dorothy, lingering over brandies and Harrods' mint crisp wafers, while they watched the election result.

'What about MS15?' Trayner asked. 'Well, get on to them straight away.' He passed a pink, plump hand over his smooth glossy hair, greying at the temples. 'David Thorndike should lead the investigation, which is good news for us,' he said glibly.

At the mention of his name, Thorndike swivelled round in his chair, sharp nose in the air, all ears. Trayner winked and favoured him with a conspiratorial smirk.

'Absolutely.' Trayner was nodding, agreeing with Kernan. 'A complete bastard – but a complete bastard who is the most likely candidate to take over from you if you get the move upstairs.' He added silkily, 'And that will surely depend on how you handle this business from now on . . .'

Dorothy had turned the sound up, and Trayner said, 'One moment,' leaning towards the living-room door as the returning officer stepped up to the microphone.

'Kenneth Trevor Bagnall, Conservative . . . thirteen thousand, one hundred and thirty-seven.'

'Not enough,' Trayner muttered tersely, shaking his head.

'Jonathan Phelps, Labour . . . sixteen thousand, four hundred . . .'

The rest was drowned in a storm of cheering from the Labour supporters in the hall. Phelps, smiling broadly, had both fists raised in the air. Trayner turned his back on it.

'Did you hear that?' he said into the phone. 'It's in David's best interests to stop Southampton Row being dragged through the mire. Keep me informed.'

He hung up. Thorndike came though, buttoning his jacket. 'Well, we'd better be going.' The two men looked at one another. Things might work out after all. The MS15 investigation, with Thorndike in charge, couldn't have come at a more opportune moment, everything considered. If nothing else, it would cast a cloud over Tennison's promotion prospects. And if Thorndike could perform a damage limitation exercise on the Met's reputation, impressing the powers-that-be, he'd come out of it smelling of roses.

Trayner patted him on the shoulder, and Thorndike

responded with his thin-lipped watery smile. 'Looks like I've got an early start in the morning,' he said.

'I'm a black bastard, I deserve all I get, I'm a black bastard, I deserve all I get . . .'

'Stop that!'

Tennison sat at her desk, her elbow on the blotter, her head propped in one hand. She tapped the ash off her cigarette and put it to her lips. She inhaled deeply and breathed out, the smoke pluming from her nostrils. The tape reel slowly turned, semaphoring plastic gleams under the lamplight with each revolution.

'I'm a black bastard, I deserve all I get, I'm a black bastard, I deserve all I get . . .'

'Tony, just stop it, man!'

Tennison closed her eyes and took another long drag.

This was worse than she had feared. Much worse. What in heaven's name had possessed Oswalde? Why had he allowed it to go on? Pushing and pressurising the boy when it was obvious that he was stricken with hysterical panic, teetering on the edge of a complete nervous breakdown? What the hell was he trying to prove? That black coppers were superior to white ones? Or that he had nothing to learn from the Gestapo?

The procedures laid down under PACE were quite explicit, and this interview was a case-book study on how to disregard every one of them. Whoever was appointed from MS15 was going to have a field day.

'A word.' Burkin's voice.

'In a minute.'

'Now, Sergeant Oswalde!'

Tennison mashed her cigarette next to the five stubs and switched off the tape.

10

Tennison had the 9.00 a.m. briefing put back to 9.15. First she wanted Burkin in, and she told DS Haskons to send him along as soon as he arrived. He came in, pale and hollow-eyed, a shaving nick on his chin, and stayed standing and silent while she tore him off a strip. The second time in under a fortnight; it was getting to be a bad habit.

'I'm not talking about Oswalde's part in this,' Tennison stormed at him. She kept on her feet, pacing, because if she sat down she'd have had the fag packet out. 'You and Mike Calder had the authority to stop those interviews. Instead, you let them continue — no, better still, you let Oswalde interview the lad on his own while you sat by the telephone waiting for me to do your job for you —'

She broke away to answer the door. It was Haskons.

'Ready when you are, Guv.'

'Right.' She closed the door and walked round Burkin to the desk. He was looking carefully at nothing in particular, as long as it wasn't her. She didn't care what he was feeling, or what he thought of her; this was a professional matter; she was expected to do her job, and she expected him to do his.

'The rank of Inspector is supposed to mean something, Frank. It carries responsibility. It's supposed to denote a certain authority.' She stared up at him, hands clasped at her waist. 'You won't make excuses. You'll face the music like a man. That'll be all.'

Burkin turned and left the office.

He went directly to the Incident Room, where Muddyman was perched on the corner of a desk, sipping coffee from a styrofoam cup. The other members of the team were lounging about, and Muddyman was saying, 'I don't understand it — we're at Harvey's bedside getting a confession and meanwhile Oswalde's off chasing Tony. It doesn't make sense.'

'His ass is grass,' said Rosper, the jive slang specialist, with a shrug.

Haskons was more sympathetic. 'It's a dreadful thing to have happened. You carry that around with you for the rest of your life,' he said.

Still smarting from his encounter with Tennison, Burkin didn't see why anyone else should be let off the hook. 'The spade should be suspended. I mean, why was he brought here in the first place?'

'You know why,' Muddyman said.

'To talk to his people,' Jones said.

'Yeah ... and now one of them's dead and it's down to him,' Burkin growled. He looked round the circle of faces, aware that not all of them were convinced. 'Look, I'm not exaggerating or nothing,' he told them stridently. 'That boy was really weird, I mean climbing the walls, screaming and shouting, like mental or something. And believe me, I tried to tell him ...'

'Yeah, course you did, Frank,' Haskons said, nodding, as if Burkin was insisting that Santa Claus really did exist.

The discussion dried up as Oswalde entered the room. No one greeted or looked at him, and he didn't seem to care either way, going straight to his desk and sitting down. He was a stranger in a strange land, no use seeking sympathy or comradeship around here.

A moment later Tennison arrived. The men gathered round. The mood wasn't one of sweetness and light.

'Morning, everyone.' Her gaze swept over them – Burkin, Muddyman, Lillie, Rosper, Haskons, Jones – and last of all Oswalde, who was standing on the edge of the circle.

'I expect you've all heard about the events of last night. Just to clarify. Tony Allen hanged himself in cell number 7 – using strips of his own clothes. I informed his parents shortly afterwards. Now, obviously we can expect some adverse publicity. I'm told we can also expect an internal inquiry led by DCI Thorndike to begin almost immediately.'

There were dark looks and a few suppressed groans. Those who knew Thorndike didn't like him. Those that didn't know him were well aware of his reputation as a cold-blooded bastard, a career policeman who'd never collared so much as a shoplifter.

'Needless to say, I regret what has happened, but Operation Nadine continues . . .'

Lillie raised a hand. 'But surely, ma'am, if Harvey's confessed – I mean, that's it, isn't it?'

'Quite frankly, I'm not convinced by David Harvey's version of events.'

This was news to Muddyman. He said, 'Admittedly there are some inconsistencies, Guv . . .'

'Inconsistencies?' Tennison raised an eyebrow. 'He said she wasn't wearing a bra. She was. He said he put a gag on her – there was no trace of a gag.'

'He could have removed it,' Muddyman pointed out. 'It could have rotted away.'

'Yes, it could have,' Tennison conceded. With the possible exception of Oswalde, she was aware that she was in a minority of one. The rest of the team agreed with Muddyman: the case was signed, sealed, and as good as delivered. She went on, 'Harvey said he killed her in the kitchen, but the fragment of tooth was found in the front room.'

Muddyman had an answer for that too. 'Perhaps there was violence in the front room – he said he hit her – before the murder took place. Perhaps he moved the body after . . .' He spread his hands. 'I mean, he did say he hit her.'

'"Perhaps",' Tennison said doubtfully. '"Perhaps" won't stand up in court. I'm not sure the confession of a dying man will stand up in court either.'

'He knew her hands had been tied with a belt.'

'Yes – and he said "my" belt.' That was something that had niggled at her. Tennison appealed to them. 'Does the belt we found look like something Harvey might wear?'

Muddyman patiently went through it, counting off on his fingers. 'She was wrapped in polythene sheeting. And there was a plastic bag buried with her. And he said the body remained above ground – which ties up with the maggots and that . . . none of those details were mentioned in the press!'

By now most of the team was nodding. It was an open and shut case. The evidence was overwhelming, whatever inconsistencies there might be. Murder was a sloppy business, not a scientific theorem.

'Look,' Tennison granted them, 'I'm as certain as you are that Harvey was involved. Most probably in the disposal of the body. But I'm not sure he killed her. We need to go over Harvey's statement with a fine toothcomb. We need to examine what Tony Allen said —'

'You won't get much there, Guv,' Burkin interrupted. 'I know, I was there.'

'You may have been there,' Oswalde said derisively. 'You obviously weren't listening.'

'. . . Sir.'

Oswalde glowered at him. 'Sir.'

'Frank,' Tennison said with a touch of asperity, 'don't you think it's a bit late to be pulling rank?' She faced them. 'Now listen. We messed up. Very badly. Which means we've got to work twice as hard from now on. Why, if he wasn't involved in the actual murder of Joanne, would Harvey involve himself in the burial of the body? Can we connect Tony Allen with David Harvey? A connection strong enough for Harvey to confess to a murder he didn't commit.'

She gave each and every one of them a hard searching look.

'I want to go back to Eileen Reynolds. I want evidence. I want corroboration. I want to solve the case.'

And with that, ignoring their muttered grumbles, she dismissed them.

*

Thorndike got out of the Rover, briefcase in hand, and waited while his driver locked the car. Together they strode briskly to the main entrance of Southampton Row. One of Esme Allen's customers, the middle-aged woman with silvery hair, was in the act of placing a small bunch of flowers on the steps. She straightened up, tears streaming down her face, and turned to go. The two MS15 officers exchanged a look and went inside.

'DCI Thorndike, DS Posner to see Superintendent Kernan,' Thorndike informed the young PC behind the duty desk. 'We're expected.'

The PC pressed the buzzer, releasing the glass-panelled door reinforced with steel mesh, and they passed inside.

Tennison felt knackered. Barely three hours' sleep made her edgy and fractious, and what she didn't need right now was Thorndike's oily, unctuous presence and smarmy twitterings. God, how she despised the man. Closer acquaintance had only increased her dislike. Sitting opposite him in the interview room, watching him fuss with his papers, she really had to control herself, fight the impulse to burst out and tell him what an officious prick she thought him.

'Southampton Row's reputation precedes it, Jane,' he said, sighing and shaking his head. He gave her a frank, accusing look. 'If you come in the front, you're likely to go out the back with blood on your face.'

'Is this on the record, David?' Tennison asked politely.

'Of course not,' Thorndike said, smiling his tepid smile. 'We're just talking . . .'

'Good,' Tennison said. 'Because that's bullshit.' With satisfaction she saw his smile drain away. 'If it was ever true, it's not anymore. I've never seen excessive force used in this nick. Oswalde's certainly not like that.'

'What with the Cameron case . . .'

She could see his game. He was trying to dredge up the past, the Derrick Cameron saga recently revived by Phelps, and use it as smear tactics. But she wasn't about to let it happen.

'Look,' she told him, 'you're here to investigate a death in custody.'

'I know why I'm here, Jane.'

'Well then, let's concentrate on the case in hand.'

'I intend to, don't worry.' He was flustered, and started fussing through the documents spread out in front of him. He had thin, bony hands that gave her the creeps. 'I think it's important for you to know I take this job seriously,' he said, putting on the stern voice of authority. 'I'm not prepared to do a whitewash.'

'No one's asking you to.'

'It's my belief that when one of the foot soldiers cocks up it's down to the officer-in-charge.'

'I accept that.'

'I don't know . . .' Thorndike gave her his fishy-eyed stare. 'Perhaps you let your personal feelings cloud your judgement.'

Tennison went cold. The same words, or very close, to the ones Mike Kernan had used. Suddenly she understood. What an idiot, that it had taken her till now to realise that it was Thorndike who had done the blabbing. This was the slimy toad who had spread the rumours about her and Oswalde.

'I beg your pardon?' she said frostily.

'It'll keep.' His eyes slid down to his papers. 'Can you ask the Custody Sergeant . . .' He pretended to search for the name.

'Mike Calder.'

'. . . yes, to step into my office, please?'

'One more thing, David.' Tennison was simmering. With a great effort she kept her voice level and cool. 'If I'm to be interviewed I'd like to speak to an officer senior in rank to me.'

Thorndike looked up. He said blandly, 'Well, that may not be possible.'

Well, Tennison thought, it had better not be *you*, or you can go screw yourself.

There was a chill drizzle just starting to fall as Tennison drove into the hospital car park. It was a few minutes after midday, and she had arranged to be there when Vernon Allen came to make the formal identification of his son. Although not strictly necessary, she felt an obligation, as a gesture of regret and condolence, to put in an appearance on behalf of the police authority. She was deeply sorry for what had happened, and felt it was the least she could do.

She locked the Sierra, and was about to start for the main entrance when Sarah Allen came through the rows of parked cars. She must have driven her father to the hospital, and was waiting for him in her car when she spotted Tennison. She made a beeline across the car park, her attractive face twisted in a terrible grimace, her large brown eyes wild with hate and loathing.

'How could you have him arrested for murder? If it wasn't for you, none of this would have happened!'

Tennison stepped back a pace, afraid for a moment that the distraught girl was going to attack her. She tried to console her, but Sarah went on in a hoarse, broken voice, 'Tony wouldn't hurt anyone, let alone tie them up, rape them . . .'

'Wait a minute . . . Sarah . . .'

'What's his daughter going to do now?'

Tennison had gone still. It had hit her what Sarah had just said.

'How did you know that she was tied up?' she asked.

177

She tried to grab Sarah's arm, hoping to calm her. 'How did you know she was raped?'

Sarah wrenched herself away. 'That's another life you've ruined,' she almost snarled.

Tennison still wanted an answer. 'Who told you that?' she demanded.

'He was going to be married this weekend ...' Sarah broke down, sobbing. Tennison reached out, and the girl backed away. 'Just leave us alone!' She turned her tear-stained face away and did a staggering run back to her car.

When Tennison got there, she had locked herself inside. Tennison tapped on the window. 'Who told you that she was tied up?'

But she soon saw that it was useless. Sarah was gripping the wheel with both hands, her head resting between them, her shoulders heaving as she wept uncontrollably. For the time being, at any rate, the question would have to remain unanswered.

*

The door opened and the mortuary attendant stood there. 'Would you like to come this way, sir?'

Vernon Allen rose heavily from the bench seat and followed him through. Tennison was sitting in the corridor outside. She stood up as Vernon passed, but said nothing and made no move as he went through the white door into the mortuary itself. She sat down again.

Tony Allen was lying on a metal table, covered to the waist by a white sheet. His eyes were closed, and but for the puckered purplish circle round his neck, he might have been asleep. Vernon gazed down at him. His eyes were dry. A tiny muscle jumped at the corner of his mouth. Very slowly, he bent forward and kissed his son on the lips.

Tennison stood up as Vernon emerged from the mortuary. He walked past her, looking straight ahead, his face empty of all expression, and went outside into the grey drizzle sweeping down from a dark sky.

When Tennison rang his office she was told that the Super was having lunch in the canteen. She went up in the lift, and having no appetite, got herself a cup of black coffee and carried it across to his table. She might grab a sandwich later on, if she felt like it.

Kernan was finishing off apple crumble and custard, watching the lunchtime news. She told him about her visit to the mortuary, and of what Sarah had said. He licked his spoon and held it up to quieten her as a photograph of Tony Allen appeared on the screen.

The announcer was saying, 'Tony Allen, who was to have been married this weekend, leaves a fiancée and a three-year-old daughter . . .'

Kernan dropped his spoon in the bowl and wiped his mouth on a paper serviette. 'You can't pull Sarah Allen in. Not with all this going on.'

He gestured at the television, which was showing 'all this' in the person of Jonathan Phelps. Together they watched the newly-elected Labour MP being interviewed outside the House of Commons.

'. . . today should have been a day of celebration for me and my supporters. Instead, it has turned into a wake as another black man dies in police custody.'

Turning away, Tennison leaned towards Kernan. 'I just want to talk to her off the premises,' she said reasonably.

179

It wasn't reason enough. Kernan shook his head. 'Too soon. Go back to Harvey.'

'He can't talk at the moment. I don't know whether he'll be able to again.'

'Well then, see where other lines of inquiry lead you. We'll review the situation in a few days.' He crumpled the serviette and tossed it down, giving Tennison a critical scrutiny. Her make-up couldn't disguise the lines of tiredness at the corners of her mouth and the slight puffiness under her eyes. 'Go home and get some sleep, Jane.'

'Yeah . . .'

'And leave Sarah Allen out of it,' Kernan ordered. 'For the moment.'

He departed, leaving Tennison gazing listlessly at the TV screen. Phelps was saying, 'With all due respect, a system where police officers investigate their fellow officers cannot be sufficiently objective. All too often a blanket of silence falls on the case . . .'

A shape moved behind the panes of coloured glass in the vestibule; the light came on and Tennison saw that it was Vernon Allen. He opened the inner door and peered out, trying to see who had rung the bell.

Tennison tapped on the glass panel of the outer door and pressed her face closer. 'Vernon, I have to speak to Sarah . . .'

He flinched, as if someone had spat in his face. 'How dare you come here! How dare you . . .'

'Vernon, it's really important that I speak to Sarah.'

'Haven't you done enough damage?' He was trembling, the outrage in his voice strained and pitiful. 'Just leave us alone –'

'But I have to speak to Sarah!' Tennison insisted. She tapped again, urgently, seeing him about to close the door.

'My wife is . . .' Vernon Allen choked, overcome at the thought of Esme's grief. The huge man seemed to be physically shrinking. He bowed his head in anguish. 'My wife . . .'

Sarah appeared beside him. 'Go inside, Pop. Let me handle this. Go on.'

He shambled off. Sarah stepped forward, tight-lipped, and stared coldly at Tennison through the glass panel, making no move to open the door. Tennison knew she had only a few seconds. She said quickly, 'Sarah, were you there that night?'

'I don't know what you're talking about.'

'Or has Jason Reynolds spoken to you?'

'I don't know any Jason Reynolds,' Sarah snapped. 'Now leave us alone! I'm closing the door . . .'

'Sarah, please,' Tennison said, 'for Tony's sake . . .'

'I'm closing the door.'

She did. The light went out. And that was that.

At first Tennison couldn't figure out what the screeching noise was, or where it was coming from.

Nearly ten-thirty, the station was quiet, and she was on the point of leaving when she heard it. Puzzled, she walked down the empty corridor and pushed through the doors into the Incident Room. All alone, Oswalde was crouched in a chair in front of the TV, the remote control in his hand. The screeching was speeded-up reggae as he fast-forwarded the tape of the Sunsplash concert. He paused it, leaning forward with a fixed, obsessive stare, his eyes glued to Joanne and Tony on the stage.

181

Tennison moved quietly towards him, frowning to herself. He pressed the rewind and played the same sequence over again, and she could see the tension in the hunched shoulders and the hand gripping the remote.

'Bob,' Tennison said, making an effort to sound casual. 'Give yourself a break.'

Oswalde flicked a glance at her and went back to the screen. 'You can talk.'

She watched him for a moment longer, then unslung her shoulder bag. She found her filofax, scribbled something on a slip of paper and handed it to him. 'Ring this number. It's a friend of mine. She helped someone who was at Broadwater Farm. She's good.'

'A shrink . . .?' Oswalde was bitterly amused.

'Sort of,' Tennison said. 'Listen, there's no shame in that. Other people make mistakes at work and the firm loses a few grand. We make a mistake and someone loses their life.' It was an argument she used on herself, whenever she made a cock-up or was feeling depressed.

Oswalde had zapped back and was studying the same sequence all over again, just as intensely as before. Tennison hitched her bag on to her shoulder and turned to go. He was a big boy, and she wasn't a wet nurse. She stopped as a thought occurred to her.

'Did Mrs Fagunwa recognise that belt?'

'No.'

Tennison nodded, on her way to the door. 'Go home, Bob,' she said, and went out.

The house where Eileen Reynolds lived was a stone's throw from the tower blocks of the Lloyd George Estate. In fact, Tennison thought, as she knocked on the door, if you threw a stone from Harvey's balcony it would break one of his sister's windows.

Eileen opened the door, her arms filled with sheets and pillowcases ready for the wash. Jimmy Young's voice floated through, quipping with a doctor about some bowel complaint or other.

Tennison smiled. 'Hello, Eileen.'

Eileen didn't return the smile. In the clear light of day her face had a hard, pinched look, that of a woman who had lived through a few trials and tribulations in her time, and survived to tell the tale. Her short bleached hair was showing streaky brown and grey at the roots.

'I've been expecting you,' she said, and went inside, leaving Tennison to shut the door.

'I wasn't lying. He was there with me that weekend. He came down a lot in those days. He had a caravan there. Sometimes he'd stay with me, sometimes at the van.' Eileen stuffed the last of the washing in the machine, straightened up wearily, and banged the door to with her knee.

Tennison said, 'So why did you say it was the anniversary of his wife's death?'

'Makes no difference.' Eileen folded her arms and gave a contemptuous shrug. 'I've spoken to a solicitor and he tells me that confession is not worth the paper it's written on. It was "obtained under duress",' she enunciated, her Scottish accent coming to the fore. 'And if my brother did it, why has that blackie killed himself?'

'Did you know Tony Allen?' Tennison asked, quietly curious.

'No, I seen it on the telly.' Eileen leaned forward,

183

thrusting her face, eyes screwed tight, at Tennison. 'Because he did it – that's why!'

'Then why did your brother confess?'

She had a sharp-tongued Glaswegian answer to everything. 'To get you lot off his back.'

'Eileen, you're not helping your brother by lying . . .'

'I'm not *lying*!'

Tennison leaned against the sink, watching as Eileen heaved a basket of clean washing on to the kitchen table. She was a small, almost scrawny woman, yet tough as old boots, and Tennison wouldn't have fancied her own chances in a scrap, even with the tricks she'd learnt from the Met's karate instructors.

She said, 'You don't have to stop loving him, you don't have to stop supporting him. But you do have to stop lying for him.'

'You know something?' Eileen swung round, blazing. 'You're a pious cow! I've done everything for that bloody man since he's been ill. I work my fingers to the bone to support him . . .'

'I know,' Tennison nodded, 'that's what I'm saying. I know you support him. I know that must be a struggle. Like taking on that loan –'

'You lot think you know everything!'

'– for him. Five grand's a lot of money.' She paused. 'How could you afford to do that, Eileen?'

'My son helps out.' She glared across the kitchen. 'All right?'

Tennison reflected. 'What does Jason do for a living?'

'You leave that boy out of this!'

'It's a simple question,' Tennison said placidly.

Eileen sniffed. 'He has a sort of . . . photography business.'

'What does that mean?'

'In the summer he works on the seafront. I don't really know. I don't pry like you do,' she said with something like a sneer.

'You mean he's a seafront photographer?' Tennison said, and a tiny surge of excitement, like electricity, ran through her. She didn't quite know why, but then something clicked in her brain, and she did.

Eileen was busy sorting out the stuff that needed ironing. 'Yeah – he used to keep a bloody monkey here at one time, okay?'

Tennison left her car parked at the end of the street and walked along the flagged pathway that led to the flats. She entered Dwyfor House and began to climb the smelly staircase. She wanted to have another look round Harvey's flat, and in particular at the photographs on the glass-fronted bureau. The ones taken by Jason Reynolds, professional photographer.

On the thirteenth floor, in flat number 136, Jason Reynolds was on his knees, searching in the cupboard under the sink. He found what he was after, a black plastic binliner, and padded through into the living-room. The place was in a bit of a shambles, coffee table on its side, ashtray and loose cigarettes spilled over the floor, nothing tidied up since they'd carted his uncle off to hospital.

He shook the binliner open and went round the sofa to the bureau. He reached for the nearest framed photograph and suddenly went still. He tilted his head, listening. There was someone outside the front door. Silently he skirted the sofa and crept into the hallway, his trainers making no sound. Somebody was fumbling with the letterbox flap. Fingers poked through and fished for the string, and started to pull it up, the key attached to the end. Jason watched as the key was drawn through the letterbox.

He looked round, instantly in a muck sweat. As the key went into the lock he nipped sideways into the kitchen and closed the door a bare crack, putting his eye to it. He held his breath, white-faced and tense, and through the crack saw Tennison pass along the hallway to the living-room. He felt sure she must hear his heart.

Tennison moved slowly round the sofa to the bureau. Along with Muddyman she'd merely glanced at the photographs in their cheap Woolworth's frames. Now she examined each in turn closely. The one she had looked at before, of Harvey and his wife. The sunset over the sea. Harvey and Eileen together. A smaller print of Eileen on her own. And one of Harvey and Jason, in a back garden, smiling, Harvey's arm around his nephew's shoulder. Tennison touched the glass. Her finger traced Jason's check shirt down to the Indian Chief's head on the belt looped through his jeans.

The surge of electricity was now a jolt, stiffening her spine.

She turned her head, feeling a cool waft of air on her cheek. Putting the photograph back, she went through into the hallway. The front door was open. Had she closed it? She was positive she had. She looked out on to the landing. She listened for a moment, heard nothing, and went back inside, making sure the door was locked.

In the living-room she took the photograph down, turned it over, and flicked up the plastic tabs, intending to take just the print itself. As the cardboard backing came away, Tennison froze. Concealed there, behind the print, were half a dozen polaroids. She spread them out on the back of the frame, her mouth dry, struggling a little to catch her breath. They were of Joanne Fagunwa and Sarah Allen, fully-clothed yet posing rather suggestively, their hands squeezing their breasts. It looked as though they were in a kitchen. And there was a close-up of Joanne and Sarah, giggling into the camera, with Tony Allen between them, pulling a funny face.

Tennison shut her eyes. This was it. What they'd been seeking all along. The link – Joanne – Sarah – Tony – and whoever had taken the polaroids. All together. And whoever had taken the polaroids was the wearer of the Indian Chief's head belt.

She went to the phone and dialled Southampton Row, and asked for DS Oswalde. When he came on the line she said, 'Bob, it's Jane. I'm at Harvey's. I've found something interesting.'

11

Oswalde was sitting on the sofa, hands laced together, the polaroids spread out on the coffee table in front of him. He nodded slowly. 'So Tony was involved . . .'

'Yes.'

As if a string had snapped, Oswalde's head dropped forward. 'Thank Christ for that.' He sucked in a huge relieved breath, then sat forward, staring hard. 'Isn't that Sarah?'

'Yes,' Tennison said. She leaned over, pointing. 'And even better . . . recognise that?'

Oswalde studied the photograph of Harvey and Jason in the garden. He looked up at her, his expression clearing. 'It's the belt . . .'

Tennison's eyes gleamed. 'We've got him, Bob – I want him picking up and I want this place turned over,' she said, gesturing round the flat, fingers clicking.

'Have you got a search warrant?'

'I'll worry about that.'

Forty-five minutes and two phone calls later the flat was in the throes of a minor invasion. A systematic search brought up piles of soft porn magazines and two shoe-boxes filled with original prints and polaroids: Jason's private collection, that no doubt he'd stored here to keep from his mother's prying eyes, Tennison thought. She sorted through it with Lillie.

Some of the early, amateurish stuff was fairly innocu-
ous – pouting adolescent girls pretending to be page
three models, quite a few in school uniform. But there
were other, later shots that Tennison found sickening
and repugnant. Naked girls bound and gagged, fear in
their eyes; real or faked, Tennison couldn't tell. Some
showing groups of two or three, using various imple-
ments on themselves. And a number of them featured
the lad himself, Jason the porno star, taking the leading
role in his own production. These had been taken with
remote-control shutter release. The wire could be seen,
trailing from his hand to the camera, as he pumped away,
face contorted, veins standing out. The girls didn't look as
though they were enjoying it.

The more professional the photograph, it seemed, the
more extreme the poses and situations became, as if Jason
was trying to keep pace with his growing technical expertise by dredging up ever more outlandish fantasies from
the depths of his sordid imagination.

Lillie held up a magazine cover of an over-blessed
blonde and the original, matching colour print from
Jason's private hoard. 'Quite the little photographer,'
he muttered sourly.

Tennison pushed the pile away with disgust, having
seen more than enough. 'Get on to Vice. See if you can find
out who publishes this muck.' She called out to Oswalde,
'Bob, get someone down to Harvey's bedside. Make sure
I'm informed as soon as he can utter a sound.'

She stood up, feeling soiled and grubby and faintly
nauseous. Turning away from the piles of magazines
and heaps of photographs, she said between gritted teeth,
'We've got to find this little shit.'

She thought, with a flutter of panic: Before he does

to some poor innocent girl what he did to Joanne Fagunwa.

Haskons had used his discretion. He'd weeded out the more explicit material and pinned up on the notice-board only those shots that might have been deemed fit for mixed company. Even so, some shots of sequences, while starting innocently enough, ended up as blatantly pornographic.

'Seems as though Jason prefers amateur models,' Tennison said, moving along them with Muddyman, who himself dabbled in amateur photography, on a more modest scale.

'Yeah, well, he doesn't have to pay them, does he?' Muddyman pointed them out. 'The polaroids are early photographs. The later ones are much better quality, thirty-five mil. Quite professional.'

'Would he develop them himself?'

Muddyman smoothed back the hair over his bald spot. 'I think black and white's pretty easy. You need more sophisticated equipment for colour.'

Tennison pinched her nose, thinking. 'I suppose he could have a studio or something . . . it's worth check-ing with any of those places that specialise in developing dodgy photos. They might have an address, a contact number even.'

Muddyman nodded and went off, back into the fray. The Incident Room was buzzing. Rosper, aided by WPC Havers, was working the computer terminal. Burkin and Oswalde had document files a foot deep on their desks, heads down, ploughing through. The other members of the team were on the phones, chasing down even the most tenuous lead. DC Jones came through the desks, looking faintly flushed, eyes blinking behind his spectacles. He held an open file.

'You were right, ma'am – Jason Reynolds attended the same school as Tony Allen. They were in the same year. When Eileen moved to Margate, to be near one of her boyfriends, Jason stayed on in London, living mainly at number 15 . . .'

'Oh, right!' Tennison breathed.

'Their Head of Year reckons they weren't friends though. He says Jason was a waster – bit of a jack-the-lad.' Jones added doubtfully, 'I suppose if they were neighbours they might have hung out together, but they sound very different.'

'Which brings us back to Sarah.' Tennison smacked her knuckles into her palm, fretting, frustrated. 'Who Kernan has ruled out-of-bounds.'

'Boss . . . ?' Haskons beckoned, and went back to frowning at two photographs on the board. They were earlier shots of an attractive blonde teenager, in bra and black fishnets, gazing over her shoulder with an invitation in her dark eyes.

'This is a bit out of left field, but I think I recognise her.'

'Go on.'

'I don't know.' Haskons was distinctly uneasy. He cleared his throat. 'I've been looking at them for ages.'

'Richard . . .' Tennison said warningly, her eyes like gimlets.

'No, I mean, Camilla's really happy there,' Haskons said feebly.

Tennison was stumped. Camilla was his eldest girl, six years old. 'What's Camilla got to do with it?'

Haskons stared at the photos, worrying his thumbnail. 'I think it's her teacher,' he said.

Miriam Todd, in charge of the third year at St John's Primary, was attractive right enough, and dark-eyed, but she wasn't blonde. She had shoulder-length black hair and was about twenty-two, Tennison guessed. Supposing the pin-ups of the girl in bra and fishnets to be have been taken five, six years ago, Miriam would then have been in her mid-teens. Near enough the right age.

Perched on tiny chairs, they sat in the sunny classroom during the lunchtime break, the cheerful clamour of kids in the playground an odd and unsettling backdrop to the purpose of Tennison's visit.

She took the two photographs of the blonde girl Haskons thought he recognised from her bag and showed them to Miriam.

'Tell me if you recognise this person.'

'No, I've never seen them before, Inspector.'

But her nostrils betrayed her. They had flared, just a fraction, enough for Tennison to notice the sharp intake of breath Miriam was trying to disguise. She tried a different tack.

'What about this girl?'

Miriam looked at the full colour studio portrait of Joanne that her mother had supplied, happy and smiling, sparkling with life.

Miriam shook her head slowly. 'No. She's beautiful . . .'

'No, Miriam,' Tennison said bluntly. 'She was beautiful. Her remains were found buried in the garden of number 15, Honeyford Road. Her hands had been tied behind her back with a belt. The belt belonged to Jason Reynolds. Do you recognise this man?' She held up the picture of Harvey and Jason together, and Miriam blanched. 'Do you want to look at these photographs again?'

'No need.' Miriam's voice was barely audible. She avoided Tennison's direct gaze.

'Tell me what you know about the photographer.'

'Jason Reynolds.' Miriam sat up straighter and moistened her lips. 'I met him in the summer of . . . eighty-six. At that time I was still at school, still living with my parents in Margate. He was taking photographs on the seafront. You know, a seaside photographer. He was charming, funny . . .' She took a breath and plunged on, 'As you know, I let him take photographs of me. For a while he made me feel attractive, the centre of attention. I stripped and posed, I dressed up and posed. Whatever he asked for, really. I wanted to get away from home. My mother was ill.'

She looked down at her hands, twisting in her lap. Tennison waited.

'He said . . . he said his uncle had a flat I could rent, that he'd look after me. I came with him to London. To Honeyford Road . . .'

There was a noise in the corridor as the children trooped in from the playground. They bunched in the doorway, one or two spilling into the classroom. Tennison put the photographs away in her bag.

'Can you wait outside, please,' Miriam called to them. 'Just line up quietly.' They went out. She turned back, brushing a few strands of hair from her pale forehead. 'I lived in the basement flat there for two months.'

'June and July?'

'Yes.'

'Did you work as a prostitute, Miriam?'

She coloured a little. 'No, not really. Jason tried to get me to go with various friends he brought round, but . . .' She shrugged. 'Well, none of us really knew what we were doing.'

Tennison looked into the dark eyes with their fringe of black lashes. Sick shit that he was, Tennison thought, Jason Reynolds must have something going for him. Some form of mesmerising power, to have snared, amongst many others, such an attractive teenager as Miriam Todd must have been back then, six years ago. She said, 'Did you have sex with his uncle? David Harvey?'

'Sometimes,' Miriam admitted. 'When I couldn't pay the rent.'

'Do you recognise either of these men?' Tennison showed her pictures of Vernon and Tony Allen. 'Did you have sex with either of them?'

'No.'

'Where were those photographs of you taken?'

'At the flat.'

'And in Margate?'

'His uncle had a caravan.'

'Can you tell me where that was exactly?'

Tennison felt herself tense up, willing Miriam to provide a name, a location, but she was shaking her head. 'I can't remember the name of the site. It was somewhere out of town.'

'Right. Well.' Tennison stood up. She fastened her shoulder bag. 'Thank you very much.'

'That's it?' Miriam said, staring up.

'Yes. Thank you,' Tennison said, and departed.

*

It was too late for a canteen lunch, and she couldn't face another sandwich, so once back in the hectic Incident Room she smoked a cigarette to fend off the hunger pangs. Her consumption was gradually creeping up again. To hell with it, no good worrying; she'd try stamping out the filthy weed once this case was finished.

'Boss – have you seen this?' She glanced round at Lillie, who was unpinning one of the photographs.

'What?'

He brought it over and laid it on the desk: a young girl ogling the camera, hands cupping her breasts. The room was tiny and cluttered, a bunk bed and a small window visible in the shot. It looked like the interior of a caravan. Lillie pointed to a calendar behind the girl's right shoulder, sellotaped to the end of the bunk bed.

'That's a 1992 calendar,' he said.

It was, Tennison saw, peering at it closely. 'So he could still be using the caravan. Try all the sites in the Margate area.' She stubbed out her cigarette and stood up. 'I want Eileen Reynolds arrested,' she informed everybody. 'Bring her in, put her in an interview room and let her stew. Perhaps that might bring Jason out from under his stone.'

Muddyman called to Rosper, 'Check all the caravan sites in the Margate area – Jonesy, give him a hand.'

There was a bustle and excitement in the room, as well as a fug of cigarette smoke. Now they had something positive to go on. They had a real live prime suspect and they were going after him.

*

Lillie opened the plastic bag and took out the belt with the Indian Chief's head buckle. He passed it to Tennison, who held it in her spread hands for Eileen Reynolds to see.

Eileen had been sitting in the interview room for half an hour or more, with only a WPC for company. She'd drunk two cups of machine coffee, smoked three cigarettes, and she was looking sullen. Tennison didn't expect her to cooperate, but that didn't matter. The woman seated opposite her, she was convinced, was the mother of a murderer, so she was in no mood to be gentle or pull any punches.

'This is the belt, Eileen, that was used to tie Joanne's hands behind her back.'

'I've never seen it before.' Eileen dismissed it with hardly a glance. From an envelope Tennison took the photograph of Harvey and Jason. She saw Eileen register that the buckle on Jason's belt was identical. But all it brought was an indifferent shrug. 'Lots of belts look like that.'

'Really. I think it's quite distinctive.' Tennison took out the polaroids and placed them, one by one, in a row, on the table. She said, 'The dead girl, Joanne Fagunwa. Joanne and Tony. Joanne and Sarah.'

Eileen stuck her head forward. 'So why isn't it Mrs-fucking-Allen sitting here?' she snarled. 'Go and arrest her. Arrest Sarah.'

Tennison said quietly, 'Because it's my belief that Jason took those photographs.'

'You have no proof of that.'

'They were found in your brother's flat, Eileen.'

'I don't know anything about that,' Eileen said shortly. Her sallow cheeks were flushed. She was putting up a stone wall, but it was crumbling at the foundations. In her eyes Tennison could see the fearful uncertainty, and thought: *She's going to crack.*

But she was not about to spare Eileen's feelings; she intended carrying on the way she had started. Coolly, as if dealing a hand of cards, she placed a set of the later, harder, more explicit shots in the middle of the table.

'That's your son, Eileen. Your son the pornographer. Would you look at them, please?' Eileen deliberately stared off. 'Look at them, please. You won't look at them. All right,' Tennison said, her back straight, her clasped hands resting on the table, 'I'll describe them to you. The first shows a girl, she's about fourteen, I would say. Your son's penis is inserted in the girl's anus. Her face shows pain . . . and fear.'

'Stop it . . .!' Eileen's whole body was straining forward, her mouth an ugly twisted shape. 'You sick bastard bitch!'

'It's not me in the photographs, Eileen,' Tennison went smoothly on, 'I didn't take them. Your son Jason did that.' She glanced down. 'The next, a different girl, slightly older perhaps . . .'

There was no need to go on.

Eileen rocked forward, covering her face, her head shaking to and fro. A strangled sob escaped from her. She was breaking into pieces. Tennison looked at her, unmoved. She said, 'Tell me where Jason is.'

'I don't know . . .' Eileen looked up, spittle dribbling down her chin, her eyes tortured. 'We should never have come south. God . . . I did my best . . .' Tears rolled down her face. 'He's no son of mine. He's . . . he's . . . he's some sort of . . .'

'Tell me where Jason is,' Tennison repeated.

'I don't know,' Eileen said in a pathetic high-pitched voice, almost like a little girl's. Tennison believed her.

'Where's your brother's caravan, Eileen?'

'As far as I know he ... he sold it.' She was sobbing, fighting for breath. 'To help pay off the loan.'

Tennison replaced the photographs in the folder. With it tucked under her arm she left the room, not looking back. All the way down the corridor she could hear Eileen's racking sobs. She wondered if Joanne Fagunwa had sobbed like that, just before Jason Reynolds bashed her brains in.

Vernon Allen was sitting at the table in the living-room, newspapers spread out in front of him. Unusually for a man who took pride in his appearance, he was unshaven and dishevelled, almost scruffy. He wore his shapeless cardigan, his shirt collar was undone, and his trilby hat was shoved to the back of his head. Rather mechanically he was cutting out articles and photographs, placing them in a neat pile. The room was in semi-darkness, the flickering blue light from the TV set and a small lamp in the corner providing the only illumination.

Vernon snipped away, added the cutting to the pile, reached for another newspaper. He looked up as a shadow fell across the table. Sarah was standing in the doorway. She was barefoot, a towelling robe wrapped around her.

'How is she?' he asked. His voice sounded dull, as if he didn't care one way or the other; he did care, deeply, but he was wrung-out of all emotion, hollow inside.

'Sleeping.'

'I don't like her taking drugs.'

'It's better than having her crying all night.' Sarah came in and sat on the arm of an armchair. She looked in silence at the cuttings and mangled newspapers. 'Pop, why are you doing that?' she asked quietly.

'They're about Anthony.'

'I know that. I just don't see how it helps.'

'Well,' Vernon said wistfully, 'if it helps me, then surely there's nothing wrong.'

'You know I'll be going back to college straight after the inquest,' Sarah said.

'Of course.' The scissors snipped. 'Is there someone who can take notes for you, so you don't fall behind?'

'Yes.' She sighed; as if it mattered at a time like this. 'Yes, don't worry.'

'Sarah, did Tony ever talk to you about ... about that night?'

'No.' Sarah got up. She folded her arms tightly across her chest, hands underneath her armpits. 'My bath'll be running over.'

Vernon had gone still, the scissors poised in his hand. His son was on TV. His Tony. It was the local news, and there was a small picture of him in the corner of the screen, above the announcer's left shoulder.

'... twenty-two-year-old Anthony Allen, who is at the centre of an internal police inquiry into the running of that station. Detective Superintendent Mike Kernan today issued the following statement, after the news was announced that the coroner's inquest into the death would start tomorrow.'

Sarah couldn't stand it anymore. She had to leave him, unable to bear the glazed, obsessive expression on her father's face. The picture switched to Kernan outside Southampton Row.

'I'm very pleased that the inquest opening tomorrow comes so promptly after this tragic event. I am confident that the verdict will fully vindicate the police . . .'

In the darkened, flickering room Vernon stared at the screen, his cheeks wet with tears. He didn't realise he had any left to shed.

The train rattled past, briefly illuminating the figure crouched beside the track. As soon as it had disappeared round the curve, Jason skipped nimbly over the tracks and went down the opposite embankment. He stopped halfway, partially concealed behind some bushes, almost level with the bedroom window of the house that backed on to the railway. The light was on and the curtains hadn't been drawn.

Sarah Allen entered the bedroom. She was wrapped in a large bath towel, a smaller towel round her head. She took down a suit that was hanging from the wardrobe door and removed the plastic cover; the suit had just been dry cleaned. She held it up to the light for inspection, and hung it on the wardrobe door.

Jason unzipped his windcheater. He reached inside for the Pentax Z10 that was slung round his neck. The camera had three-speed power zoom with auto-focus and automatic wind/rewind. He clicked it on and checked the LCD display for battery level. Then he was ready.

Sarah unwrapped the large bath towel and let it fall. No need to draw the curtains, when the rear of the house wasn't overlooked. She removed the towel from around her head and began to dry her hair.

Grinning, Jason put his eye to the view-finder and pressed the shutter.

The death of Tony Allen in police custody was a hot story, and the press and TV were there in force, milling about on the steps of the Coroner's Court. Jonathan Phelps never missed an opportunity, and he was keen to make an early statement, announcing that he personally had secured the services of a top barrister, Mrs Elizabeth Duhra, to represent the Allen family.

It was just as well he got in quick. The arrival of Tony's fiancée Esta with their daughter Cleo stole his thunder. This was the shot the media wanted, and they closed in, jostling and elbowing each other aside as she stepped out of the cab with Cleo in her arms. Esta pushed through and struggled up the steps, a barrage of flashlights dazzling her and frightening the little girl. Gratefully she accepted the help of an usher, who came to her rescue and led her inside, from pandemonium to relative peace and calm. And the ordeal hadn't yet begun.

Oswalde sat with Burkin and Calder on the witnesses' bench. To his left he could see Tennison, talking quietly with Superintendent Kernan. Oswalde's eyes swept round the packed court, then he bowed his head and stared at the floor. He couln't look at the Allen family. Vernon's arm was clasped round his wife's shoulder; she looked as though she were in a state of shock. Not even crying, just blank-eyed, drugged to the point where she hardly knew what was going on or whether it was actually happening.

Sarah was sitting with Esta, Cleo between them. Sarah was staring at Oswalde, and even though he kept his eyes on the floor, he could feel the force of her emotion, like a wave of hatred sweeping over him. No mercy there, and it didn't surprise him, when he had none for himself.

The Coroner was anxious to get the proceedings started. He waited while the court official called for silence, and then began by addressing the jury. His voice was brisk, neutral, cleansed of all nuance or feeling.

'No one is on trial. We are not investigating a crime, but a death. It is our job – yours and mine – to decide how Anthony Allen came to die in police custody. One word of warning. You may be asked to study some distressing photographs taken both at the time of the young man's death and at the autopsy. I consider the viewing of these pictures to be vital as an aid to reaching your decision. We will begin today by hearing from the Pathologist, Professor Bream.'

Bream was on the stand less than ten minutes. He stated the cause of death, from asphyxiation, and answered one or two questions from the Coroner. Custody Sergeant Calder was then called to the stand. He swore the oath, and knew he was in for a tough time immediately Mrs Duhra started questioning him. She was a slim, elegant, dark-haired woman with high cheekbones and quick, intelligent eyes; a member of a prominent Anglo-Indian family, most of whom were in the legal profession.

Calder wasn't sure that she was deliberately playing to the largely black public gallery, but she didn't seem to mind their occasional shouts and angry interruptions.

'It must have taken a great deal of force, and determination, to strangle himself in such a manner.' Mrs Duhra tilted her head a fraction, inviting his agreement. 'Wouldn't you say?'

As procedure demanded, and as he had been taught, Calder directed his replies to the Coroner.

'I don't know about that, sir.'

'Professor Bream thought so. He thought Tony Allen may have taken rather a long time to die.' She glanced down at some papers, and looked up again. 'You did

202

make your checks every fifteen minutes, didn't you?'

Calder gazed straight in front of him, the globed lights reflecting on his bald head. 'Thirty minutes, sir.'

'Oh yes ...' Mrs Duhra nodded. Her lips thinned. 'Because it's checks every fifteen minutes for prisoners at risk. And, of course, you'd decided that Tony Allen wasn't at risk, hadn't you?'

'Mrs Duhra,' the Coroner mildly rebuked her. She was making assumptions about Calder's judgement at the time without any supporting testimony to that effect.

'Why was the flap left open?' Mrs Duhra asked.

'Because the prisoner requested it to be left open, sir.'

'Why?'

'To let in some fresh air.'

'Because he couldn't breathe ... because he was claustrophobic?'

'I don't know about that, sir.'

'No, I don't suppose you do,' Mrs Duhra said, though her tone implied that any person with half a brain ought to have known. 'If, as you say, he refused the offer of a solicitor –'

'He did, sir.' Calder wanted that on the record.

'– why did you not make sure that some responsible adult was with him? His father, for example, who was in reception almost the whole time?'

'Because there was no need.'

Mrs Duhra frowned, giving him a quizzical look that was more for the benefit of the jury. 'But his mental health was of concern to you, was it not?'

'No, sir,' Calder said stolidly. 'It was not.'

This reply seemed to puzzle Mrs Duhra even more. She consulted her papers. 'But as we can see from the

'Custody record, you called a doctor at 9.15 p.m.' She glanced up, waiting.

'Yes,' Calder admitted. He'd forgotten about procedure, addressing his reply directly to her.

'So you must have been concerned,' Mrs Duhra went on, logically proving her point. 'But he didn't arrive, did he? Until after 1.00 a.m. Didn't you think to call another doctor?'

Calder's mind went blank. He said in a rush, 'I was busy.'

Mrs Duhra let the silence work for her. She said, all the more effectively because of her quiet tone, 'A boy loses his life because you were busy?'

The Coroner leaned forward. 'Please, Mrs Duhra . . .'

'Doctor or no doctor, you had it in your power to send Tony Allen to hospital. With hindsight would you not agree that you made a series of ill-judged – not to say fatal – decisions?'

The court waited. Calder finally nodded. 'Yes. I made mistakes, I admit it . . .'

In the hubbub that followed, while the court official called for silence, Kernan muttered to himself, 'For God's sake, don't cry about it, man!'

The call came a few minutes after 8.00 p.m. Tennison was in the kitchen, preparing her evening meal. This entailed removing the dinner-for-one (complete meal with two veg) from the freezer and bunging it in the microwave. She unhooked the wall phone. 'Tennison.'

'It's Muddyman. I'm at the hospital. David Harvey died at seven-thirty this evening.'

'God . . .' She sagged against the door frame. 'This investigation is turning into a graveyard.'

204

'How did it go today?'

'Dreadful.'

'Oh well, tomorrow's another day.'

She said goodbye and hung up. The microwave pinged. She took out the shallow tray, peeled back the cover, and contemplated the dinner-for-one. There were a couple of muddy shapes swimming in a sea of streaky orange-brown sauce. A dog couldn't live off this, she thought, reaching down a plate and rooting in the drawer for a knife and fork.

12

'Would you say that the interview was carried out in accordance with PACE regulations?' Mrs Duhra asked.

'Yes, ma'am.'

'You made no attempt to bully or pressurise Tony Allen?'

'No, ma'am.'

'Sergeant Oswalde, do you hold a Higher National Diploma in Psychology?'

'Yes, ma'am.'

'Passed with Distinction?'

'Yes, ma'am.'

The door at the rear of the court opened and a uniformed figure slipped in. Kernan hadn't noticed, but Tennison had. She nudged him, and they both stared in dismay as Commander Trayner slid into a seat. What the hell was the top brass doing here? Come to decide which heads were to roll?

Oswalde was standing up well to the questioning. He was keeping his answers short and to the point, not laying himself open to misinterpretation. He was an imposing figure on the witness stand, very tall and very handsome, with a natural quiet dignity. He was immaculately turned out, in a well-cut dark suit, his shirt a crisp dazzling white against his dark skin.

'It is my intention to call an expert witness in a

moment,' Mrs Duhra continued. 'A Professor of Forensic Psychology. But before I do so, I'd like to read you some of Tony Allen's last recorded words – before you had him returned to his cell – and ask for your assessment.'

Oswalde's face was a closed book. This was the part he'd been dreading, and he had to keep telling himself to stay cool, don't give her an opening, keep it short and sweet.

Mrs Duhra began reading from the transcript, holding it up in her left hand so that her face was visible to the jury and her voice carried clearly across the crowded courtroom.

'Tony: "I'm choking."'

'You: "No you're not."'

'Tony: "I'm choking. I can't breathe."'

'You: "There's nothing wrong with you."'

'Tony: "I'm dirt. I'm dirt in everyone's mouth. Choking them. My life is dirt."'

'You: "This is pointless. I'm putting you back in the cells."'

'Tony: "My life's a cell. I'm trapped. So much earth and mud. Earth to earth. Dust to dust."'

Mrs Duhra put the transcript down. She folded her arms and looked at Oswalde, tilting her head in that characteristic, faintly mocking way of her's. 'In the cold light of day, Sergeant, how would you assess Tony's mental state?'

'From that I'd say he was hysterical.'

'Obsessed with death?'

'Yes.'

'In despair?'

Oswalde hesitated. 'Yes.'

'Suffering from claustrophobia?' Mrs Duhra said,

her eyes narrowing as she scrutinised his impassive face, searching for a chink of weakness, of doubt, she could exploit.

'Possibly,' Oswalde said, realising that she was trying to drive him into a corner, and refusing to be driven.

He could feel the eyes of the entire court upon him. The Coroner on his high bench was leaning on one elbow, his chin cupped in his hand. In the well of the court, the Allen family, seated in a row, were as if carved from stone. Vernon Allen's large hands were clasped tightly to his chest, in an attitude of prayer. Beside him, Esme gazed dully into space. Sarah's eyes were filled with a cold, implacable hatred.

Mrs Duhra's voice went on, quietly, lethally, 'Yet you had him returned to his cell. His ten foot by six foot cell. You had an exemplary record, Sergeant. Could it be, that in some subtle way, you were being tougher . . . harder . . . on this black suspect because you too are black?'

There were murmurs and a few muffled shouts from the public gallery. Somebody yelled angrily, 'Coconut!'

'I'm afraid your question is too subtle for me,' Oswalde said evenly.

Mrs Duhra permitted herself a tiny smile. His reply, however cleverly evasive, hardly mattered. She had made her point. She said, 'Turning then to the attack that Tony is alleged to have made on your person . . .'

'Do you intend to question Sergeant Oswalde for much longer, Mrs Duhra?' the Coroner asked.

'Well, that rather depends on his replies, sir,' Mrs Duhra said.

'Then I should like to adjourn for the day. The court will resume at ten tomorrow morning.' He gathered his papers together. The court official's voice rang out, 'All rise!'

There was a small but vociferous group of anti-racist supporters on the steps outside, waving placards and chanting slogans. As she came out with Kernan, and they crossed the road together, Tennison heard shouts of 'Bounty bar' and 'Coconut', being directed at Oswalde, who pushed his way through, grim-faced.

Kernan unlocked the door of his car. He looked as though he was in a foul temper. 'What the bloody hell was the Commander doing there?' he asked angrily.

Tennison, walking on to her own car, turned round. 'Mike – the verdict has to be suicide,' she reassured him. 'Any other is unthinkable.'

Kernan scowled. 'Meanwhile my station is portrayed by Duhra as a hotbed of racism and brutality. Well, I can kiss my promotion goodbye. Thanks to two black bastards . . .'

Tennison stared at him, genuinely shocked. 'I beg your pardon!'

'Well . . . you know what I mean,' Kernan muttered, giving her a shifty look.

'No. I don't.'

'Oh for God's sake . . .' he said wearily, and with a heavy sigh he got in the car and slammed the door.

For once, Tennison was having a relaxing evening at home. There was paperwork in her briefcase, waiting to be looked at, but she thought, To hell with it. She wasn't in the mood to settle down to anything. The inquest was preoccupying her mind. Until it was over and done with, the verdict in, she couldn't fully focus her concentration.

After a long soothing shower she put on pyjamas and the luxurious Chinese silk dressing-gown, a special present to herself. She wasn't the kind of woman to pamper herself, but just occasionally she felt the need to splurge out on something extravagant, and bugger the expense.

She wasn't expecting anyone, least of all Bob Oswalde. She let him in, wondering if this was a wise thing to do, but the instant she saw the despondent look on his face, her heart went out to him. He was wearing a long overcoat, and underneath it the dark, conservative suit he had worn in court. He was polite and apologetic, but tightly bottled up, she could tell, from the way he stood in the centre of the room, glancing round with jerky, distracted movements, kneading his palms together.

'I'm sorry just to show up like this. I had to talk to someone.'

She gave him a searching, quizzical look. 'Someone?'

He looked at her, biting his lip. 'You.'

She indicated the armchair, and he sat down, elbows on his knees, staring at the carpet. 'I just don't know what happened to me that night. When she read that stuff back to me today, it was . . .' He swallowed, his brows knitting together. 'So obvious that Tony Allen was at risk, and that I'd been bullying him. Why . . .?'

His face was stricken. He looked to be in pain. She went to the drinks tray on the small ornate table and poured two good measures of Glenlivet, carried them back and gave him his.

Oswalde held the glass, not drinking. 'Perhaps they're right,' he said after an age. 'Perhaps I am a coconut.'

Tennison sat down on the sofa, smoothing her dressing-gown over her knee. 'Yes, I heard them shouting that. What does that mean?'

'Coconut. A Bounty bar. Brown on the outside, white on the inside.' His voice was bitter.

'I should have thought it was a bit more complex than that, Bob.'

He raised his head. 'Do you think I was responsible for his death?'

He looked so forlorn that she had to resist the urge to go to him and put her arms around him and comfort him. Instead, she said firmly, and truthfully, 'No, I don't. But it's what you think that matters.'

The pain in his eyes was mingled now with fear. He said huskily, 'I think I as good as killed him.' Abruptly, he put the glass down on the carpet and stood up. 'I've got to go.'

Tennison stood up. 'You can stay if you want.'

'No. I'd better go.'

She saw him out, and walked with him along the passage to the street door. On the step, hugging herself against the chill, Tennison said, 'Call me if you need to talk.'

'Thanks.'

Feeling somehow that she had let him down, not helped him at all, she reached up and, pulling his head forward, kissed him lightly on the lips. 'Take care.'

She watched him walk off down the dark street, shoulders hunched, his overcoat flapping around his long legs. In the shadow of a tree, directly opposite, Jason kept his finger on the button, thinking he might as well use up all thirty-six frames because he was going to get the film processed first thing in the morning anyway.

'And at 11.20 p.m. you interrupted Sergeant Oswalde and asked to have a word with him.' Mrs Duhra looked up from the notes she was consulting to DI Frank Burkin in the witness box. 'Because you were concerned about the way Sergeant Oswalde was conducting the interview?'

'No, ma'am.'

'You weren't concerned for Tony Allen's safety or well-being?' Mrs Duhra asked, a suggestion of surprise, incredulity even, creeping into her voice.

'No, ma'am.'

'Then why the need for "a word"?'

'I thought a particular line of questioning was proving fruitless,' Burkin said in a steady monotone, as if he'd rehearsed his reply, which of course he had. 'I wanted to suggest another approach to Sergeant Oswalde.'

'I see.' Mrs Duhra glanced towards the jury, making clear her total scepticism of that, and turned once more to Burkin. 'So *nothing* in Tony Allen's behaviour gave you cause for concern?'

Burkin's face was immobile, his eyes opaque. 'No. Nothing at all, ma'am. What happened was a complete surprise to me. And a shock.'

The transformation, Tennison thought, was truly incredible. Not a trace of the tattoos, the earrings, the matted hair and the five-day growth of beard. In their place, standing there in the witness box, a presentable young man with short back-and-sides wearing a neat dark suit, pale green shirt and navy blue tie. The crusty had been smartened up so that he wouldn't have known who it was if he passed himself in the street.

Mrs Duhra had a friendly witness, and she treated him accordingly.

'Mr Peters, you were in the cell next door to Tony Allen on the night he died . . .'

'Yes, miss.'

Polite too, Tennison thought. Such a well-mannered boy wouldn't dream of screaming Fucking Fascist Bastard Pigs.

'Did you see or hear anything that is relevant to this inquest?'

The reformed crusty wormed his finger inside his collar, tugging his top button open. 'I saw the body. They didn't want me to. They were trying to move me but I saw it lying on the cell floor.'

'I see. Anything else?'

'Yes, miss. I heard the prisoner sobbing. Trying to tell the police he couldn't breathe. I heard some policemen kicking at his cell door, shouting at him, telling him to shut up. Then I heard him threaten them.'

He paused there, as if, a cynic might have supposed, he had been told to, and Mrs Duhra promptly picked it up.

'Threaten them? What exactly did he threaten them with?'

'Killing himself. If they didn't let him out of the cell he . . .'

His words were drowned in the commotion from the public gallery. The court official was on his feet, calling for quiet, and the noise subsided.

'He threatened to kill himself,' Mrs Duhra said. 'Go on.'

'I heard a police officer — I'm not sure which one — shouting at him.'

'What did the police officer shout?'

Probably enjoying this bit, the crusty said in a loud voice, '"Go on, then, Nig-Nog, hang yourself."' The public gallery burst into an uproar. People were standing and waving their fists. Through it all, the crusty

213

went on, 'They were all shouting, "Do it. Do it. Do it."'

'Quiet!' The court official was back on his feet. '*Quiet!*'

It subsided again, but this time an angry rumbling murmur continued, like distant yet ominous thunder. Sarah Allen had half-risen to her feet, her father pulling at her arm. Her head on one side, Esme was weeping silently, huge tears trickling down.

The Coroner became impatient, having to wait several moments until he could be heard.

'Sydney Peters, can you tell the members of the jury how you came to be occupying the cell next to Anthony Allen on the night he died?'

'I had been arrested, sir,' said the crusty meekly. 'For being drunk, sir.'

'Mr Peters, is it true that you are a member of Narcotics Anonymous?'

'Yes sir.'

'Perhaps you could tell the members of the jury why that is.'

The crusty blinked, and gave the jury an ingratiating smile. 'Because, ladies and gentlemen, I used to be addicted to various narcotic substances.'

'Thank you, Mr Peters,' the Coroner said icily.

The Coroner's heavy-handed attempt to discredit her witness brought a fleeting sardonic smile to Mrs Duhra's face. His testimony had been heard, that's what mattered, and what had been said couldn't be unsaid.

Tennison, in her bra and slip, was rooting in the closet for a clean blouse when the phone rang at twenty past eight the following morning. She flopped down on the bed and reached out to answer it. She listened and then said sharply, 'Who is this? And why should I want to read that rag?'

Jason was in a phone booth on the sea front. It was a gorgeous day of clear blue skies, the sun sparkling on the waves and making dazzling white triangles of the sails of the yachts setting out for a morning sail around the bay.

He said silkily, 'I think you'll find something in it to amuse you. Now promise me you'll buy it.'

'Who is this?'

Jason hung up. He didn't really want to, because he liked the sound of her voice, but it could have been dangerous, staying on the line. She had a sexy voice. She was sexy-looking too. Nice figure, big tits. As a rule he liked them young, the younger the better, because they were innocent and impressionable. But he would have made an exception in her case. Give her a few drinks, get her down to bra and knickers, load up the Pentax and shoot off a roll. And after that, well, who knows? Could be her lucky day, a bit of throbbing young meat. They said the older ones really appreciated a good strong hammering.

Jason came out of the phone booth on to the sunny promenade. He was breathing quite heavily and his erection was chafing inside the tight crotch of his jeans.

He set off at an amble, his black T-shirt under his open windcheater damply clinging to him, and went looking for amusement, diversion, thrills.

Sarah Allen was on her way to the kitchen when she heard the mail drop through the letterbox. Upstairs, her nine-year-old brother David was complaining that he couldn't find his shoes and that Miss Hoggard would make him stay behind if he was late again. From the bathroom, muffled by the sound of running water, came the bass rumble of Vernon's reply.

Sarah leafed through the bills and advertising junk to see if there was anything for her. There was. She ripped open the large manila envelope and took out a sheaf of ten-by-eight glossy photographs. At first, and rather stupidly, it only registered that they were of a young and slender naked black woman, a towel wrapped round her head. Then she gasped when she realised it was her. Staring in horror and total disbelief, she looked at the grainy images of herself in the privacy of her own bedroom, taken with a powerful zoom lens.

There was some writing on the back of one of them. In such a state of shock, Sarah had to read it twice before the words sank in. Her legs turned to water. Trembling and sick with fear, she stuffed the photographs back into the envelope and pushed it under her sweater as Esme came downstairs.

Gorgeously sunny at the seaside it might have been, but in London it was pissing down. Tennison came out of the newsagent's and made a dash to her car through the downpour. She slid behind the wheel, shaking cold rainwater from her hair. She unfolded the tabloid newspaper and quickly turned the pages. She didn't have to look very far. There it was, spread across page five, a bold headline that smacked her between the eyes. 'TOP COP'S DARK SECRET.'

Underneath it, three muddy photographs that nevertheless clearly identified the two figures kissing on a doorstep as Bob Oswalde and herself; and as if that weren't bad enough, she was in pyjamas and that bloody Chinese silk dressing-gown.

Tennison slumped back in the seat. The inside of her head was like a snowstorm, thoughts whirling around. It took her a couple of minutes to get a grip, steady herself. When she had, she knew what she had to do. There was a phone booth on the corner. She ran to it and called Mike Kernan at home, hoping to catch him before he left. Thank God he hadn't. He listened to her, but didn't seem to get the full drift of it right off.

Boiling with rage and frustration, Tennison explained angrily, 'It's a threat. From Jason — he's the photographer.' She nodded vigorously, showering raindrops everywhere. 'Yes, of course I'm going to court! I wouldn't give them the satisfaction. Someone needs to warn Oswalde . . .'

At that moment Oswalde was sitting in a café, down a side street nearly opposite the Coroner's Court, polishing off bacon and eggs. He was just finishing his coffee when Burkin strode in, a snide, knowing grin on his face. He was loving this; about time that stuck-up, holier-than-thou bitch got what was coming to her. Hardly stopping on his way to the counter, he rudely waved a folded newspaper in Oswalde's face and slapped it on the table.

'What —?'

'Page five.'

'What?' Oswalde said again.

'Egg-bacon-bubble-and-beans, fried slice, two of toast, cuppa tea with, please, love.' Burkin brought his tea to the table and squeezed in next to Oswalde. 'Page five.' He said with a smirk, 'That explains it — why the boss

217

was so keen to take your side when Tony topped himself.'

Oswalde had found the item. He read the headline and stared blankly at the pictures, too shell-shocked to feel anything.

Burkin stirred his tea. 'So tell me, is she good? Does she do tricks?' He leered at Oswalde, gave him a sly nudge. 'I bet she likes it on top, doesn't she?'

Oswalde stood up fast, in the process catching Burkin's elbow and upsetting his cup. Hot tea spilled into Burkin's lap, and he stood up fast too, grinding out, '*Shit!*' When he looked up, tight-lipped, the door was swinging shut behind Oswalde's departure.

It was the final day of the inquest, and there was an air of nervous expectation as the court quickly filled up. Tennison took her seat next to Kernan, who gave her a fishy-eyed stare; by now he'd seen the tabloid splash, another nail in the coffin of his promotion prospects. He didn't know that he could ever forgive her for this, and he wasn't sure that he wanted to.

Both of them watched the Allen family filing in. Tennison wasn't keen on catching their eye, because up until today it had been plain, unadulterated anger and hatred directed at the benches occupied by the police, especially from Sarah. Now Sarah was looking directly at her with an expression Tennison couldn't fathom. Almost as if she sympathised, or at least understood, what Tennison must be going through after the seedy revelations in that morning's paper. It was baffling. Sarah should be revelling in her discomfiture – positively gloating over it – Tennison thought, and yet she wasn't, and wondered why.

Everyone rose as the Coroner entered, and settled down

again. The public gallery was packed with black faces. Total silence fell like a shroud as the Coroner began his summing up.

'Ladies and gentlemen of the jury. The time has come for you to withdraw and consider your verdict. But before you do I should like to offer you some advice. There are a number of possible verdicts, but I think under the circumstances you should focus your attentions on just three.'

He paused and stated them, separately and distinctly, so that there should be no confusion.

'Unlawful killing. Misadventure. Suicide.'

There were murmurs from the public gallery. Three possible verdicts, but only one would satisfy them, and convince them that justice had been done.

During the recess, while the jury was out, Tennison went for a smoke in the white-tiled basement which served as a waiting-room. She sat apart from all the others, needing to be alone. Besides, the Allen family was down there, surrounded by friends and well-wishers from the public gallery. Therefore it came as a surprise when Sarah came up, and after a slight hesitation, sat down beside her.

She looked at Tennison with the same sort of under-standing as when she had entered the courtroom, as if they shared some secret sorrow.

'I'm sorry about that tabloid shit.'

'So am I,' Tennison said with feeling, puffing on her cigarette.

'I received these this morning.' Sarah glanced round, and shielding it with her body, took a brown envelope from her bag and handed it over. 'From the same source, I'd say. No – look at them in private,' she said quickly, as

Tennison lifted the flap. Then she got up and returned to sit with her family.

In the ladies' lavatory Tennison took the photographs from the envelope and looked at them. Jason's handiwork, no question. Him and his phallic zoom lens, poking it where it wasn't wanted.

Now she knew why Sarah's attitude towards her had changed so dramatically. They were sisters in this, two female victims of the same ugly, sick masculine mind.

She read the message scrawled in green felt-tip.

'DON'T EVEN THINK OF TALKING TO THAT SLAG TENNISON. I'M WATCHING YOU.'

Tennison felt her fury mounting to white heat. Not because of what he had written about her, she didn't waste a second worrying about that. It was his sheer egotistical arrogance that incensed her. The swaggering bully who would stoop to the lowest, meanest, most cowardly tricks and think he can get away with it. Up to and including rape, buggery and murder.

God, she was going to nail that little shit if it was the last thing she did.

The court official waited for complete silence. 'And have you reached a verdict?' he asked.

The jury foreman rose to his feet. 'We have. The verdict is suicide.'

The scrum of reporters, photographers and TV crews was in danger of becoming a riot, fighting to get near Vernon and Esme Allen as they came down the steps of the courthouse. Esme was weeping openly in the protective circle of her husband's arm, as he shouldered his way through to the waiting cab. Behind them, spilling through the doors, came their friends and supporters from the public gallery, still angry, still booing at the verdict. The anti-racist campaigners joined in. Chants of 'Coconut' and 'Bounty bar' went up as Oswalde appeared. He struggled down the steps, being jostled and pushed on all sides.

Tennison and Kernan were largely ignored. They managed to slip through as the media pack surged after the family, wanting shots of Esta and the little girl, who were being helped by Sarah.

Vernon was doing his best to get Esme into the cab. She was hysterical, swaying and shaking her head like somebody drunk. 'He wouldn't kill himself, never,' she wailed. 'He had no reason. He was to be married this weekend . . .'

The photographers closed in, flashlights going off.

'He loved his daughter, his family, he was always a happy boy . . . he would never kill himself!'

Sarah, handing Cleo into Esta's arms in the cab parked further along the street, straightened up and looked through the crowd to where Tennison was standing. The eyes of the two women locked and held. Both of them knew that Esme, the grieving mother, was deluding herself. Far from being a happy boy, Tony had been eaten away inside by some dreadful knowledge, a secret he carried with him to the grave.

Watching Sarah climb into the cab, Tennison wondered how much of that secret she shared with her brother. How much both of them really knew about the cause and circumstances of Joanne Fagunwa's brutal murder.

Tennison drove down Chancery Lane, turned left into

Fleet Street, heading for Ludgate Circus. She'd decided that the station could do without her for a couple of hours. It was just after midday; she'd take an extended lunch break and maybe stock up with frozen dinners at Sainsbury's.

The rain was still drumming down as she waited for the lights at the intersection with Shoe Lane. Gazing through the windscreen, her eyes drifted down to the envelope Sarah had given her, lying on top of the dashboard behind the steering wheel. Tennison leaned forward, frowning. There was a postmark. Of course there was a postmark, cretin, if the bloody thing had been posted! She snatched it up. The postmark said 'CLACTON' with yesterday's date.

Instead of turning right, Tennison swung into the left-hand lane, getting a few hoots for her pains, gave them the finger in return, and drove up Farringdon Street, back towards Southampton Row.

She barged into the Incident Room, unwinding her long scarf, already halfway out of her raincoat. Copies of the offending tabloid were swiftly stowed away. She didn't show that she noticed, and if she noticed she didn't care.

'Richard.'

'Yes, boss.'

'Start again with the caravan sites. Start with Clacton and any others that come within the postal district. And then work out along the Essex coast from there. Fast, please.'

Haskons jumped to it, organising the team to begin the search.

Jason had been studying her for a good five minutes

before he made his move. She was wearing an anorak over a white blouse and a pleated grey skirt, white ankle socks and Adidas trainers. Wagging it off school, he could spot 'em a mile off. Feeding her dinner money into a slot machine. This was the fourth one she'd tried in the seafront arcade, and at this rate she'd be out of dosh in no time flat.

He circled round, closing in. Fourteen, he guessed, maybe just turned fifteen. Ripe as a peach waiting to be plucked. Firm pair of titties sprouting under that starched blouse. Nice arse on it too. He liked a nice tight arse.

He breezed up, and leaning nonchalantly against the machine she was working, started reading aloud from the tabloid he was holding, spread open at the page three pin-up.

'"Lovely Donna, from Clacton. 36–22–34." It's you, innit?'

'What?' the girl said, chewing gum. She had small, very white teeth and a soft downy complexion. Her long dark hair was pulled back in a severe, straggling bunch, but it couldn't hide how pretty she was.

'In the paper.' Jason swivelled round to show her the picture of the girl arching her back and bending over slightly so that her breasts hung down, nipples erect. 'You're Donna.'

The girl shot him a glance from under her eyelashes. 'Dirty sod,' she said, but she was laughing when she said it.

13

Young David answered the telephone. 'Hold on, please,' he said, polite as ever, and called out, 'Sarah – phone.'

Sarah came through from the kitchen, wiping her hands on a tea-towel. She glanced up the stairs, to where the sound of her mother's racking sobs was rending the air. She had been crying like that, almost without pause, for the past hour. Vernon had had to call the doctor in, and they were upstairs with Esme now.

'Who is it?' Sarah asked, taking the phone.

'I don't know.' David went off into the kitchen.

'Hello?' It was Tennison. Sarah went stiff. She shook her head, watching furtively as her father and their GP came down the stairs. She said in a low voice, 'It's not a good time to call . . .'

Vernon came into the hallway. 'Thank you, doctor. Perhaps she'll sleep now.' He opened the vestibule door to show the doctor out.

'Hang on a sec.' Sarah carried the phone into the living-room and pushed the door shut with her foot. 'Okay.'

Tennison sounded serious and urgent. 'We can't let him get away with this, Sarah. He can't turn us into his victims as well.'

Sarah looked up at the ceiling. Her mother's sobs were like hacksaw blades, slicing through her brain. She

224

didn't know how much longer she could stand it. She looked wildly round the room, as if seeking some means of escape, and then made up her mind. 'All right. But off the record. I'm not giving evidence. Tomorrow . . .'

'No, tonight,' Tennison said. 'Please.'

Sarah shut her eyes tight and breathed in. 'All right. I can probably make it around seven.'

'Thank you. Bye.'

Sarah replaced the receiver. Her hands were sweating and she was trembling all over. Above her head, Esme's broken sobbing went on, and on, and on.

The Incident Room was a cacophony of voices and jangling telephones. Each man on the team had been given a segment of the Essex coast, from Burnham-on-Crouch to Harwich, checking out every caravan site in a wide radius of Clacton. At her desk, Tennison watched over the bustle and babble of activity, chewing on a Nicorette and anxiously waiting for the first sign of a positive lead.

It was Gary Rosper who struck lucky. He banged the phone down and was up on his feet, eyes alight, scurrying across the room to Tennison, waving his notepad. 'The Shangri-friggin'-la, Walton-on-the-Naze.'

'Where the hell's that?' Tennison frowned.

'Christ knows.' Rosper didn't.

'Richard,' Muddyman called out to Haskons, who was already unfolding a large-scale map. 'Walton-on-the-Naze.'

Everyone gathered round. Muddyman pointed it out, nine miles north of Clacton, right on the tip of a peninsula of tiny scattered islands, creeks and mud flats.

'How long will it take to get there?' Tennison asked.

'This time of day, about three and a half hours,' Muddyman said.

'I want Oswalde to go,' Tennison said. She ignored the looks that were being bandied about, and went on crisply, 'Inform the local Plod. Tell them to sit tight until he gets there.'

'Why Oswalde?' Muddyman wanted to know, voicing the question none of the others dared ask.

'Because I say so.'

No arguing with that. Haskons went to phone Oswalde at home, telling him to put his skates on. After three days in a stuffy courtroom a day at the seaside would make a welcome change.

With a professional eye, Jason delved through the rack of frilly slips, cami tops and lacy French knickers. He selected a cute little number in peach, pleated sides and a see-through lace panel at the front. A crafty, calculating look in his pale blue eyes, he stepped over to the changing cubicle and swept aside the plastic curtain.

'Oi' Sandra said. Down to her bra and panties, she turned away, covering up. He'd been right. Well-blessed up top. This was going to be fun.

'There you go, Sandy,' Jason grinned, 'try them on.'

She took the pleated French knickers and gave him a long stare as he lingered by the open curtain. 'Go on then.'

Jason pursed his lips and blew her a wet kiss before turning away. His chest felt tight, his breath catching in his throat.

*

It took Oswalde a shade over three hours to reach the caravan site at Walton-on-the-Naze. Three officers from the local Essex CID were waiting for him in the site manager's office. Taking charge, he told them to stay put until he'd had the chance to size up the situation, and escorted by the manager, he walked down the sloping gravel path through row upon row of caravans to the one pointed out to him as belonging to Jason Reynolds. There was a cool breeze whipping in off the sea, and Oswalde was glad he'd put on a thick knitted polo-neck sweater and his leather blouson.

The site was on two levels. Jason's caravan, painted yellow with shiny metal strips along its sides, was on the upper level; below it, another thirty or forty caravans were grouped in an area bordering the sand dunes, and beyond them the ground sloped sharply down to the beach, a wide expanse of flat wet sand that was deserted as far as the eye could see.

This being off-season, there was no one about. Any movement, Oswalde realised with satisfaction, would be immediately spotted. He looked at his watch. It was a few minutes after six, and the light was already fading. He spoke on his mobile phone to the officers in the manager's office at the entrance to the site.

'Yeah, come through . . . one of you stay in the office and keep an eye out. The other two join me at the van, okay?'

Oswalde had a quick shuftie round, then walked up the little concrete pathway to the door. All the windows, he noted, were masked off with black curtain material. He tried the door and glanced round at the manager, a dumpy, bald-headed man with tufts of grey hair sticking out over his ears.

The manager shrugged. 'I haven't got a key.'

Oswalde went to work. In two minutes he had the door open. Inside, it was pitch black. He felt for a switch, and the interior was bathed in red light. The entire caravan had been converted into a dark room, fitted out with processing and developing equipment, an enlarger, print trimmer, the lot.

'Bloody hell,' the manager muttered, gawking inside.

'Can you wait outside, please?' Oswalde pulled the door to and poked about. Strips of film hung down on wooden pegs. There was a cork board with dozens of girlie shots pinned to it, mostly black and white, a few in colour. Three large wire trays held stacks and stacks of prints. On top was one of Sarah Allen, taken through her bedroom window. Oswalde's mouth tightened as his eye fell on some photographs of him and Tennison, kissing on her doorstep. He stuffed them inside his blouson and zipped it up.

A few minutes later the two Essex CID officers arrived. They looked at him expectantly, their faces ruddy in the dim red light.

'We'll just have to sit tight till he shows up,' Oswalde said.

Tennison did her best to make Sarah relax. The girl was so tightly wound up that at first she just sat in Tennison's office, her back rigid, hands locked together in her lap. The station was quiet after the busy day, most of the team having gone home, so there were no interruptions. Tennison bided her time. She didn't ask any questions, content to let Sarah say what she felt like saying, no pressure, no hassles.

Of course, all her immediate thoughts were centred

on Tony. They had been very close; the pain she felt at his death was like a raw wound, her grief for him nakedly displayed on her face.

Eventually, in a small, very hushed voice, she began to unburden herself, recalling how depressed Tony had become.

'I think when it was really bad he heard voices. I know he dreamed of Joanne, night after night. Always the same dream . . . that she'd been buried alive. He could hear these muffled screams.' Sarah's large dark eyes clouded over. She clenched her jaw, fighting back the tears. 'He couldn't bear to be alone. Confined spaces petrified him. If only I'd been around I could have explained . . . but Mum and Pop just wouldn't believe there was anything wrong with him.'

She stared miserably into space, overcome with guilt that she'd let her brother down, been away at college when he needed her.

Tennison allowed a small silence to gather. She said gently, 'Sarah, you could still help by giving us a statement about what happened.'

'. . . he never had a girlfriend,' Sarah went on, not listening, following the track of her own thoughts. 'No one was more surprised than me when Esta came on to the scene. I don't suppose that would have lasted if she hadn't become pregnant.'

Tennison knew that Sarah was circling round and round it, steeling herself to make the plunge and reveal the truth. But it was no good here, in the privacy of this office. It had to be a statement, freely given, committed to tape. Without it, all this was leading nowhere.

She leaned forward, gaining Sarah's attention by the force of her gaze. 'Please, Sarah . . .'

Sarah turned her head away, and Tennison's spirits sank. But then, looking resolutely away, tears standing in her eyes, Sarah gave a tiny, almost imperceptible nod. Tennison let her breath go.

As she sat down at the restaurant table, Sandra's breasts swelled above the low-cut neckline of the black velvet dress. The dress had a cutaway panel at the back too, revealing that she wasn't wearing a bra. With her dark lush hair brushed out and cascading over her shoulders, her eyes made-up with dusk-grey eye-shadow and Virgin Rose lip gloss emphasising her full lips, she could easily have passed for eighteen. Jason was dead chuffed, smugly pleased with himself. He could certainly pick 'em.

Sandra was flushed and excited, already a bit tiddly on the two Babychams she'd had in the pub. Jason ordered a pint of lager for himself and a Martini and lemonade for her. It was early in the evening and the place was quiet, not more than a dozen diners all told, mostly couples.

'Can we have some of them poppadoms?' Sandra asked, wriggling in her chair.

Jason smirked at her naïvety. 'This is a Chinese restaurant, Sandy.'

'I know,' she said sulkily, colouring up.

'I'll order for us.' He patted her hand. 'Don't worry your pretty little head.'

When the food came she didn't know how to use chopsticks, and had to eat it with a fork. Jason got another round of drinks in, even though Sandra protested she'd had enough. Her eyes were glassy, and she got the giggles. Every time Jason whispered in her ear, usually some crude sexual innuendo, she shrieked with laughter. Some of the other diners were becoming irritated. At a nearby table a man muttered to his companion that it was a disgrace, they shouldn't allow that type in the restaurant in the first place.

Jason was up on his feet, neck pumping, fists bunched. He strode across and stuck his head in the man's face.

'What you say? My type? What's "my type", eh? Eh?' White-faced with rage, he grabbed the plateful of food and chucked it in the man's lap. 'You slag. Fuckin' slag!' He gripped the edge of the table and tipped the whole lot over.

Two waiters rushed over and started yammering away in Chinese. Jason angrily brushed them off. He marched back to his table, threw down some money, and jerked his thumb at Sandra. 'C'mon darlin'.'

Sandra rose to her feet, a little nervous smile hovering on her lips. She'd never seen anyone change so quick, so sudden. He was like a different person. A shiver ran down her spine, but she did as she was told, and meekly followed him out.

In the darkened caravan, Oswalde and the two local CID officers waited. They'd made themselves as comfortable as possible in the cramped space, Oswalde taking the bench couch under the window, the other two sitting on cushions on the floor. From time to time all three looked hopefully at the mobile phone, standing upright on the sink unit. Their man in the site manager's office would give them advance word the minute Jason drove in. Then they'd be ready for him as he stepped through the door.

Oswalde smothered a yawn. Join the police for a life of thrills and excitement. They forgot to mention the endless hours of boredom while you waited for something to happen.

The embossed plastic sign in the centre of the door read: TAPED INTERVIEW ROOM. Sarah paused on the threshold as Tennison pushed the door open and bade her enter. She said tremulously, 'Was this the room Tony was interviewed in?'

Tennison shook her head. 'No, love.' She touched Sarah's arm reassuringly. 'No.'

Sarah went in. Tennison followed and closed the door.

Jason's arm was hooked round Sandra's waist, leading her to his Cavalier hatchback at the kerbside. The giggles were back. She staggered tipsily in her high heels and nearly tripped, and he had to hoist her up. His hand slid down to squeeze her buttocks. Lovely firm body on it, not an ounce of flab. That's why he preferred them young; those old slags with their arses hanging out turned his stomach. He bet this tart would go like the clappers, a regular rattlesnake.

He unlocked the passenger door and got her safely installed. He had a hard-on like a tent-pole, couldn't wait to see her stripped off and get stuck in. He had some whisky back at the van, just in case she needed loosening up, a bit of Dutch courage. He went round to his side, chest tight, grinning into the night air. He was going to give her a lot more than whisky and Dutch courage.

Sarah had taken off her coat and scarf. She hadn't bothered to change before she left home; wearing a simple dark dress and loose knitted cardigan, she sat opposite Tennison, her feet together, hands resting in her lap. Even in her fraught condition there was a noble dignity about her, Tennison decided. She held herself

232

proudly, shoulders back, and it was only in her large liquid eyes that the terrible anguish and pain she was struggling with showed itself.

Tennison started the tape. Without any prompting, Sarah began to speak in a level, controlled voice, quiet yet distinct, recalling the events of the last day of August, 1986.

'I was at home with Pop until Tony got back. That was just before nine, as arranged. As soon as Pop had gone, Tony said he had to go out for a while. Of course he wasn't supposed to, so we started arguing. I watched him go back out to a girl who was waiting for him. Joanne. Tony must have got Pop's keys from somewhere, because they went next door . . .'

'Into Harvey's house?' Tennison said, clarifying it for the record.

'Yes. Joanne was looking for a flat to rent and Tony told her about Harvey's basement. How his father owned it and all that. I followed them and watched. They went into the bedroom together. They kissed, lay on the bed together. I watched for a while. It made me feel odd. But I was thirteen, and curious I suppose.'

She stared past Tennison, a slight glaze over her eyes, reliving the memory.

'Then I saw Jason come in. Tony didn't know he was staying there . . .'

The Cavalier hatchback turned in at the gate and bumped over the rutted track past the site manager's office. It passed within a few feet of an open window, through which a storm of cheering erupted as Paul Merson headed in the equaliser against Liverpool. Leaning forward in his chair, the CID man punched the air and grinned across at the manager. Up the Gunners! Show those bleeding Scousers how it's done. He took another bite of his corned beef and pickle sandwich, and settled back with eager anticipation in the comfy armchair.

Outside, the red tail-lights grew faint, and finally disappeared from view as the gravelled track dipped down.

'I went round to the front door and rang the bell. Jason answered. He invited me in. I had quite a crush on Jason at the time ...' Sarah's eyes rolled towards Tennison, the thought of it filling her with horror. She moistened her lips. 'Tony was pissed off to see me but I wouldn't go. Tony and Joanne were dancing together. Jason was watching them, encouraging them, telling them to kiss ...'

Randy and raring to go, Jason gave Sandra a sloppy wet kiss as they staggered up the concrete pathway together. Her giggles now weren't altogether convincing. The cold night air had sharpened her senses, cut through the alcoholic haze swirling inside her head. He had bought her fancy new clothes and underwear, wined and dined her, and she wasn't fool enough not to know that he expected something in return. She wasn't at all sure that she wanted to give it.

But it was too late; she was here, at his caravan, and she didn't know how to get out of it.

Jason fished out his keys. Cuddling her, he turned the key in the lock, yanked the door open, and pushed her inside, into the pitch blackness.

'... Jason found a polaroid camera. It must have

belonged to Harvey. Jason took photographs. We were drinking Harvey's booze, getting quite drunk.'

Sandra stood blinking as the light came on. Sidling past her, Jason slapped her neat little bottom in the black velvet dress. 'Make yourself at home.'

He went to a cupboard, hunting for the bottle of White Horse. 'This is my studio . . . I got me darkroom in another van,' he told her.

Swaying a little, Sandra gazed round. She was feeling a bit queasy, and it wasn't only the drink and the Chinese food. The walls were covered from floor to ceiling with pictures of naked girls. There was a camera set up on a tripod and a battery of lights. And there was a couch, draped in a satin sheet. Suddenly she realised she was trembling all over. A horrible cold crawling sensation was seeping up from the pit of her stomach.

She jumped as he turned to her, clutching a bottle and two glasses. His fair eyebrows were raised, and there was a devilish gleam in his pale blue eyes.

Oswalde closed his eyes. He wasn't tired, didn't feel at all sleepy, but it was a strain just sitting there, staring into black nothingness, the minutes dragging painfully by. His nostrils twitched. Somebody had let one off, silent and deadly. Great. He lay back on the couch, trying to think of something pleasant to pass the time, but it wasn't easy with that reek pervading the air.

'Then Jason started making suggestions.'

'What kind of suggestions?' Tennison asked when Sarah paused.

'That we should undress. Encouraging Tony to touch

235

Joanne. I could see Jason was getting turned on by it . . . we were all turned on in a way,' she admitted. 'He ran out of film after about ten pictures but he wouldn't stop. He became more serious. More insistent.'

Sandra took another sip of whisky, just to keep him quiet. He was going on and on at her, so she did. She hoped it might make her feel better, but it didn't. The room was spinning. She sat down heavily on the couch, and then he was beside her, his breath on her cheek, his hand creeping over her breast. She tried to push him away. Somehow she didn't have the strength. The room was whirling round and her head felt hot. And all the time he was whispering, whispering in her ear in a sly, silky voice. She couldn't make sense of the words but she knew what he wanted her to do. She knew from the way his hand was kneading her breasts and tugging at the black velvet dress. And his soft voice whispering in her ear.

'When Joanne wouldn't pose topless he started pulling at her clothes.'

Tennison sat quite still, not interrupting or asking questions, allowing Sarah to tell her story. Her voice had taken on a mechanical, almost dreamlike quality. As if she was describing a film that was unrolling inside her head. A horror film from which she couldn't avert her eyes, had to see it through to its grisly end.

'She tried to stop him. It wasn't funny anymore. He was pulling at her clothes. Joanne was scared. Tony tried to stop him. But Jason got really angry. Angrier than I've ever seen anyone. He went completely wild. He punched Joanne in the face. Her mouth was bleeding . . .'

Sarah's own mouth twisted into an ugly shape. Her eyes went wide and bright with fear, watching the film unroll. A spasm shook her entire body, held rigid and bolt upright in the chair. The real horror was about to begin. She forced herself to carry on.

'. . . he broke a bottle. I really believed he'd use it. He made Tony tie some tights, they were my tights –' She faltered, her throat working. '– round Joanne's mouth. Jason took off his belt and tied Joanne's hands behind her back.'

He'd got her dress off at last. She was sitting on the silken-draped couch, shivering in her low-cut bra, staring up at him with fearful eyes as he undid the buckle and slowly slid the belt through the loops of his jeans. He felt as though he were in a state of fever. The blood was pounding in his temples. He breathed in a deep lungful to steady himself, to take the quiver out of his voice and make it sound natural as he said casually, 'Don't be afraid . . .'

Sandra stared up at him, hugging herself. It made her breasts swell over the lacy top. He could see right down her cleavage. Beautiful. Firm young titties. He was going to have the time of his life with this lovely piece of cunt; shaft the arse off it, literally.

'Nothing to worry about, eh?' he said soothingly. 'It's the punters. They love a bit of bondage.' He coiled the belt in his hands. 'I won't tie you too tight. It's all acting really . . .'

'I don't like it,' Sandra whimpered, her mouth trembling.

'Course you do,' Jason grinned, uncoiling the belt.

'I don't . . .'

'He raped her there in front of us,' Sarah said, the pain of that dreadful night frozen in her eyes. 'He held the broken bottle over her face. And we did nothing. We stood and watched. Joanne was choking on the gag. And we stood and watched.'

She shuddered.

He had her just how he wanted her. Face down on the couch, hands behind her back, the belt wrapped round her wrists and pulled tight so that it cut into her flesh. Sandra cried out then, in agony, as Jason thrust down with all his strength, forcing rear entry. She felt she was being ripped apart.

Getting into his stroke, Jason pumped away. Sandra's head bounced on the couch under the impact of his incessant pounding. She felt suffocated. She couldn't see. Her tangled hair was in her eyes and stuck to her forehead. Her cheeks were mottled and blotchy from the hot tears rolling down. She gasped as he went in, deeper. The pain was searing, tearing at her insides. She tried to scream but her head was being rammed into the couch, and what came out sounded like the muffled, terrified squeals of a whipped animal.

Jason kept at it, grunting with every thrust. Sweat from his chest sprinkled her back. His cap of blond hair was saturated. In his left hand he held the remote control. Every few seconds he pressed the button. The shutter clicked. The camera whirred to a new frame. He pounded away and pressed the button. The shutter clicked. He'd been careful in his advance preparation, made sure there was a new roll in. Five down, just thirty-one to go.

'When it was all over he went ... suddenly quiet. He warned us that we were guilty too. That he had the photographs to prove it. He let us leave. We didn't know what to do. We went home. We went to our rooms. When Mum got back we pretended to be asleep in bed. The dreadful thing was that we just left Joanne there. We weren't even sure whether she was dead or not ...

'The following night I heard noises in next door's garden. When I looked out of my window I saw Jason and Harvey digging. They were putting the earth into sacks and Jason was taking them off somewhere to dump. I guessed why, but ... but I couldn't look after that.' Her voice sank to a choking whisper. 'My nightmare was the sound of those shovels. The following morning I told Tony. We took an oath together never to tell a soul. The next time I made myself look from my bedroom window all the slabs were in place. Not a sign that anything had happened. Sometimes I could almost believe it hadn't ... until she was dug up again.'

Sarah's face collapsed. She was moaning and sobbing, tears dripping off her chin and splashing on to her bare arms. She was shaking her head, helpless and bereft. 'It was an awful secret we carried around with us ...'

She covered her face and her body slumped forward until she was bent almost double, great racking sobs shuddering through her.

'Oh God, what am I going to do ... without him? Without Tony ...?'

Tennison went quickly round the desk and knelt down beside her chair. She put both arms around Sarah and held her.

14

With a groan, Oswalde rocked himself forward and swung his feet to the floor. He wriggled his toes inside his Reeboks and arched his back, stretching. He must have been sitting in that same semi-crouched position for over an hour, and had possibly, without realising it, dozed off. His buttocks tingled as the circulation got going.

Light was filtering through the curtains. From the floor of the caravan came a bass-baritone duet of snores; both CID men were well away in the land of nod.

Oswalde twitched the curtain aside and looked out at a new day. Over the sea, the sky was a clear tranquil blue, as if it had been washed clean overnight. It was very early, not yet six-thirty. Oswalde stared dismally out, wondering what the fuck had happened to Jason Reynolds. Had he got wind of them? Or just been delayed somewhere and would show up later? The thought of having to spend all day cooped up in here with the phantom farter made Oswalde profoundly depressed.

He went outside and gratefully sucked in some of the chill morning air. He'd better give Tennison a call, he thought, rolling his head round to loosen up his cramped neck muscles. She'd want to be brought up to date on what was happening, or rather not happening.

Oswalde's head stopped in mid-roll. Below him, on

the lower level, a Cavalier hatchback was parked outside one of the caravans. It hadn't been there last night. How the hell had it got on to the site without the man at the gate clocking it?

Thoughtfully, Oswalde zipped up his blouson. Stepping lightly, he moved down the grassy slope and skirted round to approach the caravan end on, because he could see a curtain was drawn across the large picture window, blanking out the view. Arms spread to keep his balance, he tiptoed over the grass and pressed his face close to the glass, hoping there might be a chink in the curtains. No luck. He moved round to the door, pausing at another window, but that too was curtained off.

Oswalde edged up to the door and gripped the handle. In one swift smooth movement he had it open and was ducking through the doorway, eyes narrowed as he peered into the gloomy interior.

Lying on the bed of crumpled satin, Sandra's eyes rounded with terror as the tall, athletic black man burst in. She was wearing a school uniform – blouse, grey pleated skirt, white ankle socks – and was manacled and chained up for a Jason special: schoolgirl bondage. Oswalde moved towards her. Sandra pressed back into a corner and screamed, loud and piercing, and kept on screaming even when he raised both hands in an effort to calm and reassure her.

'It's all right, I'm a police officer! I'm a police officer!'

Oswalde knelt down, trying to make the girl understand that it was okay, she was safe now. Behind him, Jason crept through the narrow doorway from the kitchen area. He was gripping the empty Scotch bottle by the neck. His lips drew back in a silent snarl. His pale blue eyes with their fringe of blond lashes were wide and murderous. He swung the bottle and brought it down on the back of Oswalde's head. Oswalde went sprawling, a cascade of stars and flashing sparks filling his universe. He pushed himself back up on to his knees, groggily shaking his head. It took another ten seconds to stagger to his feet. When he looked round, squinting painfully towards the door, Jason had gone.

Oswalde stumbled outside. He touched the back of his neck. Blood was trickling down through the roots of his hair. He staggered forward a few paces, shaking his head to clear it, and looked wildly round. The bastard couldn't have got far. Then he spotted the blob of blond hair, just disappearing through the waving tufts of coarse grass that grew along the edge of the sand dunes. He was heading for the beach.

Oswalde went after him. Elbows pumping like pistons, he ran towards the broken lip of the cliff top, where it crumbled and fell away to the flat open expanse of wet sand. The blond head vanished as Jason hurtled down the steep sandy slope. Oswalde ran through the coarse grass, feeling it whipping against his legs. He reached the same spot and plunged down, arms cartwheeling as he sought to maintain his balance. He landed with a jarring thud on the hard wet sand and then he was sprinting, long legs at full stretch, the running figure in his sights, the blond head wobbling as Jason started to tire.

Got you, you bastard!

Gaining on him with every stride, Oswalde rapidly closed the distance between them. He could hear Jason's laboured breathing as he reached the shallows of the retreating tide. Jason splashed through them, staggering and sending up curtains of flying spray. He was just recovering when Oswalde launched himself. He hit Jason like an express train. Down they both went into the water. Oswalde got an iron grip on Jason's wrist and twisted his arm halfway up his back. With his other hand he grabbed Jason by the scruff of the neck, forcing his head down into the water.

Jason came up, coughing and spluttering. He twisted round, a face filled with hate. 'Coon, black bastard, jungle bunny, nigger . . .'

Oswalde rammed him under.

Jason came up again, spewing seawater, snarling, 'Rastus, sambo, fucking wog!'

Oswalde rammed him under again.

Jason came up again, coughing and gasping. 'That's right, you fucking coon, kill me as well!'

Oswalde could have done, easily, there and then, he knew it. And there was nothing in the world he'd have liked better than to drown the little shit. Rid the world of that perverted scum and have done.

Instead, with an icy purposeful deliberation, he yanked out the handcuffs and slapped them on. Fighting for breath, Oswalde gave him the full caution, as per the book. 'Jason Reynolds, I'm arresting you on suspicion of the murder of Joanne Fagunwa . . .'

The two CID men splashed through the shallows. Oswalde continued: 'You do not have to say anything, but if you do it may be given in evidence.'

Jason raised his head and spat in Oswalde's face. Hauled to his feet by the CID men, he was dragged away, still screaming, 'Coon, nigger, wog, fucking black bastard . . .!'

Oswalde sat in the water. He closed his eyes. He

could feel the warmth of the early sun on his face. It felt very good.

Tennison was waiting in the rear yard of Southampton Row when Jason arrived. She wanted the satisfaction of seeing for herself the little shit being brought in and formally charged. Handcuffed and pinioned between two officers, Jason was led inside. As he passed Tennison, he thrust his blond head towards her, leering into her face.

'Thanks for the show the other night. Just your scene, eh? Nice bit of beef ... nice black tubesteak up your stank!'

Then he was bundled through, snorting and sniggering to himself. Tennison turned away. She'd seen what she wanted to see. She didn't believe in the death penalty, but she was always open to persuasion.

The morning was damp and misty. Oswalde came along the neat gravel path, dressed for a funeral he hadn't attended; that had been yesterday, only he knew that his presence wouldn't have been welcomed, that it would have upset the Allen family.

Tony's grave was smothered in wreathes and flowers wrapped in cellophane. Oswalde carried a small bunch of flowers, but there was no card attached. He stood for a moment, looking at the headstone, then laid the flowers at the foot of the grave.

Suddenly overcome with emotion, he crouched down and bowed his head. Jane had said he wasn't to blame. She had said that when other people made a mistake, it was only money involved. When the police made a mistake, sometimes a human life was put in jeopardy. And

244

sometimes a human life was lost. He had tried to believe her, to convince himself that she was right, but it had a hollow ring, and the pain refused to go away. He would carry it with him for the rest of his life, a corrosive acid eating away at his soul.

He stood up and walked slowly back through the headstones to the gravel path, a tall dark figure that was gradually swallowed up in the morning mist.

Commander Trayner and DCI Thorndike were drinking sherry with Kernan in his office. There was an air of subdued yet distinct jubilation. Kernan detested sherry, but the occasion seemed to demand it, so he clinked glasses and forced the stuff down, hiding his grimace.

Thorndike was at his most overbearingly pompous. His voice was a pedantic drone, the corner of his thin mouth curling up in a tiny smug smile.

'This is not official, you understand, but under the circumstances it seems appropriate to give you a little taster. My recommendation is that disciplinary papers are served on Calder, DI Burkin, and DS Oswalde. I am critical of the way the station was run.' He cast a glance at Kernan, who blinked and took another sip of the disgusting muck. 'Procedures need to be tightened up,' Thorndike went on primly. 'Too many canteen cowboys. But I find no one to blame for the death of Tony Allen.'

Kernan breathed a heartfelt sigh of relief.

Commander Trayner was nodding, well pleased. 'Clearly, David, you're the right man to sort this station out.' He turned to Kernan, smiling. 'And of course, congratulations to you too, Mike. Nailing Jason Reynolds and getting the move upstairs. I shall have to give you the name of my tailor. He's particularly adroit at disguising any tendency towards the middle-age spread . . .'

'Thank you, sir,' Kernan refilled the Commander's glass. 'Do you intend to do anything about the press story, sir?'

Trayner considered a moment, and then shook his head. 'Let it blow over. Oswalde is back at West End Lane.'

'Yes, sir,' Kernan said, again relieved. He said reflectively, 'Besides, Tennison is a bloody good detective.'

'Perhaps,' Commander Trayner said, acknowledging the fact in rather a grudging tone. 'But one who has displayed a considerable lack of judgement . . . I think you know what I mean?'

The de-briefing in the Incident Room was also a subdued affair. The team had done its job well, had every reason to feel proud, but the death of Tony Allen in police custody cast a long, gloomy shadow.

Tennison had assembled all her detectives who had worked on the case; all but one. Bob Oswalde was absent, and she felt an obscure pang of guilt that he wasn't here today, even if the mood was far from celebratory. He deserved better than to have been sent packing, back to his old post, without so much as a word, some small gesture from the Super. But that was Mike Kernan for you. More damn interested in his reputation, his bloody promotion prospects.

Despite what she was feeling, she put on a bright face.

'I don't think there's any doubt that Jason Reynolds is going away for a very long time. The CPS has informed me that they are not going to press charges against anyone else.'

The men exchanged looks. There was some justice after

all. It would have been unnecessarily cruel for the Crown Prosecution Service to have implicated Sarah Allen in the murder.

'Now I don't know about the rest of you,' Tennison said, clapping her hands lightly, 'but I'm off to the pub – where I'd very much like to buy each and every one of you a large drink . . .'

'That won't be necessary, Jane.'

Everyone turned. Commander Trayner had entered. There were a few puzzled frowns as Kernan and Thorndike followed him in. Not the usual thing for all the top brass to put in an appearance, even at the successful conclusion to a case. What was going on?

Trayner said, with a faint smile, 'Perhaps I can take this opportunity to make an announcement. Mr Kernan here, will – from now on – be known to you all as "Chief Superintendent" Kernan . . .'

Mock groans from the men, a few caustic cheers, and a scattering of applause. Kernan scowled self-consciously.

'I'm also very pleased to be able to introduce his successor here at Southampton Row. "Superintendent" Thorndike.'

A solitary cough from somewhere emphasised the deafening silence. The men were looking anywhere but at Tennison. As Kernan's senior detective, she should rightfully have been next in line for his job.

Tennison felt the blood draining away from her face. It would have done so all the same if Trayner, instead of mentioning Thorndike's name, had walked up and punched her in the stomach. She stared across the room at Mike Kernan, who quickly shifted his gaze elsewhere. She didn't feel angry, not yet; she just felt numb.

Thorndike stepped forward, rubbing his palms together. 'Thank you, Commander. I realise I may have made a few enemies carrying out the investigation on behalf of MS15.' He gave a little cough, accompanied by a watery apology for a smile. 'The best thing is to clear the air straight away. If anyone thinks that's going to be a problem for them – get in the way of the smooth running of the station – then they should apply for a transfer immediately. Now, since we're all about to go off duty, and just to prove I have a lighter side, I've arranged for us to have a drink to mark the occasion.'

Most of the team brightened up considerably as two uniformed PCs came in carrying several large packs of Tennants Export and a case of Budweiser. The formal atmosphere vanished, and within moments there was the buzz of conversation and bursts of laughter as the men got stuck in. Thorndike mingled, even accepting a can, which he sipped as if it were a glass of sherry. Somebody offered Tennison a drink, which she refused. She was standing slightly apart, very pale, holding herself erect as if the effort cost her a great deal of will-power. She pushed her way through, and approached Kernan.

'So I didn't even merit an interview,' she said stiffly.

Kernan squirmed a little. 'Jane . . .'

But she'd already moved on to Thorndike. She said, politely and formally, 'May I have a word, sir?'

'Official or unofficial?' Thorndike said.

'Official.'

Kernan tried to intervene, his expression pained. 'Jane, it can wait, surely . . .'

'No it can't wait.'

Thorndike looked at her, flat-eyed. 'You'd better come to my office.'

248

Thorndike sat behind the desk, occupying what had been Mike Kernan's chair and was now his. He'd already acquired the approved manner of pressing his fingertips together and pursing his lips while he waited for Tennison, standing in front of the desk, to speak.

She said quietly, 'You'll have my formal request for a transfer first thing in the morning.'

'Very well,' Thorndike said, without a pause or the slightest hesitation. He sat, unmoving, and gazed at her.

Tennison stood. She didn't know what she was waiting for, unless it was perhaps some small expression of regret at her decision. Even of sadness at her departure. Or that she might like to sleep on it. Or to say that all her hard work at Southampton Row had been much appreciated. Or to say what a good officer she was and that they'd miss her. Or simply to say thanks, and good luck.

In the event she received nothing.

Fuck all.

She turned and went out.

Tennison went straight to her office, put her coat on and collected her briefcase. They were still carousing in the Incident Room when she walked past, a lot of raucous laughter and a babble of animated chat. Always a good feeling when a case was over. Relax, loosen up, let it all hang out.

Tennison turned right at the end of the corridor. She walked on through reception, down the steps, and into the street.

A List of Film and TV Tie-In Titles Available from Mandarin

While every effort is made to keep prices low, it is sometimes necessary to increase prices at short notice. Mandarin Paperbacks reserves the right to show new retail prices on covers which may differ from those previously advertised in the text or elsewhere.

The prices shown below were correct at the time of going to press.

☐ 7493 0942 3	**The Silence of the Lambs**	Thomas Harris	£4.99
☐ 7493 1416 8	**Wayne's World**	Myers & Ruzan	£4.99
☐ 7493 1345 5	**Batman Returns**	Craig Shaw Gardner	£3.99
☐ 7493 3601 3	**Rush**	Kim Wozencraft	£3.99
☐ 7493 9801 9	**The Commitments**	Roddy Doyle	£4.99
☐ 7493 1334 X	**Northern Exposure**	Ellis Weiner	£3.99
☐ 7493 0626 2	**Murder Squad**	Tate & Wyre	£4.99
☐ 7493 0277 1	**The Bill (Volume 1)**	John Burke	£3.50
☐ 7493 0278 X	**The Bill (Volume 2)**	John Burke	£3.50
☐ 7493 0000 2 7	**The Bill (Volume 3)**	John Burke	£3.50
☐ 7493 0374 3	**The Bill (Volume 4)**	John Burke	£2.99
☐ 7493 0842 7	**The Bill (Volume 5)**	John Burke	£3.50
☐ 7493 1178 9	**The Bill (Volume 6)**	John Burke	£3.50

All these books are available at your bookshop or newsagent, or can be ordered direct from the publisher. Just tick the titles you want and fill in the form below.

Mandarin Paperbacks, Cash Sales Department, PO Box 11, Falmouth, Cornwall TR10 9EN.

Please send cheque or postal order, no currency, for purchase price quoted and allow the following for postage and packing:

UK including BFPO

£1.00 for the first book, 50p for the second and 30p for each additional book ordered to a maximum charge of £3.00.

Overseas including Eire

£2 for the first book, £1.00 for the second and 50p for each additional book thereafter.

NAME (Block letters) ....

ADDRESS ....

....

☐ I enclose my remittance for ....

☐ I wish to pay by Access/Visa Card Number ☐☐☐☐☐☐☐☐☐☐☐☐☐☐☐☐

Expiry Date ☐☐☐☐